Beauty and the Bridesmaid

Wet Coast Publishing
MONROE

Lisa Souza

BEAUTY and
THE BRIDESMAID
By Lisa Souza

Wet Coast Media, LLC
Published by Wet Coast Publishing (USA)
Copyright 2014 Wet Coast Publishing

·

Quotes From THE BRIDESMAID'S MANUAL: MAKE IT TO AND THROUGH THE WEDDING WITH YOUR SANITY (AND YOUR FRIENDSHIP) INTACT by Sarah Stein and Lucy Talbot, copyright (c) 2013 by Sarah Maizes and Lucy Talbot. Used by permission of The Berkley Publishing Group, a division of Penguin Group (USA) LLC.

Cover Art designed by Daliborka, Belgrade, Serbia;
Cover Art Copyright 2014 Lisa Souza

Lisa Souza

———————————————————————

DEDICATION

for Mark,
my knight in shining armor and happy pants.

ACKNOWLEDGMENTS

Special thanks to Kathy Perko, M.S., P.N.P. and Wendy Coffman, M.D. for their assistance with medical situations and terminology. The Wet Coast Writers, Wally Lane, Sharon Anderson, Heide Ulbricht and Mark Souza, provided invaluable feedback and suffered through dreadful first drafts. Lisa Stowe of The Story River for much needed editing services and story advice.

This book wouldn't exist without you.

THE BRIDESMAID LAMENTS

If you've opened this book, it's likely that you have been chosen - nay, handpicked - by a close friend or relative who is a beaming bride-to-be to perform the sacred duties of bridesmaid. You are most likely filled with excitement because you will get to stand by one of your favorite people in the world on her most important day. And you are somewhat filled with trepidation, as you will devote months, if not the year ahead, to making sure that the big day and the important events surrounding it meet her every expectation. And at this point you are probably thinking, uh, now what?

--excerpt from The Bridesmaid's Manual *by Sarah Stein & Lucy Talbot, Page 1*

Lisa Souza

CHAPTER ONE

"I'm a virgin."

"Hmm?" Ginny continues admiring her ass from various angles in a three-way mirror.

"I'm a virgin, Gin." She still doesn't respond, so I figure clarification is in order. "I have not known man. I have unintentionally embraced the celibate life. I remain carnally unchallenged."

This time she hears me.

She glares down at me from her perch. "Can we stay on task, here, Dot?"

Can she comprehend how boring this is? I'm going snow blind from all the white. They use white to symbolize virginity and I am an expert on virginity. Unlike Ginny.

She should wear red. Maybe with racing stripes and corporate logos.

"You are so messed up, Dot." Ginny eyes the Vera Wang knock off from a different angle. The

5

simple white satin number clings to every inch of her till it reaches her knees where apparently it loses interest and puddles to the floor. "This may be the one."

I'd look like a Macy's Float in that thing: big, round, and secured with ribbon at the bottom. Eek.

She grins at me. "Mom'd kick my ass if I pick this one. D'you see the price tag?"

Are you getting this? Did you see how she just totally glossed over that heartfelt revelation? I don't really blame her. Ginny has always had the attention span of a gnat. And gosh, with the wedding looming a scant seven months away how could it be any different? No mock designer wedding gown selected? Oh, the horror. My predicament doesn't enter her consciousness. I'm a sex deprived manatee in sweat pants, but this pales in comparison to critical issues such as:

The ring;

The flowers;

The caterers;

Ginny's perfect ass in almost Vera Wang.

She set the hook two months ago, convincing Samuel T. Johansen III to drop to one knee and beg. Now sure, copious amounts of Jägermeister were involved (aided and abetted by an unbelievably revealing tank top), but she got the ring. Technically, he could still throw the hook, and this makes Miss Ginny Lake nervous indeed. She wants him in the boat before he can flop free. Bashing him over the head with an oar is not out of the question. Ginny's goal oriented.

Caveat emptor, Sammy boy, caveat emptor.

Consider: I, Dorothy Alana Lindell, just admitted to being a virgin in a public place. This proves conclusively that I'm desperate to switch the topic from GINNY'S WEDDING to anything else. Absolutely anything else. Yes, even my pathetic, undefiled state. And when you're painfully single, the only thing that might possibly out-bore someone else's wedding is someone else's baby.

Oh my god: how incredibly boring will Ginny be when she gets pregnant?

Her majesty turns and waves a manicured hand toward the register, ignores the assistant directly behind her. "Dress woman! You there! This is the one."

Dress woman? Ginny's such a pill.

Register woman hobbles over in three-inch heels. "Excellent, Miss Lake. And the tiara? Will that work, or would you care to see something else? Perhaps with longer veiling?"

Dress woman has a name – Tiffany. It says so on her nametag. Neither she nor her assistant offer their names. They stand like stiff little Chanel soldiers in arch destroying shoes and boxy suits, pursing their inflated lips. Maybe they got a group rate. I've seen ling cod with smaller mouths.

Bully for them, though, for not hauling off and decking her. I would have taken a swing at Ginny by now, were I not her best friend. Besides she's my cousin.

"Vera Wang simplicity sometimes suggests the need for more elaborate headgear," the one in charge counsels.

I fear her overly inflated mouth may

accidentally explode. I take a small step back, just in case.

"Ya think?" Ginny shoots an 'are you brain damaged?' look at her. Bridezilla must have stowed her Catholicism somewhere in the folds of pseudo-Vera Wang.

I take a seat on a hard, armless chair, the kind that should come with warning labels and free chiropractic care. Half of my butt fits. The chair complains loudly, causing both "dress women" to glare my way. I offer a feeble smile.

I would sell my soul for a Cherry Coke, but all this place offers is weak tea that smells like dirt and leaves. Best I keep dry.

I glance at my wrist. Nothing there. One day I'll wear a watch. The link types nip the tiny hairs on my arms and the leather ones can never quite circumnavigate my wrist.

"Ginny, what time is it? I gotta get back to work."

My cousin and former R.H.V. - that's "Red Hot Virgin" to the uninformed, barely glances my way. "I'm nowhere near done, Dotty. We haven't even addressed the footwear issue. If you have to go, call Dressler's about the flowers, 'k? Maybe you could swing by there tonight? Make sure Sam doesn't mess up the order? I'll end up with plastic daisies from Kmart if he starts checking prices."

"Can't tonight. Remember? Daters Anonymous. I have a meeting tonight." And I'll be switched if I take yet another bus to do your dirty work again today. "Later, Ginny."

Tap, tap, tap. Doc Devers is forever tapping that damn pen of hers. She's unaware of how annoying it is. It's a tiny little snapping sound, plastic against paper, a bit hollow in places.

Sometimes I'd like to slap her.

We're trapped in the meeting room of Valley General Hospital, my pathetic posse and me, holed up with Doctor Pepper Devers – A.K.A. Pepper the tapper. She's asked me not to refer to her as Dr. Pepper so I fight that urge, along with the compulsion to reach across two people and snap her pen in two.

The room is fairly small, maybe twelve by ten, all low ceilings, safety beige walls and match-the-vomit carpet. It is a hospital, after all. The chairs are three-mile-orange, the institutional plastic kind. The seats are the same molded plastic that proved too small for my ass in high school, so clearly I'm overflowing mine now. With one butt cheek hanging exhausted over the edge of the chair, Dever's interminable tapping, and the collective sighs and moans of my fellow detainees, I am miserable.

Doctor P sets the pen on her clipboard (sweet relief) and begins her opening spiel. I've heard this part before and set my brain to mute. Now it's all fuzzed out noises, like the old Peanuts cartoons with a teacher interrogating Charlie Brown: "wah, wah wah wah."

Group Therapy is weird beyond imagining.

The participants range in age from nineteen to sixty-seven. When everyone shows up there are three men and four women, sprawled on chairs, limbs dangling in varying degrees of looseness (depending on their medications).

I'd love to see the criteria Doc used to assemble this troop, but the stated purpose is "Relating to the Opposite Gender." Opposing genders. This is war.

My calendar lists it simply as "DA," shorthand for Daters Anonymous. Here's what I've learned so far in group:

Don't name your daughter Elvira.

If your brother offers to keep an eye on your wife, say no.

Meth and daycare don't mix.

Pepper's FM radio voice permeates my brain fog. "Last week, Don was discussing how his wife's adultery affected him sexually. Don, is there anything you would care to add before we move on?"

I glance over at Donald Pleasant. If Don were food, he'd be pudding. His flesh swirls around him in soft, creamy folds that coins could get lost in. He wears an ill fitting shirt in a bilious plaid paired with pants so high-waisted he's in danger of choking. If that weren't bad enough, he's also a nail biter. Eventually, he's going to gnaw off a hand. Poor Don.

He squints hard through thick glasses. Clearly he can't make out the orange chair, let alone the doctor's elegant presence. He aims his voice in her general direction.

"Well, Doctor, I think I've reached a new level of understanding," he shares between finger nibbles. His voice has the vaguely sinus-y sound of a chronic asthmatic.

Doctor Devers shifts toward him in her hard plastic chair. "Yes, Donald?"

"What's to understand, Donny boy?" Mike pipes up. He stretches back in his chair, threatening to tip it. "You're wife did your brother and tried to poison you. Badda bing, badda boom." Mikey twists his hands thumbs up, thumbs down, punctuating his brilliant observation. I'm scared to death of him. He looks like what he is: tough and wired. What Mikey lacks in hair – his head is completely shaved – he makes up in tattoos.

He's here by judicial order rather than desperation. He'd chased his wife six blocks before the cops apprehended him. At that point, he informed them that she'd escaped from their aquarium and he was merely trying to save her. The police confiscated a net of ropes he'd been swinging over the petrified woman's head at the time, (which turned out to be the hammock from their back yard) and snapped some plastic restraints on him. He later admitted to ingesting copious amounts of crack that day, yet somehow his lawyer managed to convince the court that all Mikey needed was a bit of R and R and some counseling.

I doubt his soon to be ex-wife agrees.

"I think I know why she needed Robbie. I think… I think I was being neglectful. Maybe I didn't consider her needs enough."

"That's very insightful, Donald."

"And it's…like…total bullshit." Elvira rolls her heavily made up eyes. She resembles her namesake in all ways save one: no boobs. Her chest is practically concave. Today she's done up all Goth:

long black dress, limp as a greasy lock of hair, far too much makeup in splotches of white and black – but her voice, as usual, is all peppy surfer chick. Think 'Fast Times at Ridgemont High' meets Tim Burton. She continues, "No offense, but you're kinda ugly, dude. I think it was just a matter of time till she booked." Elvira snaps her gum between black lips.

This isn't delivered as an insult, just a casual remark. Which strikes me as hilarious. I bite down hard on my lower lip and contemplate my own stubby fingernails.

When I dare to look up, Devers is suppressing a smile under her hand, but it rests in her eyes. "Remember the rules, Elvira. No name calling. Just information, observation, and assistance."

"Nothing personal, Don."

"Perfectly okay, Elvira."

Susan steps in. "Donny may be on to something, you know. Men don't pay attention. They never think about how the woman feels. It's all about them." Susan is sitting on her hands, trying to warm them. She's a single mom, a soccer mom, and she's battling a crystal meth habit she picked up while racing to keep up with an ADHD son. Since her box cutter accident a few weeks ago, she complains that her hands are always cold.

That must have been some accident. I wonder how common is it to "accidentally" slit both wrists with an X-acto Knife?

"What does it get you, Donald? So what if you were neglectful back then? What can you do about it now?" Jasper says.

Jasper is a wild card. I've no clue why he's here. He could sub for Devers if he wanted to, offering calm and sane advice. He's even attractive in a tweed elbow patches kind of way. His beard and mustache are trimmed short, the sandy brown color making his blue eyes sparkle. Maybe he's a physician. Mom says doctors make terrible husbands – and she should know, given she married two of them – so that may explain his presence in Relationships 101.

Don dislodges a fingernail-deprived hand from his mouth. "Well... I could call? Call and tell her I'm sorry about everything. Validate her feelings." He's animated, talking faster now.

A groan rises like a fart from the group, causing people to wave their hands and roll their eyes. Everyone starts bitching at once. They've heard Don's story multiple times. I allow myself to check out briefly while the doc tries to rein in the mob.

I concentrate on Peppy Le Doctor's perfect hands, pristine French manicure tap, tap, tapping on her clipboard, pausing to scribble something, thin and elegant like the rest of her. What if that pen gets accidentally snatched clean out of her hands?

I snap back at the mention of my name. Crap. What was the question?

"I asked if you recall what might have created your issue with weddings?"

"You refer to my utter contempt for them? March 5, 1989, 7:00pm, the day Melanie Fox forced my fat butt into a taffeta sausage skin while she married the love of my life."

Okay, okay, so maybe he wasn't the love of my life. Does the love of your life have to know you're alive?

Elvira scrunches up her overly made up face. "Are you serious? I was like two years old in '89. Move on, dude."

You're a little helper, Elvira.

I search for a place to rest my eyes, but when a hint of pity develops in Jasper's baby blues, I break contact.

"Remember: constructive, Elvira." Pepper aims her tapper at me. "Dorothy, how does that experience help you now? What did you learn that might help you make new choices?"

I face Dr. Pepper, the spitting image of Candice Bergen in her elegant suit. "Let's see. Never wear taffeta. It makes your butt look big and if caught between the thighs can start a fire."

There are a few muffled grade school giggles. The good doctor raises a fist to her chin, leans forward: Candice Bergen looking thoughtful. She's not letting me off that easy. "Anything else?"

I sigh. "Okay. How about 'the world has no patience for ugly people?' How about 'a crowd is more likely to laugh out loud at a fat girl than a single person might, but both will turn on you in time?' You need more? Okay, how about 'always being cast as the sidekick at someone else's nuptials sucks.' It's boring. It's expensive. It just sucks. Being ugly SUCKS!" My voice bounces in that tiny, stuffy room, a kid having a tantrum, not the calm observations of a twenty-four year old adult.

Silence. Group appears stunned.

Suddenly Elvira leans forward. "Oh my god it totally does suck!" she screams.

Who knew I'd find a champion in Elvira?

Anna Lanisovich, quiet up till now, juts out her pointed Russian chin and proclaims in her heavy accent, "Dah. It sooks."

Donald tears up, glares over at Doctor Devers, betrayed. "She's right you know. Everyone blabs on about how nice I am. How kind. What a beautiful soul. What crap! What bull pucky! Who wants to date your inner beauty?" He shrugs, defeated, "Women will let me debug their computer or pay their Visa bill. Denise was even willing to marry me 'cause I had a steady job. But when my handsome brother showed up? I was road kill."

"Almost literally, Donnie, dude. What with the poison and all." Elvira shares.

A free for all erupts, lasting for the remaining fifteen minutes. Everyone but Jasper and the Doc lament and swap tales of discrimination. This should have made me feel validated. Instead, I'm more miserable than ever. This isn't an area where I want to be right.

Maybe group isn't such a hot idea.

During the melee, I sneak out, hoping to catch the 8:05 bus. There's a bus stop on the East end of the hospital parking lot with an overhang to keep the weather off. Unfortunately, no such protection exists on the way there. I'm soaked by the time I reach it. Worse, I must have missed the 8:05, which leaves plenty of time for rumination.

Maybe Elvira's right: I should be over it. The thing is I had trusted Melanie. She was supposed to be my friend. We'd known each other since grade school. It still hurts to believe she could be so callous. Couldn't she have at least warned me?

———————◆◆———————

He called me first, you know: Gavin Dorset, Inglemoor High School's esteemed wide receiver phoned me. Oh all right. He was flunking bio and in danger of losing his position with the team. He wanted a tutor, not a love interest.

At the time though, I believed in my soul that once he met me, there would be this cosmic connection. He would sense my inner beauty, warm to my sense of humor, admire my intellect. I'd become a doctor and he'd be a surgeon and we'd have six kids.

I know. I was an idiot.

He'd gotten my name from the school's bulletin board where I offered tutorial services in biology and math, an easy way to make a buck. Gavin needed to pass bio not only to maintain his eligibility as a player, but also because his father – that would be Doctor Dorset – assumed he'd be going to med school, which was unlikely if he flunked basic biology.

When Gavin phoned, I practically flew over to Mel's to dish. Her parents house, a typical seventies rambler, was less than half a mile away. I hopped on Cherub, my rusty red three-speed and arrived panting and gasping seconds later.

She opened the door to my crazed banging. "Hey, Dot. What's up?"

"We have so got to talk." I raced ahead of the

bewildered Mel to her bedroom, where an explosion of Pepto Bismol pink covered walls, lampshade, drapes, and bedding. I plopped down on her bed, making a sizeable dent. "You will never ever guess who called me. Come on, guess!"

Melanie had her braces removed three weeks earlier, and was only now comfortable revealing teeth. Free of metal, they look huge in her tiny heart shaped face. She smiles broadly down at me. Given her tiny stature, Mel rarely looks down at anyone. "Well? Spill."

"Gavin Dorset! I'm going over to his place to tutor him in bio!"

Her bright smile dims. "Gavin? Yeah, I heard he's having some problems with that class."

"Mel, don't you get it? This is my chance! You know I've had a crush on him forever! I'm actually going to be in the same room with him. Alone."

She turns her back on me, studying a pink butterfly on the curtains at her window. "Don't get your hopes up too high, Dot. I heard he's seeing someone."

I miss the tension in her voice. I am too high on hope.

I tug on the back of her shirt. "Who cares? Let them find a new man. Let's get to the important stuff, Mel. What do I wear? I need to look hot, but not slutty. Come on, girl, help me out."

I pester her, drag her to the mall to shop for the perfect outfit. And I blow nearly every dime I'd saved from tutoring on that silly outfit. What was I thinking?

The rain slaps at the little shelter, the sound snapping me soundly back to the little overhang where I'm trapped for at least another fifteen minutes. Not a shocker, the weather, just a standard Pacific Northwest event: rain, followed by showers, rain without end, amen. In good years, like this one, the rain is warm, so I may be soaked, but I'll live. That particular year, though, my senior year of high school, we had arctic rain, rain that wanted to be snow when it grew up.

———————————

Back then, in the miserable, icy damp of that day, I huddle under the edge of a building, carefully avoiding eye contact with the wet strangers around me. A bus kiosk stood five feet in front of me, but was already jammed full of people. The lot of us could pass for a homeless enclave, lumpy outlines of bodies covered in oversized coats and rain ponchos that look like tarps, faces barely discernible. A few rogue types carry umbrellas. I assume they are Californian, since native Washingtonians rarely get caught carrying.

The rain continues its assault, snapping and popping off the ground, overwhelming the leather of shoes, oozing into socks. Water works its way up the edges of my pants from below and down my thighs from above. Diesel fumes from the buses couldn't break free of the inversion layer and remain in place, a cloud of exhaust that burnt the lungs.

By the time my bus arrives I am stone cold, barely able to climb the steps to board. I took the only available seat behind the driver and fall into a stupor, lulled by the motion of the bus and the heat which had been cranked up to compensate. When I come to, the combination of temperature and humidity fogs the windows. I take a swipe at it with my still wet arm to remove a spot to see and reveal a neighborhood completely unrecognizable. There was a moment of panic before I remember why I was making this journey. Fortunately, my unconscious cuts me some slack and it's only a couple more blocks before I reach the correct stop. I tug the rope to signal the driver.

The bus slows, stops. I, a pathetic oversized imitation of Madonna – that's if Ms. Ciccone had a slow metabolism and limited fashion sense – teeter from the bus. My pants are too spandex-y for warmth, and although the rain beads up nicely on the fabric at first, it soon seeps well into my skin. My heavy makeup, too gaudy to flatter, runs black stripes over my cheeks. Exit Madonna-wannabe, enter Alice Cooper. Assuming Alice been popping Prednisone or stuffing himself on Denny's Grand Slam breakfasts.

The leather jacket, so fashion forward at the point of purchase, is swiftly destroyed in the downpour; cheap, useless, zipper already rusting. The boots that complete the ensemble slap my sides in a plastic garbage bag. No way I could survive the trek from the bus stop to Gavin's in those things. Instead, I slosh through the damp in my sneakers.

Within minutes I spot his car – who but a football star drives a Mustang in high school? – parked at the curb outside his house. The windows are steamy so I assume occupancy, but can't see in.

That works for me. I need to make wardrobe adjustments and mentally cross my fingers that no one had seen me yet.

I lean against a stop sign in order to swap out footgear. Moisture creeps down my back. I adjust the leather bomber jacket, tug at the Lycra pants and voila: a giant, damp, black ice cream cone with very sparkly boots.

I wobble over in my silly boots and rap on the driver's side window, confident Madonna now had a rival in coolness.

Groans and a muffled curse or two filter from the car. Another minute passes before the window eases down. Gavin Dorset glares out.

"What in the hell do you want?"

I try to ignore the pelting rain as it finds its way inside the collar of the jacket and down my back. I play it like I'm just too cool to notice. "I'm Dot Lindell. I'm your bio tutor."

His head tips to one side "And I care because?"

The lack of enthusiasm puts the brakes on my response. "Um...well...it's Thursday. You picked the time, remember? You said you had practice on Wednesday, so –"

He waves a dismissive hand, "Ah, crap. I guess I did. Well, see, now –," he glances back into the car, then faces me again, "– now's not such a good time for me after all." This is greeted with high-pitched giggles.

I know the laugh; know the voice. Mel's voice. My best friend's voice.

Gavin continues, "See, tutor-girl, I'm kinda

busy at the moment."

The voice of my former best friend whispers from Gavin Dorset's car. "Tell her you're busy."

Let's get cracking on that ulcer.

I swallow a couple of times, find my spine. "Look, Gavin, I hopped a bus to be here. You want to fail bio, hey, it's your call, but you owe me ten bucks for the session." I push an open palm through the window, along with a good bit of the moisture now soaking me.

"Je-sus!" More muffled noise. Something crushes into my hand.

"Here's twenty. Get lost."

I squint: a twenty. A mountain of cash at seventeen. "Whatever. You know, you won't get into med school if you fail high school bio. Might want to give that some thought."

I saunter off, trying to look cool without twisting an ankle. The cold and wet bite at me, but my face burns as though scorched by acid.

When I am certain to be out of visual range, I drop down on the soggy sidewalk to do the shoe swap and saturate my butt in the process. By the time the first boot finally pulls free, the sky opens up and truly weeps. The intensity of the falling water obscures my vision with a shiny, oily film. I tug off the remaining boot by Braille, blinded by disappointment and rain and cold.

That's when I officially became Dorothy Lindell, the last of the Red Hot Virgin's.

CHAPTER TWO

It's May. To spite me, it's a glorious spring day, all golden sun and azure skies. Oh, what a perfect waste of a perfect day this shall be! Why? For I am dressed like the aftermath of a terrible Barney explosion, like the wrath of a vengeful, purple God.

And nothing, my friends, says 'you go girl' like yards of violet taffeta. Yes, taffeta. Again. What is this magnetic attraction between me and taffeta? Elvira warned me. Didn't she tell me to get some new friends?

Ginny selected plum and rose for her wedding colors. Plum my eggplant ass. This dress is purple. PURPLE. Seven months of planning and Ginny lands me in this chaos of a dress. Sigh.

The wedding planner, to her credit, spent days trying to talk Ginny into a more sophisticated palette. How about chocolate and amoretto? Basic black and silver? Hell no. Ginny intends for her bridesmaids to look like plump, purple sausages, explosions in ruffles and taffeta. She will then sail in, slim and chic in her simple gown, Audrey Hepburn amidst lumpy, purple-clad Oompa Loompas.

To be fair, Ginny has always loved this color. And her taste zigzags from elegance to double wide trailers, unfiltered Camel cigarettes and Jägermeister.

Regardless, Virginia Lake will wed Samuel Tibbets Johansen III of the Boston Johansens in less than ten minutes. She's chosen St. Louise's, a Catholic church in Bellevue, about ten minutes from Ginny's apartment. It's not Saint Mark's Cathedral, but it is still reasonably churchy. The smell is off though. A sea of vanilla scented candles and white roses mask the usual aromas of incense and aging bathroom deodorizers. At least the candles aren't purple. Lucky candles.

I'm being snide. Ginny is, of course, ravishing in that Vera Wang number (which she purchased over Aunt Vonda's screams of protest and Uncle Jake's sighs). And I've told her so, oh maybe a hundred or so times in the last hour. Her majesty is holding court in the crying room, grilling the wedding planner about no-shows. How else can she identify who to snub later.

The rest of us are crammed into the back of the church, sweating to the purple. Two of the groomsmen herd guests up the aisle. Those of us not yet roped into service are milling around in purple splendor.

My escort has yet to arrive. He is supposed to

be some distant cousin on Ginny's father's side. He's gay, (so said Ginny, expert on such things), and according to the pinch faced stick of a girl whispering next to me, he's wicked cool. Ginny had spoken of him with awe and a touch of annoyance: she'd tried to get him to design the wedding – and no, I haven't a clue what that implies – but he declined, citing scheduling difficulties. He also skipped the rehearsal.

Kennedy? Kennedy something? Size zero girl mentions that he's an image consultant.

And then he arrives. Or rather he glides, smooth perfection wearing, in theory, the same holy-smoking-Jesus purple suit the other groomsmen are wearing. He's tall and buff beyond reason. He's immaculately presented, totally working the grape where Prince himself couldn't have pulled it off. And clearly he bats for the other team.

Kennedy draws delicately on one of those clove cigarettes that were huge back in the fifties. It mixes with his cologne, creates a cloud of scent around him. The cigarette rests in one of those Marlene Dietrich style holders (who on earth uses those things? In a church?). He frowns over a thin plume of smoke and waves the stalk of the cig at me.

"You look beastly in that." He's got a slightly affected East Coast Prep School/almost British sound to his voice.

"Yes. Yes I do. You're implying someone could look good in it?" I cough out the smoke. Temper, temper, Dot. "Note that I didn't choose this gem of an outfit."

He releases another thin trail of smoke, considers. "Next time such an unprecedented fashion failure occurs, swing by the office. Adjustments can be made. Alterations. Corrections. Oh it will remain hideous, of course, but less so."

I look directly at him, trying to place the face which looks strangely familiar. It comes to me: the cover of Barbara Cartland's "The Ruthless Rake": same cleft chin and the amused blue eyes. That is, of course, if Dame Cartland's hero rode sidesaddle and wore a purple suit.

"You can make this offense to daytime television attractive?" I wave a hand at the front of the dress.

He inhales delicately – not easy for such a big guy – and slowly releases the smoke. "My dear, there is always a path for maximizing the positive." He pauses, smiles broadly, "Although Ginny certainly has made a game of it." His generous mouth gleams with what I assume are veneers. I'd hate to think anyone could have such nice teeth without having to pay for them. That just wouldn't be fair. His business card materializes. He slips it into my hand. Where does one store a business card in a pocket-less dress?

With few alternatives, I insert it into my ample cleavage.

"Look, Kennedy, my guess is your fees are in the platinum range. I doubt I can afford you."

His smile broadens. He reaches over and pats my hand. "Fear not. I need a project. And you, my dear," he says, taking a step back, "qualify. And of course you're family, more or less. Besides, you tolerate our dear cousin Ginny." He glances over his shoulder. Ginny is taking up her position behind us. He makes a face as though he's inhaled ammonia, coughs once, continues, "That's laudable, truly laudable. Few have survived. Just look at Johansen. He'll be on a short leash. Wonder if he's developed inner ear plugs to dampen out that stream of self-serving chatter." He takes another drag. "What do you do for filthy lucre, my dear?"

I'm too stunned to refute his summation. "I test software."

"Not for Microcosm by any chance?"

"The very same."

"I'm miserable with computers. Abominable things. My assistant Jefferson normally handles all things technical, but I foolishly let him take a vacation and now I'm lost. Not even certain what's scheduled for next week. This gives me a thought. We could arrange an exchange of services. You could track down my calendar while I..." he waves his hand at me.

"I'm sure I can talk you through it." I shrug. When I look over at him, the cigarette is gone, (no idea where) and the silver holder disappears inside his lapel with a deft hand movement. "Excellent. A prisoner exchange: my wayward technology corralled in exchange for you, drastically improved of image, yes?"

I'm about to argue. Not a fair barter. Way more work for him than me, but before I can respond, we get shushed by the wedding planner, bun so tight it eliminates wrinkles. She pushes her prissy face nose to nose with mine and shushes me before swiveling and shoving the first boy-girl team up the aisle. She offers one more glare at Kennedy and I before clickity-clacking off to reconnoiter with Ginny who has taken up her position behind us.

"Bitch." Kennedy J has few qualms about dealing with the help. "She's pushing that Kim Novak thing a bit past its expiration date."

I suppress a laugh. We're next up in the processional. I have a big stupid smile on my face. Kennedy just slays me.

The service begins. And goes on... and on, ceremony without end, Amen. I barely avoid lapsing into a coma during a chorus of "Lord, oh Lord, My Sweet Lord" and only the pain of good old Catholic kneeling keeps me from nodding off.

Kennedy makes it bearable. In direct violation of eye daggers from the priest, the best man, and that tight-bunned wedding planner, he delivers caustic observations just within earshot, causing my enormous purple dress to quiver as I fight off giggle fits.

The event finally ends. Ginny and Sam drive off in the limo bound for the reception. I'm supposed to race over to The City Club to help with gifts and cake, schlepping along in Aunt Vonda's car. That was the plan, anyway.

Until Kennedy suggests we dog such plebian responsibilities and hit a bar instead.

He knows this great place where the bartender has a thing for him. Dressed in such festive garb, we'll get our drinks for free.

"Can you imagine the potential for intrigue in these outlandish costumes? Far greater than milling around at The City Club. What do you think?"

Before I have a chance to think, I hear my voice say, "I think I'm all over it."

For the first time in my entire life, I blow off responsibility. A stupid grin pins itself on my face. I abandon my post. Blow off my cousin's wedding. And dressed in perhaps the ugliest dress ever conceived, I follow my homosexual savior to his Hummer.

"Loud car for such an understated man," I wave at the enormous silver grill.

"Sometimes grand gestures are best. Especially when it comes to ostentatious displays of success. Festive, don't you think?" He beams at the SUV. "Thing is a monster. Just eats the road, I tell you."

I rarely go to bars. Okay, never. I have never gone to a bar before. And I've certainly never been in a gay bar. Kennedy has. Before I can rethink my decision, Kennedy wraps his arm through mine and sweeps me in, where he is recognized immediately. Swarms of friendly faces surround us. Above the din of music and chatter, a handsome guy in a dress shirt and jeans points at the dance floor. Kennedy demurs, smiling an apology, motioning toward the bar instead. We take up stools and get comfortable. Four of his buddies have trailed us into the bar. They immediately vie for "best story" competition. I can barely catch a word over the pounding music, but it hardly matters. In short order I'm buzzed on my first ever Appletini. It's heavily alcoholic but I'm not driving so who cares? I'm over twenty-one.

Kennedy knows everybody or has done everybody, either biblically or in his professional capacity. There's a rock star guy with carefully spiked hair and green eyes. The three piece suit guy (oh he cannot be gay. That's just wrong!), who turns out to be an attorney. My favorites so far are the Cambodian brothers, Somnang and Sovann, currently sharing the dance floor with me. I promise to donate the dress to Sovann who wants to make throw pillows out of it. Like Kennedy, he has given me a business card. Being without pockets, and since Kennedy refused to let me bring my monster bag along, it is being held in suspension in that same sweaty niche between my breasts where Kennedy's formerly rested.

On my god this is fun!

The bar area is crowded and loud, and terribly chi-chi. I'm already wasted on my second Appletini, which I've concluded is composed of copious amounts of alcohol and something green. Since I very rarely drink, it's easy to push down the guilt demons with each swallow. Who cares that I abandoned my cousin's wedding? So what if I've casually misplaced my identity as a heterosexual? Everyone here assumes I'm the life of the party and a drag queen. So be it.

There I am, happily holding my Appletini glass by the stem (is this a fresh one?) when I catch sight of my swollen fingers. They're stubby, porcine digits with bubblegum pink nails (Ginny insisted). My stomach lurches and a wash of blood flows to my face as I stare at those hateful, fat paws with that ugly polish and catch a glimpse of obscenely purple dress. I'm about to fall straight down the rabbit hole into a sea of self-hate, when as quickly as the wave of disgust and nausea came on, it recedes.

Back to the ocean with it! Away issues of fatness, nail polish, and dress! They're of no relevance to Dot the Happy Drag Queen!

I concentrate instead on watching Kennedy make witty remarks to the bartender. Here's a guy who obviously knows how to enjoy himself. He snatched fun from a boring wedding and that's no simple feat. This is a man to admire and emulate, my new role model.

By closing time, I've danced in bare feet and Kennedy has made a date with that bartender, (an endearing fellow named Max with the chest of bodybuilder and the gentle smile of a Saint Bernard). Max the bartender offers to drive us home, but with grace, Kennedy declines.

"I must take my fairy princess home unscathed. But we're on for Friday at nine, right Max?" They share sunny smiles and a gentle touch of hands before we head off to the car.

The Hummer appears by magic – I don't recall his leaving it with a valet – but then again, I don't recall much of anything after my fourth Appletini. Or was it my fifth? Kennedy asks directions to my place and he shudders at the address.

"Listen, my dear. You really must come by the office. Let mamma fix, yes? Find the time. Tuesdays are best. Mondays are always a mess, so best to avoid them, but do what you have to do." I promptly fall asleep, waking to find we're at my apartment building.

Kennedy must have assisted me out of the car and into the apartment, (probably shaking his head the entire time). All I know is sometime during the night, I wake up still in that ugly damn dress. I strip the offensive garment off and stomp on it a few times, then flop back down on the bed, relishing the feel of cotton under my skin while enduring the sick spins that come from too much booze.

Still, my mouth tugs up in an easy smile. I had so much fun. I ignored everyone's agendas. I laughed and drank and chatted and made friends. For the first time in twenty-four years, I felt twenty-four, not fifty.

Never mind that everyone thought I was a man in drag.

CHAPTER THREE

When I wake the following morning, I reassess. Between the squirrely taste in my mouth and the deep throb at the back of my head, perhaps I should have just said no at number three. I stagger into the kitchen to play the dreaded phone messages. You'd think being a gal with zero social life I would be spared the hassle. Ha!

The first is from the wedding planner. The time stamp is from the previous evening, about ten minutes into the reception. She gives me an earful about leaving my post. Who gave her my number? I give her the phone finger and skip ahead. The next three are from my mom, her voice revealing concern as to my whereabouts, as only a mom can.

I kid, of course.

They're more like "Where the hell are you? Don't you realize you're supposed to be helping, here? You'd better have been in a car accident, missy, or there's no excuse for your selfish behavior." Etc., etc. Guilt makes my head pound harder. No wonder I rarely drink.

When I finish playing the messages, which grow steadily more threatening, the phone actually rings (argh!). It's mom. Ye-Gods is she torched.

"Where do I begin, Dorothy? What on earth were you thinking? You had a responsibility, missy, a responsibility to your cousin, and to your Aunt Vonda, - "

Ah! There's the crux of it. Bet mom got an earful from Vonda Lake, Ginny's mom.

" – and to me. Your lapse in judgment is just unconscionable. Since when do you disappear like that?"

Block, parry, counter. "Did you enjoy the reception? How was the cake?"

"How would I know? I was stuck cutting the stupid thing all night long. And it was fantastic by the way: chocolate amaretto with this Kahlua cream infilling. To die for. But did I get a chance to nosh any till after midnight? No I did not, thanks to you."

"Sorry to hear it. Would you like to hear where I went?"

"Missy, unless you were in the hospital having an emergency appendectomy, I couldn't care less what you were up to. Did you know that Vonda herself ended up tending to the gift table?"

"Interesting. So you two planned for me to handle both the gifts and the cake, huh? I must be mighty good." The thought of Vonda Lake, distinguished matron, loads of cash, few worries, schlepping at a table when a party's going on? And my dear mater, all dressed to the nines trapped at a cake table? This picture generates an odd little thrill. I'm shocked that Diva Lake didn't wrangle some unsuspecting guest into handling the honors in her stead. maybe that wrinkle free wedding planner for instance. Just the thought of her majesty stuck at the entrance to the reception hall lugging packages and acknowledging guests… Precious!

"What you are is ungrateful and rude. Vonda will likely never speak to me again. And of course Jake thought it was all too funny, which really got Vonda going."

Jake is Vonda's husband, so his name is actually Jake Lake. People mostly call him Jacko or J. R., but mom thinks that sounds too 'carnival barker', so she insists on Jake.

Time to retrieve a relationship. "I'm sorry, mom. I don't quite know what happened."

"You headed off with that fluffy man, that's what happened."

"Fluffy? He's six-foot-four. How fluffy can you be brushing against the ceiling?"

She continues reprimanding me. She's had practice. She waxes lyrical about the ramifications of my perfidy, while I take a mental holiday, wandering into the bathroom and searching for nail polish remover. Methodically, I remove the garish polish, de-pigging my toes and fingers. I head back to the kitchen and rinse a few dishes, and review my work schedule for next week.

And occasionally I say, "uh huh," into the mouthpiece.

Mom's tone acquires an edge. "Are you even listening, Dorothy? This is important."

I sigh deeply. "Mom, I'm truly sorry you were disturbed. Can we change the subject?"

The silence drags out.

After a dramatic pause, she resumes. "I'll pretend that terrible rudeness did not come from my daughter. You better not pull this stunt at my wedding."

Now I'm sighing repeatedly, echoing mom's level of drama. This is not good. "Ma, look, I'm hung the hell over and I have to work tomorrow. Can we rehash this at another time?"

The disconnecting click indicates that no, perhaps not.

Oh my god, I'm so naughty.

And it's delicious. Being bad is delicious.

People who regularly bend, twist and mutilate the rules to serve themselves can't comprehend what the last twenty-four hours have done for me. In one evening, I untangled myself from a lifetime of demands and expectations. This is virgin territory for me.

Virgin! It's a joke! Oh I make myself laugh, hardy har.

Ooh my head.

CHAPTER FOUR

I spend all of Saturday and Sunday in a happy vegetative state. I blow off my weekend chores, (vacuuming, bathrooms, dusting), and for the first time in history, nurse a hangover while watching reruns of The Swan. I don't return anymore calls from my mom.

By Monday, though, I'm just Dot again, good daughter, software geek. I'm no longer the bell of any ball, gay or straight. I'm Invisi-gal, riding the Metro to Microcosm. I pop open a Barbara Cartland romance, "The Devil In Love" and try to read. As I drift along, the hero in Babs's novel makes an appearance in my head riding his fine horse, wearing a dashing purple suit. And he's gay.

I start laughing, and suddenly I'm at work.

———————◼❚◼———————

And fourteen hours later, I'm still here, stuck at

Microcosm waiting for the completion of this software test pass from hell. The excitement of watching a scrolling screen of numbers died hours ago. Mainlining Cherry Coke isn't helping fight off the loopiness. Fellow tester Ted Wheeler arrives with Taco Time (two crisp beef burritos and a large order of Mexi-fries for me) and the two of us inhale Americanized Mexican food. The heavy food accelerates an impending bout of narcolepsy, and reawakens my thirst. Ted calls it quits - he's got a family at home - and I grab a couple of Cherry Cokes from the fridge down the hall to stave off sleep.

The computer beeps, nearly scaring me out of my skin as the regression screeches to a halt, three tests from the end. Crap crap and Cherry Cola crap. Now I have to contact the developer responsible for that chunk and request a fix. I glance at the screen and locate the person's email alias: jMiller. jMiller will be one unhappy camper when he or she learns their module crashed the regression test. Boo hoo. My problem is your problem. I locate the phone number matching the email alias from the emergency call roster and dial. jMiller is a he. I apologize, share the joy, turn off the overhead light and drop my head onto the desk for a catnap.

The nap must have deepened into actual sleep because I wake to a shadow blotting out the doorway. Not being completely awake, I make one of those horrible spasmodic moves one can only make between sleep and wakefulness, the one where every limb thrashes out to prevent a fall. The wraith speeds forward into the light of the monitor. It's just a guy.

"Gad! You scared the crap out of me." I'd thrown a hand to my massive, heaving chest, real fainting heroine stuff.

"Sorry, sis. Unintentional." Dark figure yawns and takes another step into the room. He extends a hand. "John Miller. You rang?"

He towers over my desk, and my girl brain does the math, pegs him for maybe six one or so. His name rings a bell somewhere far in the back of my mind.

Sparks fly as he brushes the clutter from my desk and ravishes me right there, amid the monitors.

I kid, I kid.

I shake his hand and scootch my chair over, waving at a similar one stashed next to the wall. With some difficulty he wedges the other chair in and we get right down to it, the business of debugging.

Developers don't make me nervous as a general rule and few resemble George Clooney. Okay they never do. They look like Bill Gates or Comic Book Guy from The Simpsons: they have bad hair cuts, and questionable hygiene. They hug themselves, and rock back and forth. They wear ugly shoes and are significantly overweight. And most are super bright, very competent types.

Wait…I just described myself. Maybe I should consider a move into development?

What little I can make out of jMiller, however, breaks the mold. At least as far as I can discern in the eerie glow of a computer monitor. He also looks vaguely familiar, like I know him. Miller's a common name...

"Didn't mean to freak you."

I inhale deeply, trying to re-oxygenate my tired mind. That proves a big mistake. A whisper of some very male cologne tickles my tired nose and slams into a weakened side of my brain, practically knocking me from the chair. Holy cow he smells good. "You just caught me off guard, is all. Sorry to hassle you at this hour, but Greg says anything that crashes the build – "

"I know, I know. 'When you crashes da build, you misses da milestone.' Greg thinks he's quite the wit." He grins, flashing movie star teeth. "Stupid catchphrase has been burned into my brain. It's like that Head-On commercial where they just bore it into you. I could slap the crap out of him."

His eyes skim over the monitor. "Don't sweat it. I have a pretty good idea where it failed. That jackass Samir probably forgot to rename his module to the new naming specs, so when I instance it here – " he points at a line on the screen, "I'm doomed."

"Doomed!" I chime in. Too tempting. Can't be helped. It cried out for repetition.

"Doomed!" He quickly follows up. We grin at each other and he shows off the superstar smile again, teeth gleaming in the dark.

And again, familiar. Some dim, lizard part of my brain recognizes him. With those teeth, maybe he's done a TV commercial. He types furiously for a few minutes then hesitates. "Do you have source control on this machine?"

I get up to stretch. If he didn't smell so fabulous, I'd collapse for certain, but now I have a mini adrenaline rush. "I have Source Safe but I don't have security access to do check-ins."

He nods, and net connects to his machine, stops, looks up again, "You don't mind me using your machine? Saves me running over to another building."

"Heck no. I've just been sitting too long."

He glances over at the romance novel cracked open on the desk and smiles at the monitor. "Power reading?"

I grimace. "Don't start with me. This test has been running since… well since forever. Pay me overtime or let me read my trashy romance in peace."

"As you wish, sis." He returns his attention to the issue at hand. The two fingered typing style works for him: his hands fly over the keys. "So easy. Seconds to compile…and done. I'll just check this in. I'll log it so Greg doesn't blow a hemorrhoid." He stretches. Fun to watch. I sense the presence of many muscles, so foreign to computer scientists. And to me personally.

"I better phone Jaime to restart the build," he says.

I stare at his shoes, as that is a safe place to look. Converse. Basic white. Old school. "He's going to kill you, you know." I caution.

"Oh no doubt, no doubt." He gets to his feet and the light from the hall illuminates him fully. I risk looking up. "But we've enjoyed our little midnight romp long enough. When I call Jaime, I'll redirect responsibility on Samir. He will in turn, point at Raul for changing the naming conventions midway through a project build. I will be the genius who averted disaster." He closes his eyes briefly, lowering the high beams. "You may as well head home. You can't retest till the next build."

That clinched it. I know him, all right. I swallow hard, shake my head slowly. "No bus at this hour. I'll crash here."

"Poor transportation choice. Stay and Greg will have you rerunning the entire regression test in a couple of hours. Think this through."

I try and smile sadly. "The trials of a software tester. I knew I should have stuck with my first career choice: high priced hooker."

He snorts a laugh.

Oh, the things which emerge from my mouth when I'm nervous.

"You need a ride? I can give you a lift."

My quota of stupid comments is not quite up. What comes out is, "That's nice of you, but I live clear out in Monroe."

"That's not a drive. That's an adventure." His turn to yawn. "Well you can't say I didn't offer, sis. I'm gonna book. See ya."

"Later jMiller."

He leaves.

When he is definitely gone, I will Google him.

But I wait for a few minutes, because I need to know for certain he won't make a surprise return. Because if my guess is correct...

Invisi-gal, Googling.

When I track down the correct John Miller, I

put my face in my hands, shake a little, take a few deep breaths.

So much for Prince Charming.

CHAPTER FIVE

What are the odds? After three disastrous marriages, I wouldn't have believed a man exists willing to take on my mom's psychic baggage. Enter Rupert Rooney, director of sales for the British bond firm Wilkes and Dunning. He and ma met up at some soiree or another, probably drawn by their respective need to let appearances dominate every aspect of their lives.

I know, I know. I'm becoming a mean spirited shrew. But wouldn't you be? This is my mother's forth wedding. Excuse me? I said fourth. I haven't had a single date in my entire life, (unless my recent outing by Kennedy J in a gay bar counts), and here my mother is walking down the aisle again.

I coaxed her out of a white wedding dress. Watching the woman who gave birth to me parading around in the flag of virginity is wrong, so I played the appearance card: told her white makes her look a tad sallow.

Now she stands next to Rupert Rooney wearing blush pink. She looks fantastic as usual.

This time there's no Kennedy J hovering nearby to prevent boredom.

We have been exchanging emails since Ginny's wedding. The most recent detailed his working with the precocious offspring of a WWF superstar gunning to be the next Julia Roberts. Thus he was not available to escort, kiss kiss.

I had briefly thought about John Miller, the hottie from work as a possibility. When the laughter-induced side cramps subsided, images of Jasper (may haps a plumber?) from group floated into view. Hmm. This degree of fantasy proves I have been reading too many Barbara Cartland romances lately.

I can see it unfold: I ask Jasper, he turns fuchsia, stares at the ground while making up some excuse about how he can't miss Aunt Brunhilde's operatic debut at the Met so he'll have to take a pass, then flees therapy forever, resulting in a lifetime of grief and loneliness for us both.

Nah. I like Jasper. No sense amping up any lingering social phobias he may harbor. One of us is plenty.

And so here I stand, the dateless maid of honor. Mom thought the notion of me acting as her maid of honor cute as hell. She believes she's doing me a solid by placing me in the spotlight, where all the eligible men can find me.

"Just think Dorothy. All dressed up and standing at the altar – that's visibility, right? Maybe Mister Right is sitting in a pew just waiting for you to walk down the aisle and into his life."

I didn't bother to argue the point. She's right, after all: what's to prevent that bronze god with the well-groomed fingernails from ignoring his hospital pager, dropping to one knee, and instantly proposing, (overwhelmed with sexual attraction by the sight of my monstrously lime taffeta ass)?

Oh, ouch. Still suffering from a bit of residual rib soreness from the previous laugh riot.

I have altar vision, so I must be circumspect while looking around. What I glimpse is a bevy of mom's cronies on one side and Rupert Rooney's pot bellied golf buddies on the other, row after row of them, sorted by degree of hairline recession. This paunch pool, according to my mother, holds my future husband.

I contemplate my destiny as perma-bridesmaid. Would any thinking person intentionally spend hard earned cash striving to look exactly as dreadful as the gal next to her? Or in my case, worse? Since more fabric is required, I can claim a higher degree of wrongness. Oh the situation could be worse I suppose… maybe toss in leprosy?

The wedding is a bold, colorful affair. Mom refused to consider having Kennedy J plan it. Rupert Rooney insisted he pay for mom to have her 'fantasy wedding' and I immediately thought of Kennedy J. Mom's stuck her lip out like a stubborn two-year-old.

"Dorothy, I've been married three times already."

"Well aware, mom. I was there for two of them. Your point?"

"Well… each time, somebody foisted their opinions on me. First Timmy's mom Gladys bullied her way into every decision from dress to flowers. I told you I got stuck carrying daisies, didn't I? I hate daisies!"

I nod. Heard the daisy story before. Many, many times.

"Well she was paying for everything as she reminded me every single second of every day. She wouldn't spring for roses, the tightfisted old – "

"Ma! It's okay." I pat her arm.

But she's on a rampage. "Then Curtis. Well of course he planned every single thing down to the flatware pattern. Beautiful, I'll admit, but I had nothing to do with it."

Curtis was her second husband. Sweet guy. He stuck around just long enough to finish design school. Now he lives with a lovely man named Nathan down in San Fran somewhere. Mom refuses to believe he's gay.

She should. He is.

She's still rambling, " – and I don't even want to get into the whole Conrad thing. Well that was all just a fast Vegas mess."

Couldn't agree more. Especially since ole Connie Jeffers routinely scarred my soul with his verbal backhanded comments. Lord she's still talking.

" – so I'm doing this one right. Just for me." With a satisfied bob of her head, mom snatched up the phone. Next thing I know, she and Vonda Lake were off to the races. I wisely pled a full work schedule, but promise to do whatever I was told.

The resulting cacophony of sight and sound is a combination of Vonda Lake, the opinions of a bridge club, and the bold vision of my thrice-married mom.

After leafing through perhaps a thousand wedding magazines, (most geared to the barely pubescent bride), mom spies an ad for a tropical honeymoon getaway. You know: palm trees, tequila sunset. God help us all, she was inspired.

The result stuns. Mom's gone with a Hawaiian theme. There's even an entire roasted pig for the reception. However, before I can escape into a coconut and pineapple haze of Pina Coladas, (this alcohol thing is far more medicinal than I had previously known), I and the cast of the 'Bridge Over Troubled Waters Card Club' must first meander down the aisle to Don Ho's ukulele and the crooning warble of "Tiny Bubbles."

Super.

Mom's aged bridesmaids sulk in taffeta of such an intense lime green it could fry your retinas. I'd laugh at them, but I'm in a coordinating lime green taffeta print. Mine's made more conspicuous by enormous hibiscus flowers tattooed all over it. The bow at the back could hide illegal immigrants. I fear retaliation for wearing something this garish in a house of God so I lit a votive when I came in just in case.

Now, holding a single hibiscus that somehow manages to clash with the dress, I watch ma make the big walk.

I'm stunned: she looks fabulous. Her pink gown appears surprisingly appropriate in the dim church lighting. She holds some sort of pale green foliage, thin and grass like. There are pale apple green ribbons dangling from it. She looks all of thirty and I assure you she drove past that number decades ago. Her skin glows when she takes Rupert Rooney's hand. I brush aside tears and mess up the new base makeup Kennedy J emailed me about. My mom looks like a goddess.

I pull a Tammy Faye, tracking mascara on both cheeks.

The ceremony is sweet and touching and the reception is an absolute blast. Who would'a thunk it? The roasted pig tastes a dream. I find myself in a line of the smiling elderly dancing to "Conga" by Gloria Estefan, trying not to upset the paper umbrella in my drink on the crowded dance floor. Did I mention I've taken up alcohol?

It totally destroys my efforts to remain in a funk.

I bump into Richard and Delilah Driscoll and we exchange updates. They used to live two houses down from us when mom was still with Conrad, so I spent a lot of time hiding out there with their obnoxious son, Sean. He used to practice his karate punches on my held up palms. Shocking we didn't end up an item, right? Delilah slyly mentions that Sean is visiting between tours. Perhaps I should give him a ring?

Bless her, she's mental. Sean's a poster boy for the Marines – I mean an actual poster here: the one where you see this hot guy looking too cool for school piloting a helicopter on a recruiting sign. That is, of course, when he's not off saving people in undisclosed locations as part of a special ops group. Last time I talked to him, probably five years ago, he still spoke in grunts and hand motions. I suspect this resulted from always getting his way, so he never had much use for speech.

My hands start to ache and throb just thinking about ole Sean.

The Driscolls have ocular issues or they'd never consider me for their son. When I knew him, he had hooked up with a dangerously thin Goth girl sporting a ring through her lip.

Just thinking about flat stomached girls threatens to bring on a wave of depression, so I escape politely from the Driscolls. Still distracted by visions of anorexic vampire chicks with multiple piercings, I smack hard into Jasper Atkins, (Mr. Elbow Patches himself) from group.

He's wearing this sharp suit, a conservative navy pinstripe, and the shoes match. Fashion wise, he's made a major forward leap from the tweed thing. In these duds, I'm thinking CEO, not plumber. Maybe a surgeon? He's even trimmed up the facial hair. Very nice.

He catches me staring and blushes, but not quite the fuchsia I'd feared him capable of. He surveys his feet for a moment before giving the conversational ball a toss.

"'Yo, Dot. You look…"

"Oh don't bother searching for an adjective, Jasper. Nothing quite captures this." I roll my eyes. "Nice to see you, though. What brings you to the wide world of weddings?"

His blush darkens to a charming pink. "First

date." He tugs his head to the right, indicating a waif of a girl with insufficient mass to classify as a woman. The only thing keeping her earthbound is an abundance of red-gold hair and flawless skin. She's deep in conversation with an equally underfed girl. They're exchanging diet secrets is my bet.

My hand itches to slap her but Jasper's still talking.

"… not my choice for a first date. It seems way too… serious. You know? Bringing someone to a wedding? But my mom had her heart set on it and I couldn't bring myself to talk her down."

"She's very pretty, Jasper."

He shakes his head in denial. "She's whiney." The fine lines at the corner of his eyes crinkle, making him appear confused. "She's got these fingernails like Wolverine's." He holds up his hands, makes a claw fist. "You know, the guy from X-Men?"

Secretly, I'm thrilled to hear this little stab at Penny Perfect. "Trying to get voted out of group?" This seems to go over his head. I switch course, "So how'd you meet?"

"She does my mom's hair. Apparently that makes her perfect for me. Perhaps because we're both unmarried and disease free. Well, I am anyway. A slam dunk, right?" He drops his voice a notch. "She has two kids by two different men and a ring through her belly button. She scares the crap out of me. And she brought her friend. She asked if she could bring her BFF along for company. I thought it was a book, or some weird breed of pocket dog. Instead she brings her girlfriend along."

He sighs heavily, shakes his head.

Note to self: introduce these two to Sean Driscoll ASAP. "So does your hairdresser know Rupert Rooney or the bride?"

"Neither as far as I know. My mom belongs to the bride's bridge club. She sent me as her emissary while she's off in Mexico on a cruise."

I nod. "Ah, the 'Bridge Over Troubled Waters' gals. Your mom's a player?"

He stifles a laugh. "That's not an expression I would normally equate with my mother, but yeah, that's her group. I take it your mom's with them too?"

I grin. "My mom's the bride. Thus, the shocking fashion faux pas." I wave at my dress.

He grins back. "No kidding? You know, Dot, she looks amazing. Really."

Damn it she does. Which is great, honestly. Nothing quite says wonderful like your mom looking amazing at her forth wedding. A muscle in my cheek tenses up. "It's nice of you to say so." Everyone always does. Bless them.

The redhead struts over and drops a proprietary hand on Jasper's arm. She snaps some chewing gum, an oddly infantile behavior in the face of this aging population. "You ready, Dr. J?"

I raise both eyebrows at Jasper. "Doctor? Do you play basketball or carry a stethoscope?"

He finally achieves that fuchsia shade I feared. He dips his head toward the girl. "Tiffany, this is Dot Lindell. Dot, my date, Tiffany Bunch."

I want to say something snide. I really do, but thank god for social niceties. "Nice to meet you,

Tiffany."

At that moment, Aunt Vonda sends out the stink eye from over at her position near the cake table. Rats. No time to grill my new friend Tiff about Jasper's medical credentials. "Gotta go." I pin Jasper with one last look, trying to read a profession there. Nothing. Clearly my career as a psychic has stalled. I do the hitchhiker thumb over my shoulder, aiming in Vonda's direction. "Duty calls."

"Nice seeing you, Dot." He nearly stumbles when Tiffany tugs him off toward the bar.

From my spot behind the cake table, where I remain Velcroed by Aunt Vonda's frequent glares, I observe the new couple do the honors. Mom and Rupert look like teenagers rather than a dignified married couple. Rupert Rooney, (who I've secretly been calling "Lord Rooney" given his stiff upper lip style), wipes smashed cake off his face and beard, eyes crinkling with laughter, while mom giggles behind her hand like a geisha. I'm struck by a sense of possibility. Maybe this one will work for her.

I know, I know. It's the spiked punch talking.

Still, what if this is the real thing? What if this time mom has found that Vaseline covers the lens and she Rupert are running through a field of wildflowers into each others' arms? What if this is real? I take a mental snapshot of them: Rupert's hand a gentle brace in the small of her back, she leaning slightly into him, acknowledging the touch.

I swipe a fist at my damp face, leaving a thin trail of mascara on the back of my hand. No one thought to add pockets to the hibiscus dress, so I'm stuck without a Kleenex. I wipe the mess onto the side of the dress, leaving a dark smudge on the already vile fabric.

Good riddance.

I serve cake for hours. For days. Forever. My hands continue to push cake, but my brain takes a holiday, creates little mini movies. In one, John Miller sweeps in, demanding I dance with him. Magically, the loud dress I wear disappears replaced by some Barbara Cartland inspired ball gown. Like Barb's heroines, my body in that dress appears waif-like, delicate.

Then Jasper Atkins – that's DOCTOR Jasper Atkins – swaggers onto the dance floor wearing hospital scrubs. He drags me from John's arms. The two face off, scowls of testosterone fueled anger on their faces as they prepare to fight for my hand.

So I'm a bit startled by Tiffany Bunch's open palm shoved in my face. I lurch back, worried she plans on punching me out, before I come to: she wants cake. Her vacuous gaze makes it clear that she doesn't recall our brief meeting, or more likely, chooses not to recall it. I'm just the help and she wants free cake. Give it.

I slap a broken piece on a plate, happy to note that it is a bit short on frosting. I shove it unnecessarily hard into her hand. It's a paper plate. Maybe she'll tear a nail? A girl can dream.

Eventually the new couple makes their exit, an exodus of their friends and family in their wake. I schlep behind the partygoers, tidying up so mom doesn't lose her deposit. That's the price for not helping with wedding plans. I pay the caterers with checks Rupert Rooney filled out in advance. I make a quick pass around the floor using an enormous mop head designed for the purpose, but refuse to go the extra mile and search for a dustpan. I cut the lights and lock the door behind me.

I'm alone in the dark in a sweat stained, mascara marked taffeta dress. There's no one around to offer me a ride.

I have to ride the bus home in this damn dress.

THE BRIDESMAID REVOLTS

You might even feel like the bride wants you to look like crap. While, in fact, there are stories of brides who have confessed to choosing poorly cut dresses and ridiculous hairdos on their bridesmaids in an effort to ensure the maids don't outshine them on their big day, a bride who is a true friend will want you to look and feel your best. She just won't have time to show you how. That's where you come in.

excerpt from The Bridesmaid's Manual *by Sarah Stein & Lucy Talbot, Page 102)*

CHAPTER SIX

Another neutral day in my beige office. I barely register as a sentient being. Watching numbers in a table increment hardly qualifies as living. This is the bare bones of an existence, tasteless, odorless, without texture. I guzzle my third Cherry Coke of the day – liquid sugar heavily spiked with caffeine – and my body disregards the rush. I'm that numb.

The rerun of my automation suite finishes. I stretch, yawn, and dip my hands into the pockets of my sweats. There's something crammed in there: a battered business card. 'Kennedy J – Image Consultant.' I don't recall putting it there. We email each other once in awhile. The guy's hilarious when kvetching about his latest escapade. He's even funny when badgering me for free computer advice, or to come in for an overhaul.

I stare at the card.

Crumpled from its stint in my pocket, his card still conveys elegance with its simple script. A hint of scarlet takes it just over the top. Like Kennedy J himself.

"Watcha got there?" Ted pokes his head in the doorway. He's giving me a ride home tonight, (bless him), and his long face is welcome. Ted broke down and bought a minivan yesterday and is so eager to put miles on it, he's willing to drive to Monroe. He wanders in, hangs over my shoulder. His narrow face and equally thin frame remind me of a praying mantis, a sweet tempered insect in glasses, hovering.

"It's a business card from a guy I met at a wedding."

He pulls back and faces me. Behind his specs, his brows do the woo-woo that presumes an interested suitor, "Fish on, D. A. Lindell."

I roll my eyes. "He's gay, Ted."

"Oh. What business's he in?"

"He's an image consultant."

Ted bends his insect head to the side. "What exactly is that?"

I push out my lower lip. "Hell if I know. Pretty funny guy, though. And he sure knows how to dress. He dresses people, I guess. Picks their clothes. Chooses their accessories and such."

"You're thinking of hiring this guy?" There's a hint of laughter in Ted's voice.

Now that's an excellent question. "I don't know." I logoff. I'm done here. "You ever feel stuck, Ted? Like this frigging beige-a-topia," I pass a hand around the room, "is all there is? I keep waiting for something to happen, something to change, and then it does. It rains harder."

"You need a vacation."

"Clearly. From what? To where? I don't think a vacation is going to magically solve my problems."

"What needs fixing?"

I snort. That comment earned a snorting. "Are you friggin kiddin, Ted? Look at me. I'm a mess. I'm a relationship black hole. There's nothing even remotely attractive about me." I actually said that out loud. Shouted it, to be fair. To a coworker, for goodness sake.

He assumes a schoolmarm stance, complete with crossed arms. I believe he's just created a new insect: The Praying School Marm. "What's not to like? Everyone likes you, Dot. You've been watching too much reality TV is all."

My jaw drops. "Everybody likes me? Are you brain damaged, Ted? Oh my god, you've been married to Tiffany for what is it – five years? You have your high school sweetheart and twin girls and that goddamn new minivan. You're a developer, not some second rate tester. What do you know about being a loser? Being lonely? Being second rate?"

Can you imagine this? I'm brow beating a guy who drives a mini-van. I have lost my mind. Poor Ted fidgets there, all insect-y nerves. Sorry, bug man, I think. I inhale deeply, trying to lower my thermostat from ornery down to supportive fellow employee. No more word burps! I have to work with this guy. My breath shoots out as a heavy sigh. "I'm sorry, Ted. Maybe I've been putting in too many hours on this regression."

Ted blinks behind his specs. "Don't sweat it. Sleep helps. Heard it blew up in the wee hours and you had to call in the big guns."

"That so?"

"Heard you zapped jMiller over in Building 17. That guy is wicked cool. I couldn't believe he got caught on a rookie mistake. I howled, kid you not."

Wicked cool is the ultimate compliment. It suggests jMiller writes solid code, free of logic and syntax errors. Bully for him. I don't want to swap yarns about Mr. Wonderful, either. I slide my laptop into the oversized plastic beach bag I use in lieu of a purse. "Listen, thanks again for the ride, Ted. I'm full on done with public transportation."

He shakes his head. "You should buy a car, Dot."

CHAPTER SEVEN

Thanks to Ted, I get home in record time: it's only seven thirty, in time for Jeopardy. After a rough evening in game show land, (geography, sports and Grammy Awards are hardly my categories), I take a long shower and wander, dripping, into the kitchen. Still wrapped in an enormous towel, I take a second to peruse my Gary Larson calendar. May features a cow smoking a cigarette. That cow has a more active social life than I do.

I flip from May to June. The entire month is empty, save work. No little penciled in to-do's, no appointments, just day after day of work recorded in pencil in case my shifts get changed. For the first time in forever, there isn't even a wedding listed. Not even in June. This is my whole life, empty squares on a grid, scribbled in pencil.

The cold hits me. Cold's good. Shivers distract me from a crying jag that threatens. If it gets underway, it might never end. I dig through the pantry and retrieve a 12 pack of Hostess Ding Dongs to accompany my Cherry Coke. Without bothering to lose the towel, I head for the sofa, throw my enormous tattered comforter over myself and flip the tube back on. Don't want to hear myself making sniveling sounds.

Fortunately, I'm distracted by some of that reality TV Ted mentioned earlier. It's a rerun of Extreme Makeover. A bat-faced wallflower appears on screen, complete with humped nose and pudgy, gelatinous body. This girl won't be competing for America's Next Top Model any time soon.

Footage of bat girl petting a horse runs while her overdubbed voice describes being teased and tormented. She talks about high school and the abuse she suffered in the halls. Now she's shown split screen, side by side, in profile and from the front. The images rotate as they show a list of procedures she'll undergo, the things she's willing to subject herself to in order to fix the mess she so clearly is. They're going to gut her like a fish.

They cut to commercial: Eat Taco Time it proclaims. Bring it on, says I.

Poor batty's back. She's cut, stitched and stapled, scraped and peeled away in layers. She looks like she fell out of a fourteen story building. The visible parts are mottled black and blue, the remainder of her is bandages. Egad!

Then it begins in earnest: they diet, detox, toughen and surgically alter her. But then, a miracle: at five minutes to nine she's unveiled for her family and friends. And what they reveal is an entirely different person, unrecognizable as bat faced girl. This girl is…attractive. Her family cheers. My heart swells.

They cut to another commercial.

Suddenly the Ding Dong I'm noshing on tastes unpleasantly waxy. Didn't even realize I was eating it. Nor did I note the other three, (which clearly I have eaten, given the foil wrappers littering my coffee table). I stuff the remains of number four in my mouth and click off the TV.

I'm consumed by thoughts of bat girl. She could be my twin. Her "before" picture anyway. And the problems she had in high school, we certainly share that legacy.

My high school yearbook is buried on the bottom bookshelf. I remove Data Abstraction and Problem Solving in C++, and Steve McConnell's Rapid Development to dig it out. I'm a little surprised it's still there. I should have burned it. I flop down Indian style, grunting a bit to get comfortable.

I flip open the yearbook and it cracks at the page where the binding has broken, falls open flat on the ground in front of me.

My photo is the far left at the bottom of the page. Obviously demented, at the time the picture was taken, I believed I looked lovely. The girl in the picture has a permed helmet of hair, her features barely discernible through the heavy makeup and rolls of flesh. And artwork had been added to the picture, boldly drawn. In the margin next is a large W scrawled by Jack Weston. He used a Sharpie.

I take a breath, and wonder if it will still hurt as

badly.

—————————◼◼—————————

Just before the picture was snapped, I sit on the floor in front of my locker. The senior class has been given three hours for yearbook signing, and the decibel level in the halls is intense. Boys snatch yearbooks from the hands of their secret crushes, daring a "have a great summer" in bold script. Girls send out scouts to perform the same task. A girlfriend would grab the yearbook of the target boy, hand it to her friend where the two would collaborate and giggle for fifteen minutes on exactly what words convey the right message: very interested, but not a stalker.

Ginny already signed my yearbook the day before, eager to get it over with. No one should see a cheerleader consorting with the likes of me. Mel and I were barely speaking at this point, but she scribbles a token "have a good summer" over her picture in an attempt at sainthood. What a gal. Since those two signatures sum up my entire high school experience, I plan on getting to my feet and getting the hell out of Dodge.

I am about to close the yearbook when someone snags it from my hand.

"Couldn't let you leave the building without my words of wisdom, now could we Snotty?" Jack Weston has my yearbook in his hand. His face twists into his usual Grinch inspired grin. I might find him attractive... had he not made my life a living hell. His features are angular, his eyes narrow but an intriguing snake green. Under the circumstances, however, beads of sweat begin a slow slide down my back. I half expect those emerald eyes to be slit vertically.

"Let's see... something memorable, noteworthy. I wouldn't want you to forget our special times together..."

He refers to fine times like the day he brought binoculars to school and shouted "Whale Spotted!" whenever he passed me in the hall. Or the time he brought a harpoon to school. He landed a two day suspension for that stunt, but was spared expulsion by virtue of his value to our football team. One doesn't trifle with a starting wide receiver when in the running for a state title. The faculty felt his skills clearly outweighed his offenses against me. After all, he didn't shoot me.

There were a lot more "times." I've tried to block them out.

He trills his fingers across the face of the yearbook, a dull drumming sound that I clearly hear over the din in the hall. "What to write, what to write." He leans back against a row of lockers. No hurry, no worry for Jack Weston.

If I had paid for that stupid yearbook with my own money instead of asking mom to spring for it, I'd abandon it, leave it behind and high tail it out of there. Nothing terribly memorable took place in High School that I wouldn't just as soon forget. Instead, I get clumsily to my feet.

"Give it back, Weston." I attempt a bored expression.

"Now, don't be impatient, Snotty. It doesn't become you." He looks off at the ceiling, waits for the muse to direct him. Suddenly he shouts above the din, "I've got it!" This catches the attention of the hall crowd, (always a priority for good ole' Jack) and even over the general chaos, a number of heads turn expectantly to find out what Jack Weston is up to. He takes a minute to record his thoughts.

Then, to my shock, he returns the yearbook to me, smiling, "That oughtta do it, Snots. You are sooo welcome." Jack the Jock turn to a thin girl wearing enormous shoulder pads. He snaps her bra strap as she passes and she pulls away squealing. He chases after her and the giggles faded out down the hall. The crowd quickly loses interest.

Compared to earlier encounters, this is tame. Few people witness the exchange. Jack used words for weapons this time, (unlike two weeks earlier: who knew a finger could be so painful? He snuck up behind me, poked a finger sharply into a roll of fat on my back and screamed, "Help! I'm sinking! Get the jaws of life!"

Oh, he is a card, our Jack, a real cut-up.

This time it's just some Weston-ian words of wisdom, just some scribbles in a yearbook. I can handle it. I leave High School without cracking it open. I don't even peek at it on the bus. I read my Barbara Cartland (The Taming of Lady Lorinda) to pass the time till I'm safely home.

But when at last I'm home, the door to my room closed, I have to look. Like a car accident. Like a canker sore you have to worry with your tongue.

I start at the back, scroll forward past pictures of the drama club and chess team, leaf through the senior photos till I find my picture, overwritten in Sharpie pen. He'd added sow ears and a snout to my photo. A budding artist, our Jack. He had added the caption: "You're an ugly, fat ass, Snotty, and this photo proves you don't take the cake, you ATE the cake! And donuts, Twinkies, and the Space Needle! No dessert for you! J.W."

———————◄◗►———————

I glaze over. I'm not sure how long. I sit there with that dreadful cartoon of myself and realize that is what I see whenever I look in a mirror. Or in someone's eyes. That is what I see.

Zombie-like, the phone is in my hand and I am dialing the number from Kennedy J's business card. I have it memorized, and some dulled part of my brain is surprised by this. No one is answering of course – it's nighttime – and I endure the recorded message, relieved at having a moment to collect myself. The voice on the recording isn't Kennedy, but a smooth sounding male FM radio voice suggesting I leave a detailed message and that the call would be returned as soon as possible.

I hear my voice, which sounds nothing like I remember. "This is Dot Lindell. Dorothy. For Kennedy J. Kennedy, I met you at Ginny's wedding. It's important I speak with you - professionally." I leave both my home number and my cell number. No playing hard to get. This is war.

I stumble toward the bathroom tripping over the comforter and dropping the towel. I glare at myself in the mirror, then take a good, hard look. I haven't looked at myself in years, not on purpose anyway, and I'm scared shitless now.

At first I'm shocked. I mean it. I'm grossed out by the roundness of my face, my piggy little eyes. I've had skin problems for as long as I can remember, but now I record each and every rupture, forcing myself to see what others see. Oh my god, my skin sucks. I work my way down. My nose got fatter. I've never been skinny, but I don't recall my face being circular. The mirror face has extra chins, or a spare neck, or both. My head appears to be melting into my shoulders. I don't look like the terrible image enhanced by Jack Weston in my year book. I look infinitely worse. And that's just from the front.

I turn a bit so I can see over my shoulder what my backside looks like. I despise that extra roll of skin on my back, my 'back bacon,' Jack Weston's location of choice. It's a puzzle how I cram all the flesh into a bra. It only gets worse from their down.

I inhale deeply. Well, we've certainly gotten a handle on the problem areas.

But my hair's good. Mom calls it "Pantene hair": shiny, super straight and incredibly thick. Currently it hangs in damp ropes to my waist, but even wet, the color is darn good, sort of a copper color. Normally hair this thick is course, but not mine. Usually I just rope it back in a ponytail or bun, away from notice. The hair is good, though. I take comfort in the hair. One of the biggest mistakes I ever made was perming it back in the eighties. The hair is okay.

Mouth isn't bad, but a bit lost in my fleshy face. Still, women pay big bucks to have their lips look like mine. Heck, I saw a gal plump hers up on Extreme Makeover just a couple of weeks ago.

Physically, that's about it. The positive side of the balance sheet is a bit light.

The phone rings and I jump two feet in the air. No one calls me but work and my mom and neither has a reason to call tonight. I pick up in a panic. Someone or something must have died.

"Dorothy, Kennedy J. here. I must be a tad psychic today, because I just had to check my messages – shut up Jefferson – and there it was. The time has come."

In my head, I see Gene Wilder rapidly sliding his hands back and forth across each other, doing his mad scientist impersonation from Young Frankenstein.

"Giselle will clear my schedule for the next few days. So first thing tomorrow, yes?"

I backpedal. "I'll have to check with work. Make sure it's okay."

"Tomorrow. Make your excuses. You're ill. You're cat died."

"I don't own a cat."

"I'm surprised yet relieved. You miss the point. No stalling. Tomorrow."

"You're sure?" I hear him make a growling noise through the phone. "Right. Okay. So I'll call work and tell them I need to take a couple of personal days. I'll come by tomorrow."

CHAPTER EIGHT

I've never been to this part of town before. I've lived in Washington State for twelve years, and within forty-five minutes of Seattle for most of them, and rarely have I ventured downtown.

On one street, I witness terrible decline: trash lined shop fronts, fading paint, questionable types hovering near the entrances. A block further and everything's revitalized: fresh facades and scrubbed entries punctuated by oversized sculptures and planters, briefcase carrying types hustling by. I pause in front of the new library, Ren Kuhlhaas's anthem to coolness: steel diamonds interlock to form an exoskeleton – sort of an oversized erector set. A guy taps my shoulder, invites me to donate to a Gay Rights cause. In honor of Curtis Mayer, (dad number two), I fork over ten bucks and the stranger rewards me with directions, sending me past the enormous Hammering Man statue and down toward the water. By the time I reached the granite entry to

Kennedy J's salon, I am both intimidated and winded despite the fact that the climb was downhill.

The entry is flanked by two enormous columns. Miles Davis plays soulfully from a speaker somewhere, and I consider remaining here, enjoying Miles and the pretty mosaic floor tiles for the remainder of the day. I chide myself for being such a chicken and head inside.

The reception area is a semi circle of mahogany, illuminated by delicate pendant lights suspended on fourteen-foot cables that draw my eyes up. It smells wonderful. Vanilla? Citrus? I can't place it.

"May I help you?" A smoothly coifed receptionist asks.

And could I feel more gauche in my sweat pants and running shoes? "I'm Dot Lindell. I'm here to see Kennedy J. I phoned ahead."

"Welcome, Dot. I'm Giselle, Kennedy's assistant. Let me get you something to drink and we'll send you right in." She brings out an Asian tea service and talks me through the choices. I'm branching out today, so rather than decline her offer, I select Green Tea. I manage a single sip before Giselle retrieves the tiny cup and leads me to a back room.

Talk about intimidation. Rack after rack of clothes crowd one wall. A three-way mirror flanked by a carved bench takes up a second, and a third is floor to ceiling trinkets and baubles hanging from clear hooks I later learn are glass. It's the antithesis of my office, utterly foreign. I stand like a stump in the middle of all the glam.

Kennedy J floats in from somewhere, hands on hips, eyebrow raised in true diva fashion. "I see you dressed for the occasion, darling." He glances over his shoulder at the receptionist, and motions toward one of the benches. "Thanks Giselle. Leave the tea, dear, and hold those calls."

Giselle sets the cup on a coaster and disappears behind the enormous wooden door. It closes behind her with a soft 'snick.' My stomach does a dive forward roll.

"Tell me you aren't wearing pajamas."

"They're sweat pants."

He puts a hand on either side of my face, looks earnestly into my eyes. "They're flannel, Dorothy. Flannel for the love of God." Kennedy moves his hands to my shoulders and marches me over to face the three-way mirror. This proves more painful than my recent experience at the house. This time, someone else will see me.

"First, we assess."

Did that yesterday. Don't want to go there again. Kennedy begins a stealthy visual inventory. I notice him whispering into a hand held recorder, misting words over the tiny device. His gaze is so intense I briefly forget he's gay. Those feel like heterosexual man eyes on me, which is a foreign experience. He's compiling a laundry list of my faults and failings, something I've experienced practically every day of my life by everyone who meets me. For the longest time, though, I've tuned it out, let it fade into the background. The commentary continues, but now Kennedy's speaks loudly enough for it to register.

"Hair. We love the hair. Just needs styling. Face? Well, my…there are some issues –Becker, I think. Doc Becker ASAP; eyes…they're practically AWOL. Maybe after some of the weight comes off. Mouth, fantastic. Very workable. Chins: one is nice, three's a crowd. No neck…we need a disguise. Power breasts – amen to that! Still, need some lift…"

He goes on like this clear to the ground. I mean he literally makes me take off my shoes and checks my toes, clucks his tongue and records the need for a pedicure. I've never had a manicure or a pedicure.

"I haven't seen your closet, but judging by what you're wearing to see me today, I'll assume you have not one stitch of salvageable clothing." He points at my running shoes. They're New Balance cross trainers, broad enough to house my orthotics and brand spanking new. "And those shoes! Unforgiveable!"

"My arches fell. They help."

His face gets close to mine, "And yet, so ugly. Your arches have fallen because of your excess weight. We'll get you some inoffensive footwear immediately, but I suspect that once the trainer gets a hold of you, your foot problems will fade." He ruminates some more, chews a pen that appears to be made of lapis. My eyes need a place to park, so I check out his manicure. I've never had one. His hands look immaculate, but still masculine.

He gives me a little shake, forces me to reconnect. "You will be a masterpiece. You will be the makeover equivalent of Elton John's Goodbye Yellow Brick Road." He throws a hand up in the air for emphasis, "I waive my fee!"

"That's nice of you, but I considered all this, Kennedy. It's okay – "

"Save your thinking for that vile software company of yours. Trust me you'll need your money. There are a host of professionals waiting for you. Unlike me, their fees will be in stone. However, insurance may cover some of the work. Giselle will do some research."

His hand remains on my shoulder. This feels oddly comforting after being taken apart inch by inch. "You have gifts that are being trampled. We shall... unsquash them, yes?"

"Okay." Suddenly, I come to. "Professionals? What professionals?"

"Well a dermatologist for starters. Surely you know your skin is for shit?"

"Oh, that sweet sugar coating, Kennedy. Yes, I'm aware there's a problem."

"Well Doctor Bhintu Becker is your first stop. She's cutting edge. She'll micro-laser-dermabrasion the living daylights out of that mine field of yours. Then Nancy Meiser."

I scrunch my forehead. "Why do I know that name?"

"She's a master nutritionist. She's on the news all the time. Maybe you've caught her stint on Northwest News? But that's just for starters. Aren't you glad I'm waiving my fee?"

"More than you will ever know."

"Nancy will put together your menu plan for the next few weeks. You'll need to drop about fifteen pounds before we even bother with Doctor

Tam."

Now my eyes bug out, and not in a good way. "Lee Tam? But he's a plastic surgeon?"

"That's the one. You know him? What have you had done?"

"Never met him. I overheard a bunch of women talking about him at work a couple of months ago. They got together and talked him into a group rate. He lipo'd 'em all at a discount. Have you ever heard of anything more twisted?"

He laughs. "Dear, that's sensible, not bizarre. Especially given what Dr. Tam charges. Heartbreaking that you weren't able to get that bulk rate." He gazes off into the distance, a hand under his chin. "But gad he's marvelous. Top notch, really."

The door flies open and a coffee colored dream of a man flies in wearing a gray silk suit and turquoise tie.

"What's this I hear about you not taking calls? Have you lost your mind?" He pauses to acknowledge me politely, "Hello my dear," he says with a heavy British accent. A real one this time, not the slightly East Coast affected version of Kennedy's.

"Hello." I answer.

Kennedy crosses his arms. "Jefferson, don't be sassy. I just need a few days to work with my new project. Dorothy Lindell, my assistant Jefferson Barkley." He turns to me, hand to his face, an aside, "He's imported and testy, but that smile is all about American Dentistry."

Jefferson scowls at Kennedy, bows elegantly

over my hand, "A pleasure Ms. Lindell." He returns to his original mission, glaring through amazing greenish eyes at Kennedy J. "Revealing my secrets just makes me peevish, Kennedy. We have no less than three formal affairs coming up this week and I am being inundated with calls from that twitchy Dame Adams. You need to free up four hours this afternoon to catch up."

Kennedy sighs and begins rifling through his suit pockets. "Three. Tell Giselle. I'm creating." He retrieves a pack of clove cigarettes from his breast pocket, extracts one, making it clear that he's done with this conversation. Jefferson turns on his heel and exits. Kennedy strolls to an elaborate burled wood desk adjacent to the three-way mirror. A low humming noise catches my attention.

He laughs at my confusion. "It's an air filtration system. Jefferson despises smoke, so I had a system installed to protect his delicate sensibilities." He waves his hand toward the desk where a crystal ashtray rests. "It sucks the smoke right out of the air. Isn't that clever? Otherwise all my couture would reek. And that," he taps the butt neatly on the edge of the tray, "would be bad."

He smiles broadly, genuinely. "Oh the fun we're going to have."

CHAPTER NINE

Doctor Devers wiggles her pen back and forth against her clipboard. It looks like butterfly wings.

"You hired an image consultant?" Jasper's eyebrows attempt to hide in his hairline.

"More of a prisoner exchange. I got his computer working and he waived his fee. Which is hardly fair to him. All he needed was Adobe Acrobat installed and bam, problem solved. It's a free download for goodness sakes. Took maybe three minutes. It'll take months to get me overhauled."

Group stares.

"Yes. I hired him."

"Isn't that a little…you know... tragic? Having some stranger dude decide what you're going to look like?" Elvira's problem is not shyness.

I bite down hard on my lower lip to keep from spewing with laughter. "Possibly. But no one's come begging for my style secrets. Whereas

Kennedy win awards for his." I shrug. "Seems like a sensible solution. Calling in the professionals. Like they do on TV."

Anna shakes her head. "Unnatural. Having some man do dis to you."

Jasper considers. "People wear braces to straighten their teeth. They take medicine for medical conditions." He directs his gaze at Anna, "People kick nature in the ass plenty when it serves them."

Dr. Devers swings toward me. "This isn't TV, Dot. The money and the pain won't be a thirty-minute blip with commercial breaks. They'll be real. So my question is, where are your boundaries? Have you decided what's sacred? What you'll protect?"

"Nothing's sacred, Doc. At this point, I intend to follow Kennedy's suggestions to the letter and let the chips, the pounds, and the fashion faux pas fall where they may. I have little to lose."

She frowns. Apparently that's the wrong answer.

"Look, you might want to schedule some private sessions, Dot. Doesn't have to be with me, I can recommend some people."

"Sorry, Doc. My money is going to be tied up for some time. Oh, and that reminds me, I won't be coming to group for the next few weeks."

I'm flattered at the chorus of no's from my fellow cast offs.

"Just for a few weeks. I have all these appointments that Kennedy set up and with all the bus trips –" I let myself trail off, stand up to leave.

Donald and Susan shake my hand. Elvira cracks an eerie black smile and wishes me luck. "Come back and show off the new look, right?" She shoves a card into my hand. Oh my heavens the girl has a business card! I push it into my pocket.

"Thanks, El."

Anna clucks her tongue disapprovingly. "I vish you vould retink dis decision. But I hope all vill be vell wit you." She surprises me by jumping up and giving me a quick peck on the cheek.

Mikey isn't there (back in the pokey again), so that leaves just Jasper and the doc.

Jasper's face is unreadable, which is frustrating. "I'm going to miss you, Dot. You're coming back, though, right? After the 'few weeks' is up?"

My turn to feel pink hit my cheeks. "That's the plan at the moment. Things are pretty up in the air at the moment, so I'm trying not to make too many promises."

He looks thoughtful. "I see. Well, I wish you all the best." His eyes lock on mine. He looks like he's about to say something, then drops his eyes.

I walk out.

I wonder if he's really a doctor. Or a plumber. Or a figment of my imagination.

At the bus stop, I strain to read "The Race for Love," by the poor light of a streetlamp which would be book number ninety-two on the Barbara Cartland countdown to romance. Fortunately for me there's no rain (yahoo), but it's nippy and dim and the sounds of voices approaching makes it difficult to concentrate.

The voices grow more agitated and soon the unmistakable surfer-Goth cadence of Elvira cuts through. The other voice isn't familiar, just the grunts of some young Neanderthal. I duck into the shadows of the overhang, fading into the darkness, and dog-ear the page of my book.

" - waste of fuckin' time," grunts a guy about my height. He seems beefy and squat next to the lean line of Elvira. His clothes are all dark, but the streetlight occasionally winks off one of the piercings, marking his proximity.

She crosses her arms over her nonexistent bosom. "No one holding a gun to your head, dude."

I do like that girl. "Hey, Elvira."

She starts a bit. "Oh, how-dee, Dot. You shaved a few years off me."

"Sorry about that. Didn't want to intrude."

The troglodyte wheels on me, a cold look in his eyes. "Yet ya did." He rams his shoulder into Elvira's stiff form as he turns on his heels, the force of it causing her to take a step back into the bus stop. I catch her before she falls over. "Fuckin' outta here. I'm heading to Burger King."

He huffs off in the darkness, leaving Elvira and I holding our breaths at the bus stop.

"That one's a keeper."

She shakes her head, her enormous eyes shimmer with unshed tears. "He's not usually such a dick." She sniffs and digs into a big bag for a tissue. "He can be really nice. Sweet, ya know?"

What kind of a monster would start a fight with

those eyes? "Sure. Everyone has their bad days. Was he your ride?"

She nods.

"Not to worry. The bus will be here soon."

Her mouth twists sideways. "Not sure it's even my bus, dude."

She has a point. "True. But it'll get us out of here."

Lisa Souza

CAN THIS BRIDESMAID BE SAVED?

It is obviously more challenging to look fabulous when all of these decisions are completely out of your hands. An unflattering cut dress in a color that makes you look jaundiced can present even the most natural beauty with new challenges.

excerpt from <u>The Bridesmaid's Manual</u> *by Sarah Stein & Lucy Talbot, Page 102*

Lisa Souza

CHAPTER TEN

Dr. Becker is a doctor. She's a bindi-sporting dermatologist supermodel. She's a dramatic looking Indian woman whose white coat doesn't completely disguise a flame orange dress. She wears very high, very narrow stilettos, the kind that could puncture a car tire. Her voice matches her face, lilting and lovely. Her skin is flawless. Gad.

I didn't need a designated driver for these visits, thank goodness. Dr. B scheduled me for a chemical peel and two facials, and hasn't ruled out the need for a micro-dermabrasion, but I bus to each appointment.

This is heroic. Having your face burned off with acid is no walk in the park. Sure, the medical assistant holds a little fan to your skin to theoretically cool it - but please. Then having to bumpity bump your way back home – by BUS – with your face on fire? Makes a girl reconsider the critical importance of smooth skin

At Kennedy's advice, I made all my dermatological appointments for Friday afternoons. Turns out your face continues to cook and peel for a day or so after each visit. Eeck! By Sunday morning? Disgusting. But absolutely mesmerizing, how the skin bubbles and peels, a horror of a face. And this is better than the zits?

On my way out of Doctor Becker's office, I spot my Elvira's skeletal body draped over the bus bench. Her eyes glow black from a ghoulish white mask. She's wearing these fantastic plugs in her ears that appear to be made of mother-of-pearl with some sort of dark wood inset. They're huge. Her dress is (surprise!), black. The only splashes of color are a single red mesh glove on one arm and a large red band-aid that has been hastily painted on near the hem of her boot length skirt. The boots look like they belonged to a cartoon witch, narrow heeled and laced up. There's a glimpse of black and white horizontal striped tights between boot and hem. She is a unique vision.

"Elvira? That you?"

She startles, takes a hard look at my face. Her eyes saucer and her black lips form an 'O'. "Oh my gawd, Dotty, dude. What happened to your face?"

This is why I recommend you have this procedure done on a Friday. "Nasty, huh? Believe it or not, I'm creating perfect skin."

She bites a slender pinky. "Via industrial accident? Or maybe a car fire?" She reaches out the gloved hand as if to smooth my hair, an oddly comforting gesture. "Does it hurt?"

"Not nearly as bad as it did about twenty

minutes ago. Whatcha doing?"

She flails a hand behind her, the one covered in the fingerless mesh glove. "Had to sign contracts over at The Firehouse. We play tonight and I keep forgetting to sign all their shit. Wouldn't accept email sig. Crazy annoying. I'm gonna be back here again in a couple hours. Are they friggin' Amish? Ever heard of the Internet, dude?" She shakes her head to clear it. "And you, Dottie? What's on your ta-do? How do you plan on following up the facial toasting? Someone going to take a swing at your teeth?"

"My mentor, Kennedy J, seems to have my life planned out for the next year or so. Today, though, I just hope to get home before too many people see my scary face."

"It's like you fell asleep under a sunlamp, dude."

"It'll calm down by Monday. A shade too pink for normal, but not bad. Where I work people don't see me anyway. They email. Even if they're sitting two feet away, they email. I don't have any face-to-face meetings till Wednesday. By then, the worst of the peeling's passed."

"You get bored tonight, come and watch the band. Now that I've John Hancock'd that stupid contract, we storm The Firehouse at nine."

I was about to beg off when a noise in my pocket sounded the alarm. I had forgotten all about the food Nazi.

Elvira eyed my purse quizzically. "Your bag's ringing, Dotty."

I dig around in my monstrous bag for the cheap

Casio watch I'd been forced to purchase and silence the alarm function. "Yeah. Yet another appointment. I'm meeting with the dietician in about fifteen minutes."

Elvira shook her head, sending black strings of hair into motion."You are wicked dedicated, Dotty dude. Best of luck to you."

I waved her off and hoof the three blocks to the nutritional center. It's housed on the fourth floor of a generic brick medical building, as sterile as one would expect.

Nancy Meiser, food Nazi, ushers me back to her little office. Unlike the building, Nancy's office drips with all the colors of a Jackson Pollack painting: butter colored walls, the soft blue ceiling, and the bold splash of a monstrous canvas. The painting of over-scaled bell peppers against a black background hypnotized me. I didn't realize bell peppers came in that many shades: purple, sunshine yellow, alligator green, and glossy flamenco peppers.

Nancy uses a massive wooden table as a desk, but it could barely be seen through baskets of full of grapes, cherries, lemons. The walls not blanketed in peppers disappear behind floor to ceiling bookshelves painted bright white. They are crammed full, the book spines creating an additional riot of color. No beige here. This is promising.

"You must be Dorothy, right? Please have a seat."

But I could be wrong. You can practically hear the Wicked Witch of the West shouting that ugly name. The chair in front of the table is solid wood number, like the table. I take the stumpy chair while she sinks into the comfortable looking upholstered job. Which annoys me. Nancy annoys me. Oh, she's nice enough, don't get me wrong, but everything about her rubs me the wrong way. Her hair bugs me: a sea of Ramona-the-Pest's-arch-enemy curls in constant motion. Her body irritates me: she's always sleeveless, preferring that you see those perfectly rounded shoulders and her smooth, subtle, achieved outdoor tan. Her eyes madden me: beady, black marbles that dart around like a lizard's, missing nothing. And she's short. She's a tiny, hyper elf person with scary eyes.

And she's a stalker.

"As we discussed last time, I've made a thorough study of your home to see what you eat. I've visited your office. I've copies of the menus from the café in your building. And of course, I have the nutritional information from your old standby, Taco Time – "

(Here, she shakes her head dispiritedly, a move common to sixties TV parents)

" – and you and I discussed your food preferences. Using that information, I've compiled menu plans for the next few months. Sticking precisely to those menus is work. But I'm hoping you are up for the challenge."

She shoves aside the basket of lemons and offers me a sheaf of papers. I accept them without taking my eyes off her. Those black eyes burn holes through me.

"Changing food habits is tough, Dorothy. It's perhaps the most difficult change a person can make. We're talking about rewiring your brain. To be successful at this, you are going to need to commit to this process like you have never done before.

"To begin, we detox you. By eating in this very strict way for the first few weeks, we change how you perceive tastes. That makes the rest of the process much easier. But don't panic. You won't be starting that till next week after the Pantry Purge."

(Pantry Purge?!)

She continues smoothly. "Don't be fooled, though. Taco Time and Cherry Coke will be screaming out to you for years to come. Hopefully, though, by the time they try and sneak back in, you'll find that your trouble foods don't quite taste the same."

I frown. It's easy to frown with Nancy in the room. "That's not exactly encouraging. You make it sound like I'll be jonesing for fast food for the rest of my life."

She nods, sending curls flying. "Possibly. And the thing is, unlike alcohol, you are unlikely to go cold turkey off food, right? But the good news is there are some tricks and techniques that make the process manageable."

She pushes another basket out of the way revealing a CD case. "This is a self-hypnosis tape. I've had it made specifically for you. I want you to listen to it twice a day for the next twenty-one days while awake. After that, you can listen to it as you're drifting off to sleep. You don't even have to pay attention. Just have it running."

"You're kidding, right? You want me to

hypnotize myself?"

She smiles her cheerleader smile. "Oh I'm quite serious. This is one of the more powerful tools we now have in our arsenal. Hypnosis allows you to train yourself at a subconscious level to develop habits that create a healthy body."

Did I mention the "we" thing disturbs me, too? "How do I know it won't having me barking like a dog when I see a Taco Time sign? Honestly, I seriously doubt I can be hypnotized."

"Then why worry? It certainly wouldn't hurt , right? But listen to it while you're wide awake anyway. Hear the information. The suggestions on the CD are simply the changes you told me you wanted to make. That's all that's on it. The decision to listen to it, however, like any other suggestions made here, is yours. You decide whether or not to listen, to practice, to engage."

I fight skepticism. It's all so new-age-y and ridiculous. But this is all about change, right? So maybe me 2.0 needs to consider all possible options. Think swan. "Can't hurt, right?"

Her face softens. "Yes. About hurting. I want you to consider an appointment with a therapist."

Fight the eye roll, Dot...

"A therapist? How exactly does this pertain to nutrition?"

"It doesn't. It has to do with health – mental health. You listed on your goal sheet a desire to be healthy."

I had to write down something. My first thought was 'I want to get laid before I die,' but that sounded a trifle desperate.

"Mental state has an enormous impact on all phases of health. It's what helps a fit person decide to lace on running shoes. Or to choose salmon and a fruit cup over Taco Time."

Always with the Taco Time slam. It's not the only place I eat. Honestly.

"Please consider it. Menus and planning and hypnosis will work, but only if you choose to engage your brain in the process. You've got to choose to cooperate, Dorothy."

CHAPTER ELEVEN

Nancy arrives a week later, right on time – 6:30pm – with a large box and a roll of plastic garbage bags for the Meiser Pantry Purge. She sets the box down on the counter, then begins rifling through cupboards and fridge, scooping items into black bags obviously brought for that purpose. Ominous.

Her bright blond hair bobs around in those pesky boing-boing curls so energetically I want to deck her. Thank goodness we'll normally be communicating via email. Miss Nancy is certainly here today, though. And I'm scared.

She pauses, and her happy curls suddenly seem to droop. "Dorothy, I hate to be brutal, but I haven't found a single acceptable food item." She waves a hand toward the fridge. "A freezer full of Ben and Jerry's? A mountain of Hostess? Cheese?" She shakes her head, sending the curls into overdrive and practically shudders. "You have nothing but processed food and junk."

The hell you say.

She begins ticking off 'no' items as they disappear into the bag: "No more Cherry Coke. I hereby dub you 'water girl.' No more Hostess. Stick with fresh vegetables and fruit, nuts and grains. Make it simple: if it came in a bag, a box or plastic, don't eat it. And if you get desperate for sweets – "

Oh, I think we can count on that happening.

" – make a fruit Smoothie."

Puh-leeze. I sigh audibly.

"If you insist, you can try Diet Jell-O. But I'd strongly caution you against artificial sweeteners of any kind. They're toxic."

She bulldozes through my remaining food stocks, curls bouncing and a bright enthusiastic smile pasted on her face. "Always tough at first, but within a few weeks, your mind and stomach will adopt this new way of eating. You'll feel so much better eating this way you'll chose to do so."

Resistance and seething anger simmer in my head as she continues to unload all things edible from my space. I lose it. "Or just maybe I'll eat your way because I haven't a thin dime for food after paying the nutritionist who gutted my pantry."

Uh-oh: word fart.

Her smile thins, tightens. "Look, this is the hard part. So you go right ahead and use humor if it helps you."

I clam up.

Nancy continues bagging and tossing till the place is bare. She takes a minute to retrieve the box she brought with her – the replacement foods I am allowed to eat – and restocks my pantry and fridge. I ignore that part. There isn't much to see. She reiterates her belief that I would benefit from counseling and leaves me to contend with broccoli-rabe and mung beans.

———————————◆●◆———————————

The next evening, I return home trembling from anger. A run in with a surly programmer from the building next door combined with low blood sugar made for a rough day. My stomach sends memos about the two meals eaten that day, cobbled together from the odd assortment left by the food Nazi raid. I'm crazed from sugar and caffeine withdrawal. I stagger on autopilot for the cupboard anticipating a parade of Ding Dongs, Ho Ho's and Cupcakes in neat containers, a veritable sea of self-medicating foods, having completely lost sight of the fact that, like old Mother Hubbard, I'm in for a bit of disappointment.

Staring at the pantry, I see no correlation between the contents and food. There are a couple containers of dry protein powder, boxes of herbal teas, stacks of canned tuna and canned salmon. I guess that would work if you were a body builder… or maybe a cat. I turn to the fridge, silently praying for a better outcome. Nope. There's just a couple neat Tupperware containers of walnuts, peanuts, pistachios, and an entire shelf of bottled water. There's a section devoted to every flavor of fat-free sugar-free Greek yogurt ever created, and sticks of low-fat string cheese. Oh, and there are eggs. I guess I should be grateful for small favors.

Of course the crisper is a green grocer's dream. If you like that color. But where's the food? I scan the counters and see bowls of fruit. Admittedly, they are visually stunning: bold oranges, shiny green apples next to matte gold pears, swollen purple grapes, bright fleshed lemons. Lemons? What the hell am I going to do with lemons? The only use I know of for them is as a garnish on the side of a glass and I only learned about that a few weeks ago.

I want to weep. That may seem melodramatic, but somewhere between overwhelm and fury is a place where your leftover crisp beef burritos are supposed to be. Nancy the Nazi stole them yesterday. I deliberately chose not to stop for takeout after working because I knew those leftovers were waiting. Now what am I supposed to eat? Tuna and a green apple does not Taco Time make.

While glaring at the tuna I'm supposed to eat, I phone Nancy to find out what I'm supposed to do with the lemons. Didn't I remember? I'm to add a squeeze of lemon to my morning mix. Didn't I read the notes?

My what?

Ah yes. I scan the Nancy manifesto and sure enough, I'm supposed to be drinking a glass of water with lemon, cayenne and ginger – preferably warm – each morning prior to breakfast. I'm sure there's a reason.

And yet so there is so little interest in that reason...

Two days later – excuse me: two caffeine-free

days later – I develop such a piercing headache I can barely stand. I had failed to consider the affects of dropping a powerful Cherry Coke habit cold turkey. Pain stabs at my ears and my poor eyes feel in danger of exploding. I practically crawl to work, sluggish without my morning sugar infusion.

By day four of this new regime, my emails take on a Unabomber craziness, rambling and irate. I rip apart software products and the evil people responsible for them. I test with an intensity reserved for Texas Marshal Sam Gerard hunting Richard Kimball.

By the evening of the fifth night, I nearly buy a car, the better to purchase Hostess Twinkies at 7-11. I'm now officially obsessed by images of sweets. I stop watching TV because the fast food commercials make me drool like one of Pavlov's dogs.

By the end of the week, my experiment in transformation has failed. Despite being a good girl and eating like that she-beast Nancy told me to, I dropped only a pound. Did you hear that? One friggin pound. Now I'm not only fat, I'm stressed, starving and depressed.

As she reviews the results, Nancy suggests we (we?) ramp it up a notch. Clearly my metabolism slows at the slightest threat to the status quo.

Solution? My new nemesis, Trainer Joe.

CHAPTER TWELVE

Trainer Joe. A fine, upstanding Dogpatch name if ever I heard it. And oddly enough, I heard it bright an early the next day at 7:00am, which is when the phone rang, and I think we can all agree that's far too early for this sort of pestering.

"Dot? Good Morning! Trainer Joe here. Wanted to make sure I caught you before work. Nancy Meiser tells me you are ready to make the move to fitness. That's fantastic, just fantastic, darlin'."

A cliché with a drawl. At least he didn't call me Dorothy. Annoying cornpone enthusiasm tries to bench press its way through the phone. "You ready to do some work?"

"Absolutely, Joe. You understand, though, that I can't come to a gym. I need to do this at home."

"Not a problem. I have plenty of clients who workout at home. My fee is one-fifty an hour. We'll meet three times a week till I feel you're underway, usually a couple of weeks, then twice a week for a bit. Then we'll discuss a maintenance plan to keep you honest. What days are you free?"

I'm still stuck back at the $150 an hour. Where will that materialize from? The functional part of my brain shouts that actually it's $450.00... for the first week! Holy Hannah. Where's the excuse to stall? A cursory calendar check confirms that sadly, I'm free forever. "Can you do Tuesday, Thursday, Saturday?"

"Can and will."

Thus, Trainer Joe is added to the list of whip wielding inquisitors.

Trainer Joe delivers. And what does he deliver? Exercise. And what does exercise deliver? It delivers an entirely new flavor of hurt, a hurt with brand recognition, its own ad campaign and a hunky spokesmodel, Trainer Joe.

Joe is the powerfully handsome, and – oh let the joyous news be spread! – heterosexual Joe Towner. He's well over six feet, deeply but smoothly muscled, and shaped like... well, not so much the Incredible Hulk as Michelangelo's David. When he arrives at the door for the first time, warning bells clang in the back of my brain. Do NOT trust Trainer Joe and his bright smile and thick hands! That forewarning is completely ignored because I'm infatuated with change, and entranced by the vision that is Joe. Bring it on! Feel the burn! First day of the rest of my life and all that crap. Jane Fonda will salute me. Richard Simmons will hug me! Pump it!

He introduces himself in a lovely baritone, then

points over his shoulder at a full sized treadmill he has somehow lugged up the stairs. I step out of the way while he drags the monolith over the threshold and positions it in front of my sofa. None of that hurt at all. That part, watching Joe set up the treadmill, was worth the full one-fifty.

For this first visit, he insists on photographing me for a 'baseline' image. Other than weddings, where one cannot escape, I have successfully ducked being photographed for years. It's easy if you plan for it: just stand outside of camera range, behind someone a shade taller than you, or behind a substantial arborvitae.

Joe's dreaded Cyclops of a camera, with its winking red eye, threatens. I let him snap a shot, but only after he coaxes my crossed arms down to my sides and assures me, in that glorious gravely man voice, that I am not required to tape this picture to my refrigerator.

Taking my photograph is distressing, but it doesn't hurt. Much.

Despite the distraction of a chiseled jaw and that sensual mouth, I am focused on my goal of attaining beauty. I don't waste time, for example, studying in detail the fine curve of Joe's biceps, the expansive wall of his chest, the honest-to-goodness six pack beneath the navy T-shirt.

Heck no.

Staring at Trainer Joe does not hurt. Nor does gawking.

I'm on task.

He whips out his next instrument of torture, a measuring tape. The truth of my current dimensions is humiliating. Humiliation stings.

"I don't trust your scale, so we'll use the doctor's weigh in number as our jumping off point," he says. He shares this troubling number, writes it down, repeats it out loud to me, a number reserved for truck scales. This hurts outright.

It's just information, I tell the part that whimpers.

He slaps the clipboard down on the counter. "So let's get moving!" Joe waves a hand at the treadmill. This and hand weights, he explains, are my new best friends.

Well, Elvira did say I needed some new friends.

I do as instructed: hop on the treadmill and move. The warm up's not too bad, similar to the usual waddles between home and the bus. That much I can handle. Several minutes later, Joe's meaty hand reaches over and tinkers with a couple of buttons. The machines slowly tips and now I'm crawling uphill at a faster pace. Sweat trickles down between my shoulder blades. I fight a Monica Seles-like urge to grunt.

I complete thirty minutes on the treadmill. I'm proud of myself. I didn't think I'd pull it off. I'm sweaty, but done.

Then a massive hand comes down on my slightly damp shoulder. "Let's not bring on an aneurysm the first day, right?" He points at a notebook he's brought. "We'll work up to fifty minutes a day of cardio: fifteen to warm up, twenty at training heart rate, fifteen for cool down. Then it's about building muscles with weights. For now, we're going to ease into it so you don't get injured."

I shake my head. "You don't understand. I don't have the money to ease into anything. I am ready to change my life. And before I go broke, I need the tools to do that."

Trainer Joe grins from ear to ear. "Then grab those hand weights! No time like right now!"

That is when the hurting began in earnest.

CAN YOU SEE ME NOW?

Your job as a bridesmaid is to be part of that overall picture, the vignette, a stage set. How you look as an individual doesn't really matter. I know, I know, that's horrible! It's a travesty! Well, it's the truth.

excerpt from <u>The Bridesmaid's Manual</u> *by Sarah Stein & Lucy Talbot, Page 103*

CHAPTER THIRTEEN

Crippled. All this health crap is turning me into a cripple. This is my third session.

Trainer Joe's shouts of, "Don't be weak! Just one more!" cause an echoing shout from the adjacent apartment, usually followed by a couple of thumps on the wall.

I don't feel truly supported in my journey by the guy in apartment F2.

Perhaps he doesn't appreciate the struggle to lift a trembling leg in just one more fire hydrant raise when the tiny muscles of the inner thigh vacillate like hummingbird wings. Body parts previously dormant have been surprised into forced labor and they are not pleased. Poor lower body.

But today is the upper body.

"Gad, Joe, I...I..," And that's it. That's all the sound I can muster. I wanted to suggest a cessation of all activity, but can't, because oxygen conservation is paramount. My sweats are soaked.

They stick to the back of my knees and in that divot in the small of my back, (not a good look). From the land of crabby, sore and angry, I no longer appreciate Trainer Joe's beauty. Because he is a mean, mean man.

Mean Joe kneels on one knee in front of me to watch my technique for performing seated biceps curls. To avoid staring at him – because he's mean - my attention wanders to that thick rope of muscle, his quadriceps, genuflecting in front of me.

Ummm…quadriceps.

Pretending to not appreciate T.J.'s beauty? Barefaced lie. It is incredibly helpful to witness Joe's broad smile when I complete a set or when he drops those meat patties that pass for hands on my shoulders.

"Now that was excellent work. Remember that tomorrow is the stretch routine and treadmill only, forty minutes each. Then Thursday, it's lower body and abs."

Behold! One hundred and fifty bucks just hurtled out of my wallet!

In addition to the very real possibility of acquiring an Aleve addiction, I believe I would sell my soul to Satan for a Cherry Coke. Still, one must think positively, right? The work is getting done. And I'm still standing, albeit on very twitchy, incredibly sore legs.

CHAPTER FOURTEEN

The next day. I wake up to the compelling EHHH! blasting from my alarm clock. Normally, one rolls over and turns it off.

Argh!

I don't recall being recently bucked off a bull, but clearly it happened.

Somewhere between pressing my pectorals, curling my biceps, pulling my triceps, and a cornucopia of other movements both hostile and harsh, nothing above my waist works. I'm internally bruised and swollen. All my parts throb – and not in a good way. I'm forced to endure the clanging of the alarm clock an additional five minutes before I can finally reach the button.

I surmise that my core – and Trainer Joe is all about the core – is trashed beyond recognition. The battery acid that replaced my blood courses through me like that Alien monster.

Someone should tell off Trainer Joe. I'd do it

myself, but couldn't possibly lift the receiver, so I let the notion pass.

I'm so paralyzed by muscle soreness I can't strip the foil from my yogurt. In desperation, I take a knife to it. The knife gained weight overnight. Opening bottled water brings on tears of frustration.

———————●●———————

Thursday - it's the lower body's turn.

With my upper body still paralyzed from Tuesday, Trainer Joe shows up to decommission me from the waist down. And for the next three weeks of training, there is nothing but absolute misery. Even on days when I didn't train, the pulsating pain from the previous day controls my thoughts.

During this same time, the comfort of food, sweet, fatty, crispy, naughty, and so expected, so familiar? Denied. Have you ever tried to change a minor habit? Like chewing your fingernails? Well there was nothing minor about this. Someone trying to quit smoking must experience a similarly global change. Every minute I have to remind myself that I chose to change, wanted to make things different, that this was my idea.

Wasn't it? Had I really been so unhappy? I'd flashback to the taste of a sweet chocolate donut, melting in my mouth at that first bite. I'd linger on the memory of the salty, crisp crunch of the first, hot Mexi-fry. And I'd sigh deeply over how much I missed relaxing on the sofa watching reality TV without the inconvenience and torture of the treadmill and weights.

To my great annoyance, Trainer Joe wouldn't

weigh me, insisting that no measurements take place until at least a month had elapsed. But after twenty-one days? I wanted information. More than that, I needed some reason to continue beating the holy crap out of myself every day.

When I brought it up, he put a gentle but lion-sized paw on my shoulder and tipped his head down to eye level. "Research indicates that a habit takes twenty-one days to establish, which means we're just getting you habituated. I want these new habits to really take hold, to change your life permanently, not mess up your metabolism. I'm giving you the opportunity to let your body embrace a new way of living. But to do that, you have to be realistic.

"If you hop on a scale or get measured every day, you'll only be seeing what's happening in the short run. It's like watching your stocks: you spend too much time tracking every blip up or down and those wild waves of the market will make you nuts. One day you're thrilled, the next day, not so much, maybe the next day it's completely in the toilet. But over the long haul the market performs fairly consistently. That's what we're aiming for here. We're going to get you over the hell hump, this initial phase of change when every single movement's a mountain, every decision, momentous. Then and only then will we start measuring. At that point, the fun starts. Then we'll pick a date to send you back to Kennedy for your first fitting. Then momentum propels you forward - like drafting on a bicycle. It gets far easier. So hold off for just one more week and we'll do some checking." Then he smiled that golden boy smile and left.

Easy for him to say. He wasn't the one trying to alter every facet of his life.

———————◄█●█►———————

Finally a full month of "Trainer Joe days" has elapsed. When he arrives for my session, my heart was pounding as though sex were imminent. Joe pulls his trusty scale out and sets it up. "Remember, far more important than pounds is muscle mass. We want you strong, not weak."

Right. Whatever you say. Just let me know…

I step on that stupid scale like Marie Antoinette mounting the steps to the guillotine. I let Joe do his thing and hold my breath.

"You've lost…eight pounds! Great work."

That's it? Four weeks in hell and I've only lost eight pounds? Trainer Joe's still talking so I try and tune back in.

"…and you've already lost an entire three percent off your body fat! That's what I like to see – not just losing pounds, but losing fat pounds. You're the success story I like to write about! Picture time."

What?

Sure enough, he whips out his digital camera again and points at the wall, the same wall where I stood a month ago. What the heck. Maybe eight pounds is okay. I stand tall and let him snap away.

A HERO'S SAGA

A pear shape is smaller on top and larger on the bottom. An apple is thicker in the midsection. Understanding if your body falls into either of these categories is key to dressing fabulously. Okay, maybe you're a swimsuit model and you look good in everything. Well good for you. You can sit your skinny *ss down and eat a brownie. We'll get to you later.

excerpt from The Bridesmaid Manual *by Sarah Stein & Lucy Talbot, Page 93*

Lisa Souza

CHAPTER FIFTEEN

It took three and a half months to lose the twenty pounds Dr. Tam required before he'd perform the first of my surgeries. Do you understand what I just said? It's not like TV. I didn't just wait for the commercial break and come back twenty pounds lighter. It wasn't like that at all. I watched an episode of The Biggest Loser once where a guy lost twenty-six pounds in two weeks. Two weeks! Not me, though, hell no.

But thing is, I feel good as I walk into Dr. Tam's office – after yet another double Metro transfer. Waiting for Dr. Tam to step into the room, dressed only in blue paper, my mood is decidedly better than it had been in…well ever.

There's a light rap and in comes Dr. Tam. He's a diminutive guy, compact, efficient. The odd thing is whenever I speak to him, there's something about his hands, the way he holds them, that speaks of a tremendous artistic streak. Maybe it's wishful thinking. After all, he's going to inflate me like a Macy's float, gut me like a fish, then sew me back together. One would hope that the person doing so would have a sense of the aesthetic. Then again, Picasso was also an artist. I shiver.

Dr. Tam smiles and it reaches his dark, Asian eyes. "Well look at you! Good morning, Dot. It appears you took my request seriously. You look wonderful. Sure you still need surgery?"

"Ha ha, doc. Yes, I'm still sure."

Dr. Tam takes photos, too. Why is it when you are at the apex of your uneasiness about your appearance, everyone seems to want a photo? I'm allowed paper undies. Lucky me. I stand in front of a large screen, apparently placed there for just this reason, while a series of very precise photos are taken. It reminds me unpleasantly of mug shots. Naked mug shots. Hope that artistic streak kicks in soon. Side, front, back. I'm allowed to peek at the pictures on a monitor. Why bother to look? Because I can't help it, that's why.

Dr. Tam draws directly on the screen with a stylus, pointing at my hips and inner thighs. "This area here, and here…we'll merely be sculpting, taking just enough to smooth and contour. Now here," he points to two sections on my back. "We'll be more aggressive. This area, too," now he's flipped to the front section and indicates my lower belly. "I think we can avoid doing a tummy tuck. That's a terribly invasive and very painful operation from a recovery standpoint. I think I can do a modified version I developed where we'll tighten these muscles here laparoscopically through an incision in your umbilicus – belly button – then do some heavy lipo sculpting with the Vaser. You'll get an excellent result with less recovery time and without the scarring."

I ponder his proposal. Sounds better than what I read in my library book. The tummy tuck photos looked ghastly, showing an enormous incision from hip to hip below the belly button closed with a horrific railway of black, Frankenstein-like stitches to keep their intestines from spilling. I went online and found chat rooms where women dished about their surgeries, where paragraph after paragraph detailed the pain of tummy tucks. Oh, they were nearly all thrilled with the results, but the theme of pain seemed universal. Only a few insisted it wasn't bad. And I think they were former Soviet Cosmonauts.

But no more worries. Cisterns of water have been guzzled. Omega rich salmon consumed. Sit-ups, curl ups and lunges performed on command, all to reach some elusive place called pretty. Now the end zone hung just out of reach, and it resembled, to a remarkable degree, a short Asian guy in a white coat.

Global change on planet Dotty. Bring it on.

"Sign me up."

CHAPTER SIXTEEN

Surgery, like moving, uncovers true friends, the kind of folks willing to drag your three hundred pound sleeper sofa down the stairs, or willing drive you to the airport, the ones you can count on in a pinch.

I don't have any.

You think I'm exaggerating, but this is for real. Surgery is a huge deal, a monster step up from dropping you off at SeaTac. Only a true friend would suffer the discomfort and inconvenience, the creepiness of being at the hospital, and the hassle of a whining patient.

I just didn't realize how few friends are in my life until I scheduled that first in-hospital surgical procedure. All my surgeries require that I designate someone who will drive me home, so I had no choice but to suck it up and phone Ginny.

Over a damned bottled water (I despise paying money for something I could be drinking out of a hose for free), and after an hour Ginny dishing in excruciating detail Sam's inability to comprehend the staggering adventure that the arrival of children would bring, I popped the question.

"So, Ginny, will you be my surgery pal? I need someone to lug me home from the clinic after the lipo."

Her eyes grew big as plates. I was instantly sorry I'd agreed to pick up the tab for her double-tall skinny latte. "You've got to be kidding, Dot. You know I can't abide those places."

My mouth dropped. "Excuse me? You had Botox injections three times last month. I went with you."

She rolled her eyes. "Well of course I've had Botox. Hell, I named the friggin Chihuahua Botox. That doesn't mean I want to spend my free time hanging out at a hospital."

"Surgical center, Ginny, not a hospital. As usual your resemblance to Mother Theresa amazes."

"Don't be snide, Dot, I don't even know the woman. What about Mel? Or your mom?

"Ginny you know Mel and I haven't said a word to each other since she married my imaginary boyfriend. And mom's in London with Rupert Rooney. Look, I really need you for this."

"No can do, toots." She scooped up her to-go cup. "Gotta book. I think I may have Sam talked into that first baby. We can only hope. I'll let you know what happens."

I watch her exit Starbucks. My face wants to scrunch up in frustration, but thanks to Dr. Becker's latest, that's out of the question. My skin may glow with good health but clearly I have a problem.

I hop a bus back to Redmond then take the connecting shuttle to my building. Too bad Microcosm doesn't offer connecting shuttles to the clinic, since no obvious solution presents itself. For a moment, Elvira's elf face floats behind my eyes for consideration, but then the bus reaches my stop.

I'm so lost in thought I pass the door to my office. I'm about to U-turn when a brilliant thought strikes and my legs propel me past two additional doors to land at one of the larger offices in the building. It belongs to my lead, Greg Larson. The rattle of fingers scuttling over a keyboard filters out into the hallway. I rap once at the open door jam and walk in.

Greg's fingers are tanned spiders, all over the keyboard. He is, as ever, a uniformly nut brown color and wearing shorts. This is unusual for a white boy computer scientist. Geeks aren't known for experiencing daylight first hand. In Greg's case, the forecast could be sixteen degrees and snow, yet Greg will not waver in his fashion choices. He likes his 'man-pries,' the label our group assigned to his slightly-too-long mid-calf shorts. He is lean, intense, busy. He doesn't look up from the screen. "Whazzup, Dot?"

"Gotta minute, Greg? More like fifteen?"

Greg pauses dramatically over the keyboard, hits a few more keys, swivels his office chair to face me. "Closed door?"

"Definitely."

He nods and I shut the door behind me. "Talk to me."

You know, at moments like this, I really like men. Their brevity comes in handy.

"You know I'm taking a bunch of vacation days, right?" He nods. "I'm having a bunch of surgeries done. My ride home just fell through. No ride home, no surgery. Any chance you could give me a lift home from Swedish on Wednesday?"

Greg swivels back toward his monitor, brings up his Outlook schedule. "Time?"

I consider. "Between 3:45 and 5:00. It should be closer to 3:45, but you never know with these things."

He blocks out the time in his schedule. "Good to go. You need a lift there, too?"

Any sensible person would shout, "YES YES," right about here, but I don't want to press my luck. I can bus it in, right? "No, I'm good, thanks. I really appreciate it."

"No worries. Swedish, Wednesday, 3:45. Just check in at the front desk?"

"Yeah. They'll send you down to the recovery room."

I back out of his office, fighting the urge to genuflect and head back to mine. Once there, I burst into hysterics, laughing till my cheeks are wet. Continual swipes at my eyes are required to see. All that laughing weakens me. I drop into a chair to catch my breath.

Imagine replaying that conversation with anyone on earth other than Greg Larson. Wouldn't you have some questions? Perhaps wonder at the reason behind the need for surgery? Nope. Not Greg. Greg's a linear kind of guy. He figures if I want to share, I'll share. He has zero interest in people's personal business.

And this is the guy I talked into picking me up from six different medical procedures.

———————◆◆———————

To be fair to me, I had no idea how messed up I'd be after surgery. I hardly catch a cold, let alone go to the doctor, so this is an entirely new arena for me.

It didn't help that I ended up piling on multiple surgeries at the same time, something that the doctors were very much against, citing concerns about fluid levels and such. I countered with desperation and only having so many vacation days available.

On Wednesday morning, I'm up at 4:00, since it takes three different busses to get me to the surgical center. Thank goodness busses run on schedule. I check in at the desk where a round woman wearing a shapeless pastel smock and white shoes stands ready.

"Good morning, sweetie. You're here for surgery?"

"Yes, I'm having procedures done by Dr Tam and Dr. Marcus."

She smiles up at me. "Oh the full meal deal! I have a friend scrubbing in on you. You need to take off all your clothes and put them in this bag." She hands me a gray garment bag, points at a room behind her. "No jewelry, right? Good. Then into the gown and footies and right back to me. You have someone to pick you up after your procedures, right?" She looks over my head, sees no one.

"Yes, I have a friend coming."

"Name?"

"Greg Larson." She scribbles the name on my chart. "He'll need to be here before we release you. Do you need to call him and let him know?"

"No, he has it scheduled. I told him not to come this early so he wouldn't get stuck waiting around for hours."

She frowns, considering. I head off to change before she can stop me.

My steps slow as I approach the room. My heart beats loudly enough to disturb nurses on another floor. Nerves kicking in, I guess, which is silly. I won't feel a thing, right? I disrobe and throw on the gown.

I step out of the room, wearing the scary, backless, hospital gown. There is a strange change of status that comes over a person wearing this badge of frailty. I hand over the garment bag with one hand while holding the barn door of the gown closed with the other. I may not be much to look at, but I'm not giving it away for free.

The woman at the desk fights a smile at my fashion issues. "A little airy back there?" Deftly, she reveals a cotton blanket and wraps it around my exposed backside. Better.

She walks me past a room full of beige recliners, where my fellow Hari Krishnas lounge, each with an IV bag hanging next to them. Each patient comes complete with a companion seated in a hard metal chair. Krishnas and companions all look like they're working on ulcers. No comedians in residence.

I'm escorted past them to a starkly beige room and told to take a seat. Doctor Tam and Doctor Marcus will be in shortly to do their 'markups.'

Doctor Marcus comes in first – he's doing my face. Oh didn't I mention the face thing? I had thought my face was fine, too – well, other than the skin thing. But Dr. Tam suggested I might want to have Doctor Teddy Marcus take a look at that bump on the bridge of my nose. (Bump? What bump?).

Doctor Marcus is around sixty, portly and bald with the soft, limp handshake of a surgeon. He looks like he'd be comfortable driving a golf cart, but nothing more athletically challenging. Hopefully that's the sign of a good surgeon. Suddenly I'm worried that my handshake may be too strong for me to become a surgeon.

He lifts my wrist and looks at the name typed on it, nodding. He asks me to stand directly in front of him. He's exactly my height, so we're eye to eye. He stares hard, but his hands on my face are gentle. "Okay, Miss Lindell. Let's just be quite clear on our goals. Narrow the nostrils just a touch, drop the bridge a smidgeon. No deviated septum to contend with. Pretty straightforward stuff. Go ahead and lie down for a minute. I want to double check my lines from that position."

I lay down on the raised mattress while he checks his lines. A rap on the door behind him and Doctor Tam comes in, a head shorter even than Doctor Marcus. They exchange pleasantries and Doctor Marcus says he'll see me shortly and he leaves.

"You ready for some more lines?" Dr. Tam smiles.

Actually, they make me feel like a beef carcass awaiting the butcher. Gulp. "Oh sure." Before he starts drawing, like Dr. Marcus, he grabs my wrist and checks the name on the band.

He sees my puzzled look. "Wouldn't want to work on the wrong person now would we? Always double check."

Unlike the straight lines of Doctor Marcus, Doctor Tam is all about circles. Circles around my belly where his modified tummy tuck will happen. Circles on my hips and thighs for lipo. Circles on my bootie and back.

Polka Dot!

Oh gad, I'm truly losing it. Punning before a surgical procedure is wrong.

I look ridiculous and I oughtta know, since there's a full length mirror right in front of me. Despite my recent weight loss, and with the addition of a sharpie, I am an albino Holstein.

Doctor Tam finishes his art work. He pops the pen in his pocket, takes my hand. "Dot, you did everything I asked. Now I'm going to go to work and put some finishing touches on all that hard work. And I'm very good at this." He pats my hand once, then leaves. I don't doubt him for a second. If I did, I'd flee the building, naked butt cheeks flapping.

The nurse returns with a clipboard and we do some paperwork. She leads me back to Krishina lounge land and has me take a seat. "We're going to start your IV. There will be some medicine in it to help your nerves, then Jason will wheel you down to surgery."

I get my own recliner. Whoopie.

There's nowhere to look, except at the other lounge lizards. No one sits in my metal companion chair. Every wall is painted some muted shade, beige into a gray into muted green into pale blue. They should consider adding some color. This can't be healing, all this drab stuff. There's nothing to listen to but the thrum of electronic equipment and other people's tense conversations. So of course I'm eavesdropping.

"- Jeremy stop being such a whiner. The doc says lots of people have hernias."

"- but I thought it would only take two hours! What am I supposed to do for daycare?"

" - It's your fault, after all. We wouldn't be in this predicament if your mother had listened when I told her –"

" - Don't you worry for a second momma, we'll have you outta here in no time."

Nurse Angela interrupts my rude intrusions into other people's lives by sticking a needle into my hand. I know her name because it is on the white badge clasped to her collar. She has a crown of blond braids and a 'no nonsense' manner that match the Teutonic hairstyle.

Whatever she injected me with stings and then runs cold. The stuff is supposed to calm me down. That's not the affect. I want to run in a circle like a nervous dog, chasing my tail. I know that would annoy my fellow recliners, so instead, I try slow, even breaths.

The breathing comes from the self-hypnosis CD that Nancy the Nazi gave me. Controlled breathing is an important part of the process. In through the nose, out through the mouth. Still cold. Still nervous. I tug the blanket a bit tighter. My kingdom for a space heater.

Nurse Angela introduces me briefly to Jason who walks my IV and me down the hall to surgery. Since my medical experiences have been limited to occasional episodes of ER and old reruns of Quincy, I'm surprised that I walk to the surgical suites. I always assumed they'd wheel me in on a gurney.

Instead, I follow Jason past deep, foot controlled sinks, electronic equipment on rolling carts, metal cabinets. Jason enters the operating room and points to the sheeted mattress. "Let's have you face up for now," he says. The room is bitterly cold. Or maybe it's just me from having that icy medicine pumped into my veins. I'm so friggin cold.

"How do the surgeons work without shivering?"

Jason smiles. "You get used to it. I need you to scooch up a bit…just like that and then your arms go on these pads..." I'm shaking in earnest now, while Jason places straps on my arms. With limbs splayed out, I feel like I'm being crucified. "Take a couple breaths…"

I slept.

CHAPTER SEVENTEEN

Is it time? Are they going to cut me? Will it hurt?

A face hovers over me. I can't see very well.

"Dot? You awake? Go ahead and talk so we'll know you're awake."

"Ishit time?" my voice sounds garbled, thick and stupid. I feel inflated, my body and face blown up like a Macy's float.

"All done. You're in recovery. How's your tummy? Any nausea?"

"Don't know." I try to care. Suddenly, I'm on a brisk ride downhill from euphoria to raging upchuck. "Owww. Dizhy."

The face above me nods. "Just the anesthesia. Bad news is it can make you nauseous. Good news is it will keep the pain down a bit longer. Your friend's outside in the waiting room. We'll let him visit in a bit. Just want to make sure you feel less sick to your stomach and check some vitals."

I wouldn't recognize this woman again in a photo lineup. My eyes are so swollen I can barely make out an image. I assume this is courtesy of my nose. Ahhh my poor nose.

Within an hour, I'm assisted into my post surgery clothes. Thank God almighty I packed an EZ on shirt and drawstring pants. Even so, it's Abbott and Costello trying to dress body parts wandering off in strange directions while comical sounds emerge from me. My range of motion has taken quite a beating over the last few hours. I make the big effort and swivel my puffy eyes toward the clock. At least one of them is successful. 4:45.

Poor Greg. He has no idea what he's gotten himself into.

I'm eased into clothes and between yelps and groans assisted into a wheelchair. I'm thinking the pain isn't too bad when my newly stitched stomach heaves. There's nothing's to pitch, as I wasn't allowed to eat for hours before surgery. I settle for groaning some more. At this moment, Mr. Stomach hates anesthesia.

(A few hours later, I would discover that anesthesia is a fantastic, wonderful, powerful magic. People who give it to you should be knighted. When it wears off, you miss it badly. I had no idea that boatloads of pain control still floated in my system).

I'm wheeled briskly down the hall where I can just make out a man hunched over his laptop, typing furiously.

"Mr. Larson? Dorothy's all ready to go."

The guy looks up and it's not Greg Larson. It's

Ted Wheeler, his jaw dropped in a monstrous 'O.' "Holy shit, Dot! What the hell happened?"

Please don't let me laugh. "ust a itta ip and tuck." Nice. "Jus get me om."

Ted's eyes snap from me to the nurse. "You've gotta be kidding. You're going to let her go home like this? Was she in a car accident?" He still resembles a praying mantis, but now he's a very concerned mantis.

"I assure you Dorothy is doing very well. The bandages are to keep all the sights clean and free of infection. Let me walk you through her discharge requirements."

"-ere's Greg?"

"Called into a Quick Fix on a network problem. He asked if I could fill in."

Ted hesitates for a heartbeat and then snaps shut his laptop. The nurse rests one of those ubiquitous clipboards on the low coffee table, lecturing him on the various places I'm oozing, crusting, and draining. Here's a drain, there a drain, be sure and clean the drain, drain. Still a bit wonky with the anesthesia, I ignore the occasional glances of complete panic Ted lobs my way. He signs the forms in front of him then tells me he's going to pull the car around to the front. If I was less stoned, I'd have been worried he was going to take off.

Good news! He returns. I'm wheeled out to the side of his minivan. Which is strange, because I thought he drove an Explorer. Then I remember that Greg Larson has the Explorer - this is Ted's car. God bless the minivan. I try to imagine climbing into the old Explorer. Not pretty. It takes both the nurse and Ted several minutes to load me into the back seat. I don't want to be upright. I don't want to lie down. There's no happy medium. When Ted snaps the seatbelt across my lap, I howl (yes, howl). Poor Ted. His eyes beg forgiveness. And he got roped into this at the last minute. Eventually I hear the soft snick of the driver's side door closing and we're off.

Dear God who paves these roads? I'm being tortured by each bump, divot and crack in the pavement. The seatbelt is killing me and I try and pull it lower, down onto my lap.

No dice. It snaps back to its previous position causing a sharp 'ahhh' that freaks out Ted.

"Do you need me to pull over? Are you okay?"

I have become lucid enough to speak without sounding like a mental patient. "Seatbelt got me. Sorry to scare you. Thanks again for doing this Ted."

"Look, Dot, you have someone staying with you, right?"

I've practiced this lie for a few weeks now. "Don't sweat it. I'm good. Some friends are going to swing by and take turns. I just had a cancellation on the ride home." Which is hooey. I have taken considerable care to make my apartment invalid friendly. And I have the phone number to a nursing service loaded into my cell phone just in case.

We arrive about forty minutes later at my place. It takes Ted and I another fifteen to get me, doubled over with pain, from his van, up the stairs and inside. I've never been happier to reach my own apartment and never more frightened to be left there alone. Ted, ever the good father, takes a minute to look around. "I don't feel right about this, Dot. Do you want me to call your mom or something?" Watching him ring his hands fails to dissolves the bug image.

"Just one thing, if you would. Could you get this prescription filled? It's for the pain meds. No one is going to be by till later and…"

"No problem." He glances around and shakes his head. "I'll be back with it in a minute. Is there anything else you need?"

"I think I'm good."

Ted cross his arms, scouts the room nervously.

Never have I been more appreciative of my powers of planning than at this moment. See, I knew I'd be essentially trapped in my own apartment for the next… well who the hell knows how long, so I did a little preliminary remodeling. My bed sits squat in the middle of the room, flanked by a wheelchair and a mini fridge. The fridge acts as an end table, a spot to hold the remote control and bottled water. The TV has been repositioned to the foot of the bed. An absurd number of pillows have been placed at the head of the bed. I figured who knows what position will work post surgery? So I planted extras.

Neatly piled boxes of protein bars line the other side of the bed, along with mountains of books and magazines of all sorts: Dean Koontz, Stephen King, Vogue, and Cosmo. I included programming manuals and a book on SQL, knowing full well I'd ignore them in favor of Koontz and King. The thought was there, though. Okay, I had hoped Greg would make a mental note of my dedication to computer science.

I doubt praying mantis Ted noticed.

"Well, let's get you settled." He puts a hand to my elbow and guides me to the edge of the bed. This is the rough part, I know, having recently negotiated leaving my hospital bed and a mini-van. The getting in and out of stuff will kill you, I swear.

Anyway, ole Ted helps me advance on the bed. I remind myself of the mummy in the old Johnny Quest cartoons, covered in bandages, advancing with my elbows locked to avoid jogging stitches more than necessary, moaning with each step. I fight the urge to yelp when my belly stretches a fraction, cry out for real when I finally hit the mattress. Liposuction? I had forgotten all about it. But now the happy anti-ouch meds have left the building.

Ted puts a hand behind my back and eases me back onto pillow mountain. He adjusts pillows and fusses with the blanket. He withdraws the pile of release forms and instructions from his pocket and sets them on the mini fridge, smoothing them with long fingers. Finally he turns on the table lamp stationed there. You can tell he has kids.

"You don't happen to know where the pharmacy is, Dot?"

I had previously programmed the number into the phone. Am I not awesomely organized? I foolishly try to wave toward the phone. Huge booboo! Enormous mistake! Movement, BAD! I gasp, then try using my words. "The number's programmed into the phone. Just hit 3. It's on speed dial. They can give you directions. Phone's right there on the bookshelf."

Ted grabs the receiver and dials. If I didn't hurt so friggin badly, I might just laugh at the vision of ole Ted, his long, thin frame rocking from one foot to the other. He reminds me of a recently toilet trained three year old who desperately needs to potty, yet won't take five precious minutes to use the bathroom. If that three year old was an insect.

"Okay. Okay, I'll be right over."

I'm beginning to wonder how Ted survived Mrs. Wheeler's three pregnancies. While he's certainly solicitous, it's becoming apparent that my less than stellar physical condition wigs him out. "Thanks, again, Ted."

He waves absently and leaves.

With him gone, I can finally assess the magnitude of mess I've made. As I said, I'm a planner. However, I really didn't anticipate how eyeball-poppingly painful this process of being invaded with sucking tubes, sharp knives and tapping hammers actually is, until now, now that the anesthetic is gone for good and true from my system, leaving me crystal clear on every stabbed, prodded or sutured spot. Mini tummy tuck my incredibly sore ass.

I reach – carefully – for the mirror I've strategically placed on the bookshelf and take my first hard look. Holy Cow! Barely visible beneath the bandages, I can still make out my face, grotesquely swollen, eyes blackened like a prizefighter. You'd think it had been days rather than hours since my hair was washed. I had braided it into a ponytail, thinking low maintenance, but already the strands that emerge from the bandages are clumping together in greasy ropes.

There's worse to come, though. The tummy tuck and lipo are my current concerns. The people in the hospital somehow squished me into what are called 'compression pants,' hospital lingo for a neoprene body girdle. It's black, feels suspiciously like the material from my second dad's fishing waders, and makes it terribly difficult to breath. Also it makes me sweat. To be fair, breathing is bad idea anyway. Every single inhale seems to tug at something and I feel bloated as a toad. The good news is the puncture wounds from the lipo and the scary gut mark from the tummy tuck are covered by this garment, preventing me from getting a firsthand look at the bruising and scarring. But I'll get to see it fairly soon. Because one way or another, I've got to use the bathroom.

CHAPTER EIGHTEEN

Ted returns from the pharmacy. Like a proud parent, he extends his gift – a white paper bag loaded with Oxycodone and a stool softener. "The pharmacist says you're supposed to take one of the white ones with a whole glass of water and a light snack right away. Maybe toast or something. And the brown one before the end of the day." Ted wanders off to pour a glass of water. When he comes back from the kitchen, he stares in dumb surprise as I reach for the glass. His attention is rapt on the piece of toast on the plate in front of me.

"What?" I say, all innocence.

"I'm just impressed. You even moved the toaster?"

"Well, Ted, I'm a planner."

"So I see." He hands me the pill. "Anything else I can do for you?"

Can I have a drum roll? "Well, now that you asked, there's just one more thing. See, they have me in this thing to keep the swelling down. I need to get it off to use the bathroom, then put it back on again."

Mr. Ted Wheeler, father of three and coworker, steps back from the bed, drawing his insect arms together in front of him. "Come again?"

I don't have time for this. I just want to get 'er done. "Don't be coy, Ted. I need to do this like yesterday. Just help me get the thing off." And thus endeth any vestige of dignity.

We struggle for maybe fifteen minutes to free me from bitter body bondage. I whimper and grunt and moan the entire time, since every twitch makes my stomach ache. We have it down a full inch when we find the zipper. There's a gosh darned zipper on this thing! A quick pull and it's finally off. I wanna scream some more. Seems the pressure from the garment was actually helping. In its absence, I'm a naked, bruised, rapidly swelling lump of flesh. I drop the long T-shirt before Ted passes out from embarrassment. Good news, though: the process took so long, the narcotic has kicked in. I have flown from hopeless to Olympus. I suspect myself capable of amazing feats.

"Let's rock, Ted. Just twelve steps to the bathroom and we're done. Help me up."

Skin white with horror, Ted uses his superhuman insect power to ease me upright. I only scream a little, and God help him he nearly drops me in panic. That strikes me as hilarious and I start giggling. Dropping me would be bad. And, THAT, my friend, is some powerful medication, and I'm glad I took two. Ted assists me into the wheelchair and like magic we're at the bathroom door.

"Amazing," Ted says. He's staring over my head at my recently revamped powder room. It hosts metal grab rails around the toilet (they came in a kit), Costco sized cases of toilet paper stacked on the counter, even reading material within reach. I went to the extent of removing the bath mat, fearing it might impede the wheelchair. Pretty happy with my choices.

My brilliance doesn't prevent me from gobbling like a Thanksgiving turkey when I make the big move from the wheelchair to a standing position. I follow that with animalistic grunts when switching from standing to squatting. Who knew things could hurt so much? And why didn't someone mention it to me?

Pain makes me irritable, and I snap at the hapless mantis, "Close the door, for goodness sake!"

The door shuts hard.

Somewhere in the back of my brain, guilt sulks in a corner. I ignore it. I'm too sore to mess with guilt today. Instead, I focus on the near nirvana combination of Percocet and a good pee.

Oh, would that I could remain completely in the moment.

Minutes later, I shout for Ted. "Hey, Ted. Teddyyy, I'm ready!" My words ring, echo off the tight quarters of my powder room. "Oh, Ted, I could use a hand, here, buddy."

Uh oh.

CHAPTER NINETEEN

Eventually, I figure it out. Poor old Ted, like Elvis, has left the building. My own fault, of course. I mean Ted is a buck private who got drafted. He's probably in his mini-van trying to figure out how he got conscripted into this chauffeuring gig in the first place. I'm fairly certain that nowhere in his job conscription did it mention nursing a fellow employee to the john. Still, I had hoped he'd stick around until I got that damn compression suit back on.

Instead, it takes me nearly fifteen minutes to navigate my way back to the bed. This is followed by an additional twenty minutes or so getting into those stupid things. Layers of stomach muscle and fat, so recently stitched together, protest such massive effort. I make one last effort to pull the zipper up. This time, I yank too hard and overshoot, tapping my nose on the way past. I scream for real and pass out.

———————◖●◗—————————

I wake up with freezing feet. They are clear the hell at the other end of the bed, far below those damn compression pants. You'd think this is easy, right? Just throw on some socks, pull up the blankets. Easy-breezy. Unfortunately, those actions require the use of your stomach muscles.

Prior to my tummy tuck, (I know, I know: my "mini" tummy tuck), I vastly underrated the importance of internal and external obliques, the mighty pull of the abdominus rectus. Sitting, standing, leaning, hell even curling up into the fetal position requires that your stomach muscles play ball.

My sheepskin slippers taunt me, just inches from the bed, in clearly view. They lay there on the floor. I will them to levitate.

No dice.

After my landmark trip from bathroom to bed, I'd landed smack in the middle of the comforter. The likelihood that the comforter will drape itself over my legs is only slightly less likely than the levitating slippers. I feel a weeping attack coming on, but then I see it, just below the foot horizon: the extra blanket I'd placed there. My port in a storm.

In six additional minutes I fashion a retrieval tool from a coat hanger (I'm a veritable McGyver) and snag that bad boy. And I did it. Oh the pride! This is the second time today that I am swept up in powerful gratitude for simple pleasures. I am reconnecting to a physical self I'd ignored for years.

Okay, Forever.

Eventually I discover that the designer of the special compression garment anticipated that the wearer might want to dare a visit to the facilities. It has a hook and eye crotch flap. There was no need to remove it.

Are you kidding me? And to think, I completely destroyed my relationship with a coworker because nobody told me.

Sorry, Ted.

———————◀●◐▶———————

Dr. Devers smiles. "That's quite the heroic tale. I'm interested in your choice of words, the notion that you are 'reconnecting to a physical self.' It implies a previous disconnect. Talk to me about that."

Damn doctor makes me think all the time. There's nothing more painful than thinking about feelings. I miss work-style thinking, all clean and analytical. "I stopped being aware of my body a long time ago. I stopped caring about how it looked or how it felt. And pretty soon, I didn't really have much sensation in my body. And that was okay. People are too superficial anyway. I told myself that only shallow people deal with the physical stuff. I was above such concerns. In the head. But it was crap, really. I just got tired of being beaten down."

"Beaten down?"

"Sure. Every single day, someone would remind me that I didn't fit in. My dad, for starters. That's bio dad, not mom's present love meister, Rupert Rooney. Every single damn day he'd have something to say on the matter. 'You fat tub-a-lard, your mom must have backed into a pig when I wasn't looking' and so on. Like I chose to offend him with how I looked. No one seemed to get that my physical appearance was a husk I couldn't shed. And I hated it. Oh God how I hated it. Hated being called names and hated not being pretty. And the envy! Oh my god when pretty people got asked to be someone's friend or go to a party..." I took a sharp breath. "So at some point I unhooked. I just stopped experiencing my body altogether. Went cold. Barely gave it a moment's thought. I concentrated on my mind."

I look at her, brisk and coolly beautiful in her cream wool suit. Her clipboard hangs, poised.

"Do you get it? Do you see? No more outside. Just the mind. Just good, clean thinking. I speak French. I can program computers in several languages. I work for the biggest software firm in the world. Hell, I could have been a doctor - "

"Yet you never finished college. You mentioned that you stayed in the testing group when a promotion was offered. You never travel. And you never went to medical school."

I grunt like an animal, exasperated. "That makes it worse. Even I don't buy into my own bullshit. Can you imagine how confusing that is? I try and tell myself every day that what I am is enough, that I am is okay. But I don't believe it. I try and tell myself that I'm bright and literate and capable of doing great things in the world. But why should I believe that? I have absolutely no evidence to support it.

"What I do have is this hard, cold voice, which

sounds suspiciously like my dad, always willing to tell me how worthless I am. Sometimes the voice becomes a tangle of voices, kids from my neighborhood or at school. School bullies." I close my eyes. "It's pathetic. I study and train and work and try to do better. It doesn't matter. I go to the interview and they're disgusted, just grossed out. You can see it in their eyes. No matter how smart I am, they see only the shell, not what I know. To the world, I am what I look like. My mind, body, and feelings refuse to synch up and play as a team. There seems to be a rule against just being happy."

She sets down the clipboard with a wooden thunk. "Says who?"

For ten hours, I sleep, waking up at around two-thirty in the morning desperate to pee again, God help me. Stupid pain meds have worn off and doing the up-down thing by myself threatens to tear a stitch. Good news, at least I found that special booty flap.

Desperate times. I break down, scroll through the rolodex next to my bed and make a call.

CHAPTER TWENTY

The clickity-click on my porch signals the arrival of the Manolo Blanik cavalry.

"Come on in, Ginny." I holler. I have wisely unlocked the door following my last trip to the bathroom.

Ginny trip traps in, which passes for stomping in high heels. "Tell me there's a reason I'm here," her voice shows up before she does. When I do see her, it's the usual pursed lips, but her hair has been dyed a deep auburn with bright cinnamon highlights. She stops, stares hard at me – a bandaged whale beached on my bed. Her mouth drops open. "Oh my god you look like absolute shit. What have you gone and done?"

"Practically everything. Nose job. Laser resurfacing. Lipo. Modified tummy tuck. Doctor Tam says he should have thrown in a set of steak knives."

"Ya think? Why exactly am I here?" She tosses

aside a Chanel handbag.

"Simple. I need you to help me to the bathroom."

Ginny's eyebrows defy her Botox injections and ascend up beyond her bangs. "You have got to be kidding."

"Oh how I wish I were. Look, it's not rocket surgery. It's really difficult getting there and back into bed. My stomach was recently bisected and won't cooperate."

Ginny swishes her currently auburn head in denial. "But I don't want to. I'm no Mother Theresa. You said so yourself on countless occasions."

"I lied. You're a friggin' saint. You just don't know it yet. This is your ticket into heaven" This will be good for both of us. You'll break out of your selfish, insular, egocentric world, and I'll get to use the john. Everybody wins. "Please?"

Nurse Ginny is not pleased. I know this because her forehead tries to crinkle up. It can't, of course, because of all those Botox appointments, (each and every one of which I sat through). And since I have now had several treatments myself, perhaps later we can have a frown off. I crack myself up, but oh, I dare not laugh. I swallow the mirth.

"Come on. Be a buddy. Think Nike. Just do it."

Ginny stayed long enough to get me in and out of the bathroom. Then she ratted me out to Elvira, who's psychedelic business card had been hastily thumbtacked to my bulletin board. She forced me to cough up a name while hooking the flap of my squeezy pants. Hers was the only one I could conjure up, other than mom, Trainer Joe, and several doctors. That's how Elvira Wentz (whose last name I didn't know at the time), ended up on my doorstep, dressed like a vampiric Pippi Longstocking, fully prepared to nurse me back to health.

"That was a dangerous thing you did."

"What? The surgery? Calling Ginny?"

"You should have arranged for someone to be with you for the first few days after surgery."

"You really don't get it do you? There was no one. No one. I'm lucky that Ginny bothered to show. And I'm crazy lucky that Elvira has a heart twice the size of her head.

CHAPTER TWENTY-ONE

Elvira watched Ginny sweep past her out the door. "And a merry afternoon to you, too," she offered to the closed door. She hesitated on the little square of my foyer holding a black, plastic garbage bag in one hand and a guitar case in the other. It reminded me of the scene in The Sound Of Music where Julie Andrews arrives, bags in hand, at the Castle of the Baron Von Trapp. Except Julie hadn't been wearing a hat with ear flaps, a leather biker jacket six sizes too big for her small frame (black of course), and a tutu dotted with skulls. I'm also positive that Miss Andrews never wore tights banded in black and red stripes. If she did, she wouldn't have paired them with high top sneakers.

"Miss Thing says you went through with the surgical morph. Wicked." She dropped the bag and stepped closer to my modified living/bedroom. "You and me seem to have, like, a GPS for attracting society's finest." She thumbed over her shoulder, "That one's a peach." She let the bag drop and took a slow look around. "Interesting design decisions. Function over form, right?"

Hugely grateful for the running dialog, I gave her a pathetic thumbs up. What do you say to someone who has shown up like Dudley Do-Right when you really need them?

"Thanks for coming over."

She gave a dismissive wave and dragged a chair from the kitchen over to the bed. "I needed a change of scene. Karmic, really."

"I'm all about karma at the moment, El. Well, that and Vicodin. I'm a bit about that, too."

"Clearly."

"What karmic issues are plaguing you, divine Ms. El?"

She bit at a piercing tucked in the corner of her lower lip – a silver ring. Her enormous eyes, like those annoying Precious Moments statues my mom collects, liquid shimmer at the lower rims.

Oh crap she's going to cry.

CHAPTER TWENTY-TWO

She did cry. Sobbed. Fortunately, my post-op arsenal included Kleenex, and I shoved the box her way. I'm not a 'hug strangers' kind of gal, but had I not been mummified, I would have thrown an arm around her. She was that miserable. Besides she's a fellow D.A.'er.

Eventually the flow dwindled and she could speak between hiccups. "There was this guy I met at a gig. Uber hot, ya know?" She swiped a wadded tissue across her nose. "Figured I didn't have a shot in hell, but he said he dug my music, and that is, like, huge. We hooked up and I've been seeing him for two weeks, which is, again, a world record for me. I even considered dropping out of Dater's Anonymous. Figured I was sorta cured."

"Sounds like you earned your way out."

"Ya'd think, right? But I had this gig yesterday and he showed up with this urban posse of his. When I see him, I gave him the look right? You know 'hey, bro!' But it's like he's suddenly lost my business card and totally doesn't know me. Like, hello! I'm the entertainment, but suddenly I'm forgetting entire chord progressions because he is so not acknowledging I exist and that is so not helping my self-concept, and Dr. Pepper – I mean Dr. Devers – she says I need to value myself and work on my self-concept. And I've been really doing the stuff that Dr. Pep– that the doc said to do. Like working my strong points. And the band has really taken off, ya know? So it's like working, right?

"But now I feel like a complete doofus. Like the whole time I thought this dude got me, that the two of us are tight, but he's laughing at me." Her voice cracked hard, but she rallied. "He is so fucking laughing at me that it's fucking resonating off the fucking walls. Oh, sorry 'bout the fucking language, dude." She sniffed hugely, a gross, mucus-y inhale.

"Not a fucking problem."

She laughed a hard, short bark. "So the night was an epic fail. My mates helped me settle enough to finish the set and make it home." Devoid of most of her makeup which had been swiped off with her fists, her eyes had the pitiable look you find in shelter dogs, that terrible mix of confusion and hurt. "And he was there. At my place. Fucking troll. Acting like I should drop my drawers because he happened to be in the neighborhood." She stopped for a second, staring down and the wad of Kleenex in her hand. Her voice became tiny.

"Dottie, I let him. I let him in. And after he was uber mean to me. Because... well he was hot, right?

But he..." She slipped off the hat, turned her head to the side revealing what appeared to be a purple handprint. "He just wasn't the same, dude, know what I mean? And now I'm afraid of him showing up at the club or my place again and I... I want to be sure not to be there, ya know? To not be available." She seemed to deflate, the remaining strength dropping away from her as though her plug had been pulled. "Does that make any sense?"

What do you for someone in that position?

"Protein bar? It's not booze, which you clearly could use, and it's not dope, since I don't do that, but it's what I have."

CHAPTER TWENTY-THREE

It took a full three weeks before I could move around without grunting. Doesn't mean I didn't move around, heck no, it's just that I made terrible noises while doing it. Elvira ensured I got sufficient exercise. She also emptied out drainage tubes, (while wrinkling her nose, "dude! Gross!"), and zipped me into and out of compression pants, (popping gum and laughing the entire time), insisting that circulation would help with healing. "Madam Yola – she's my psychic? She's like all about circulation."

So circulate I did.

I'd never had a roommate before, but Elvira proved to be that golden goose of roommates: she ate like Calista Flockhart, wrote songs quietly all night, slept till noon, and when awake, offered comic insights on any subject that wandered by.

Oh! And she had a car: a pathetic 1993 Mazda Protégé named the Rubiyat Rubaiyat of Omar

Khayyam ("like it's ruby red, right?"). None of the original side body molding remained and someone had replaced a door, but God bless, it ran. When my three weeks of vacation ran out, she gave me a ride into work to celebrate my return to civilization. Not riding the bus? True extravagance.

My nose is still a bit swollen at that point, but not nearly as much as I had feared. Most of the discoloration around my eyes had faded and other than the deep twinges from scar tissue when I stand up, my stomach had healed. I've lost over fifty – seven pounds between the diet and surgeries. My nose is changed. I have a waist. My skin is amazing.

And thanks to Kennedy J, I even have my first makeup consultation.

The first time I see myself tricked out in full Kennedy J form, I don't recognize myself. My mentor insists I come back downtown to the salon for retrofitting after the surgery, but I stall at first, claiming my stitches still pull and the bus ride would be uncomfortable. Elvira rolls her eyes at that.

"I'm headed to Seattle next week to drop off a demo tape. I'll drop you at K.J.'s."

Traitor.

So I suck it up and the day before I was due back at work, Giselle greets me at the reception desk without a glimmer of recognition in her eyes. When I speak, her jaw drops, she squeals, and inches around the desk in her four inch heels to hug me. She grabs my hands and steps back to get the full effect and I notice her nails – a delicious shade of pearl, perfectly shaped and lustrous. Suddenly we are chatting about her manicure, about the surgeries, about how much fun Kennedy would have dressing me.

Small talk isn't a strength, but jawing with Giselle suddenly seems easy breezy. Kennedy swoops in, ready to squash me in a bear hug, and then he hesitates, catching my shoulders in his large hands and holding me at arm's length.

"You look absolutely marvelous, but are you fully healed, my dear? Wouldn't want to crush any of your hard work."

At my nod, he squishes all air from my lungs.

"Excellent! I'm giddy as a well-hung school girl!" He twists toward Giselle, "I'll drag her out when she's done. I know you've been looking forward to this one." He grabs my hand and we race to the back room.

Inside, there are two additions: a chair and a glamorous, black mountain of a man in a robin's egg blue silk shirt. Built like a linebacker, enormous through the shoulders and even taller than Kennedy J, (which puts him well over six-four). I'm riveted by his eyebrows: they're perfection, black delicate swoops over his shiny agate eyes. I barely notice the unnaturally smooth skin I'm so mesmerized by the brows. You rarely see such perfectly groomed brows on a woman, but you absolutely do not see them on a man. Then there's the eyeliner. I'm fairly certain this is the first man I've encountered wearing it (outside of TV). His eyes are groomed like a forties femme fatale.

"B. J., this is our project. Dorothy, let me introduce Bubba Jackson, perhaps the greatest hairdresser of our time. It wouldn't be Oscar night without him, I assure you. B.J. understands the dilemma, and he insisted on flying in to help. Gratis. You're a doll, B.J."

"Yes. I am. But when Kennedy sent me your picture... well let's say I could see that all that wonderful hair deserves the very best, which is me. And since I have a salon opening in Seattle in two weeks your head shot will simply make the place." He patted the chair back. "Come, take a seat. And tell me about what you normally do with your hair."

I fight the urge to giggle. "I normally pull it back into the impressive pony tail you see before you. After a good scrubbing of course."

Bubba shudders. "Do not scrub your hair. Treat it respectfully."

He pulls a plastic poncho off the sideboard and drapes it over my shoulders. He stares at my reflection in the mirror for an instant, considering. "Mister K, have you a Polaroid nearby?" After a quick beep to Giselle, Kennedy produces a camera. Bubba takes several head shots. He paces around me, asking questions, fluffing a section of hair on this side, pulling it down in straight lines on either side of my face, lifting my chin with one hand, turning my head into profile with the other. He grills me: do I wear it up? Do I use a curling iron or blow dryer? How much time am I willing to spend? Do I use any products? Am I willing to?

Mostly I toss out no's: no, I rarely wear it up, no to the curling iron, maybe I blow it dry once in a blue moon. I don't own hot rollers.

"We're keeping the length of course." He

throws this information over his shoulder to Kennedy J, who echoes, "Of course."

"You're lucky. With such a symmetrical and oval face to work with, virtually any style will work. It comes down to lifestyle and personality." He paused dramatically. Swooping eyebrows drawn. "I'm going in."

Facing away from the mirror, B.J. cuts it dry. The few times when I've had it done at a real salon, the hairdresser washed your hair first, or at least misted it with water. This guy hacks away, leaving great chunks of hair flying. I hold my breath in terror, fearing that the one god-given feature I like about myself is being manually detached. Eventually his pace slows and his movements become precise, surgical. He steps back, crosses his hands over his chest.

Kennedy wanders into view, throws a well manicured hand to his chest. "Mr. Jackson, you are gifted."

Bubba Jackson wears a Mona Lisa smile. "Yes."

The door swings open behind us. Giselle's slender back comes into view and places an enormous tea service on the sideboard. "Sorry to barge, Kennedy, but I just had to get a look." She turns to face me, then her chin drops and her eyebrows raise. Her head turns slowly from side to side. "That's crazy. That's just phenomenal. I mean you looked okay before, don't get me wrong but…" She angles her head towards where she assumes Kennedy stood. "Oh and Marcy'll be here any second. She stopped to get a Starbucks."

She doesn't finish the sentence when a diminutive woman in black appears at her elbow, tugging off a red felt beret. "Nice do, B. J."

"Sissy! so good to have you!" There is a series of air kisses as Kennedy introduces his sister (soul sister that is, no relation), Marcy Allen. Marcy has been summoned to lacquer finishing touches on me. She and Bubba obviously know each other and exchange additional compressed air kisses. Marcy notices the Polaroids on Kennedy's desk, and shuffles through them.

"You're Picasso, Bubba. You gonna do mine next?"

"Just as soon as you grow me an inch of hair to work with, dear."

"Ah, you're just chicken." She runs a hand over her black buzz cut, smiles big, white Chiclet teeth at me. "Let's rock."

She spends only minutes creating a face so flawless it appears retouched, but it takes her a great deal longer to walk me through the techniques and tricks that got it that way. By the time she is satisfied, my eyebrows look nearly as good as Bubba Jackson's. She completes her crash course in multi-level lip coloring, (don't forget just a tap over powder over the tissue to set them), then steps back and signals to Bubba Jackson who snaps another Polaroid. "Now that is an "after."

MAID OVER

A little levity could be a quick fix.

excerpt from The Bridesmaid's Manual *by Sarah Stein & Lucy Talbot, Page 72*

CHAPTER TWENTY-FOUR

I return to work a swan.

Or at least a sharp dressed duck.

It's hard to accept that the attractive woman I glimpse in mirrors and windows might be me. Easier to swallow 'imposter.' Whatever remains between body, hair, makeup, and wardrobe, (including a new bra which creates cleavage I am not entirely comfortable with), I am no longer Dot Lindell, sad loser. I'm swan girl.

Which, given where I work, proves useless. Prince Charming doesn't work at Microcosm. I am surrounded by very busy frogs. On the positive side, no one recognizes me, not even my truant boss, Greg Larson, (he who boldly opted out of transportation duties). I went to see him immediately upon my return to work.

A quick rap on the wall outside his door resulted in a bark.

"In."

Greg hunches over his desk, the usual pose. He's a big, meaty guy, hairy arms, over-scaled for his desk. He wears his glasses today, so he's been at his monitor too long.

"Just wanted you to know I'm finally working in-house again. Jeff sent over the packet and Suni and I already broke up the different modules. I'm taking all the U/I and any SQL, and Suni will cover the rest. Anything else?"

"Nope. Good to have you back. Don't forget the team meeting tomorrow at 2:00." Greg's eyes remain fixed on the monitor, fingers whistling over the keyboard.

"I'm off then." I stand there like an idiot, internally twiddling my fingers.

Finally, he glances up, and his fingers halt in mid-movement. "May I help you?" Then he makes the connection. His hands fall away from the computer and he stares hard. "Well I'll be double damned-duh. Things change, people, change, taxes rise. What exactly was that surgery you had, Dot? Perhaps I'll sign my girlfriend up for some. Hell, do they do men?" He grins, a fairly unusual event for Greg. Good to see a face still capable of crinkling up on command.

No Botox for you, Greg? Good man.

I let myself smile, showing off my new "Zoom Whitened" teeth. Just a warning: it leaves your teeth sore. "It all hurts. They leave that part out on TV."

Greg shakes his head slowly. "Well worth it. You've changed, Dot."

I bite my lip. "There's something I need to ask about if you have a minute." This was the part I'd been secretly dreading. It seems so trivial a thing, but... but I'd made up my mind and now was the time. "I've decided to start using my middle name. It sort of... marks a new beginning, you know? Alana. That's the name I want to go by now. So if you could put a blip in my personnel file, or make a note? I'd appreciate it."

I take a breath. I'd almost forgotten to breathe. "And maybe let operations know I'll need a new email login? That would make it more official. I'd appreciate it."

His narrow gray eyes widen a bit behind those black-rimmed glasses. He raises one hand to his mouth, elbow resting on the arm of his office chair. He picks up a pencil from a stainless cup on his desk, leans back, begins to wiggle it, creating a bowtie in the air. "You know you'll get crap about that, right? I mean certainly I'll notify personnel, but people are going to call you what they call you. We aren't exactly Emily Post compliant around here."

A slightly deeper breath causes that tug at my midsection reminding me why I'm playing this game. "I understand. That's why I'm asking you to help remind people? This is a big deal, Greg." Silently I try and burn thoughts into his brain: you owe me big boy. You dumped responsibility for getting me home from a frigging hospital on someone else. Now you owe me. And you'll help me with this.

He drops the pencil back in the cup. "Okay. I'll send an email and voila, they will all comply, as I have waved the mighty wand-o'-management' over them. So let it be written. So let it be done. Let the name 'Dot' be stricken from every obelisk and all that."

This is what I want, right? "Great. Thanks, Greg."

I'm pot committed.

I leave his office and return to mine, a space now shared with a nice contractor. It smells at once familiar and foreign, like it did my first day here. I settle down, using my as yet unchanged email alias and retrieve about six million emails, along with a nasty-gram from operations warning me that "my mailbox is full," and I better delete some messages or they'll do it for me.

It hits me: I've really gone and done it. I altered my face, my body. Now, my name is gone. What the hell is left of me?

CHAPTER TWENTY-FIVE

I have been back at work for about three weeks. Microcosm being the big M that it is, I spend the lion's share of that time bug hunting – searching for programming errors – in complete isolation, an unlikely setting for a Barbara Cartland heroine. When I hit on a bug so nasty it required reproducing it for the programmer, it came as a blessing. Elvira returned to her own apartment last week and who knew who much I'd miss her company?

In any case, it was off to meet the programmer. In rare cases like this, you need to show the steps that create the problem on the developer's own machine, since it might have a slightly different version of software. I don't care why. I am just glad for a change of pace.

Veteran employees of Microcosm modify their offices to suit their personalities. This guy is clearly a lifer. Towers of soda cans and paper in cartoons litter the eight by eight space. It's a mess. There are posters, action figures, and the piece de resistance, a life-size blow up cartoon doll, (no not that kind of doll). The inflated creature has pointed elf ears and a mop of red plastic hair with a horn protruding from it. It's smiling, which I find slightly creepy, and from the smile protrudes a single, lopsided fang. A tossed salad of debris rests beside the garbage can, clearly a miss.

Later I will learn the identity of the monster doll as Jin the Wind Master from Yu Yu Hakusho. The occupant of this particular cell has a jones for Manga, Japanese cartoon books, collecting anything and everything associated with Japanese cartoons.

To me, the space appears to be collapsing in on itself, a black hole of stuff. I am hardly surprised that the developer lead who occupies the space was a 'him.' He doesn't look up from his monitor. Then he does.

I freeze. He obviously doesn't recognize me from our meeting months earlier. And most certainly he doesn't recall our far earlier acquaintance in high school.

But this time, I am not sleep deprived. And I have the benefit of a Google search to confirm my suspicions.

The guy is definitely John Miller, former star running back of Inglemoor High School. He was our school's answer to Brad Pitt, boon companion to my arch enemy, Jack Weston. My vastly diminished stomach lurches and I swallow bile.

Led by Jack Weston, team terror never missed an opportunity to take a verbal swipe at me. Their torture squad of jocks seemed singularly devoted to me. The thought of intentionally entering his office, no his lair, for a fresh round of 'how fat is she?' would have required a whole new level of crazy. Instead, I'm paralyzed. And I cannot believe I didn't recognize him instantly the first time.

From a million miles away I hear, "Whatcha need, sis, I'm on the clock?"

Revelation: John Justin Miller hasn't the outside of a clue who I am. 'Cock-rot Dot' from Inglemoor High bears no relation to Software Development Test Engineer Alana Lindell. Special shout out to Greg for changing my email alias. A boatload of plastic surgery probably muddied the water a bit as well.

I am incognito.

"Rock 'n roll, m'lady. Time's money and all that."

I will myself forward the three additional feet into his office. I issue a silent prayer of thanksgiving to Jimmy Choo for creating elegant patent leather flats. Had I been wearing heels I would have doubtless toppled over.

"A Lindell? For the bug, yes?"

I'm rendered speechless at hearing my new email alias. I nod.

He drops his chin but raises his eyes, the ones I recall from years back: unearthly, silver blue under sooty eyelashes, the eyes of a Vegas hypnotist. "Prove it, sis."

To calm myself, I study the room, offering an editorial review. "Quite the shrine, jMiller." Anyone can toss an email alias around. His answering smile is dangerous and familiar. How on earth did I fail to recognize him? What if this is a mistake? Perhaps there is an identical John Miller, a doppelganger, wandering the earth. Maybe they were twins separated at birth. Heck, John is a common name.

Besides, the swaggering high school football player I know would not have been caught dead playing with little cartoon action figures. His associates at the time would have shaved his nards for such childishness.

The blue crystal of his eyes questions.

Oh it's him alright.

But I am no longer a tormented high schooler. I have graduated from the Kennedy J Boot Camp of Self Confidence. Make him proud. Show no fear. And most importantly, ignore the overwhelming physical presence of John Miller.

Disregard his blue black hair. Pay no heed to that light, musky scent. Should he direct a question your way, gaze at the monitor and concentrate deeply, but avoid Satan's eyes, those wicked, blue crystal shards. Remember the pain. Be vigilant, alert for the verbal backhand. Do not let your guard down.

John Miller shoves the latest copy of Shonen Jump – more Japanese cartoon stuff – off his guest chair, which I take to be an invitation. This places me too near my old nemesis. I take a deep breath and inhale that lovely cologne.

The work, the work, the work, I chant inwardly. Without prevarication, I reproduce the bug on his machine.

He seethes. "Damn." He rubs at both eyebrows.

They are nearly black, like his hair. Very George Clooney. They make him appear deeply thoughtful, incredibly sexy. "I guess this is where I'm supposed to genuflect, thank my lucky stars that QA saved my bacon and gracefully code a fix."

"Cash donations accepted in lieu of praise."

"Shameless exploitation, that's what it is." He flashes ultra white teeth. "But I'll spring for cheap cafeteria food if you have a solution?"

"Why shucks, partner, I just might."

"Liar!" He swivels the office chair, takes a hard look at me. And I mean he really looks at me: Dot-lite, new and improved, Version 2.0, created by Kennedy J and a staff of hundreds, but modeled by yours truly. My deodorant fails spectacularly. Epically.

"Seriously, you've got a fix?"

I blush clear to my hairline. "I think so." This guy seems so removed from the monster in the letterman's jacket, the one who laughed in unison with his buddies. The work, I chide myself. Focus on the screen, open up the source program, review the lines of code. "Check the host open routine. I'm pretty sure it's... here. See? All the names are local. Maybe they got put in during a self-test and didn't get swapped out. See? Right there?" I point a finger at a line of C# code on the monitor.

His brow wrinkles. "Shit on a... Excuse me. I mean, that's it. Give me ten minutes to fix this and get it compiled and you'll get your bragging rights. Or at least cheap cafeteria food." He makes the corrections using only two index fingers, typing at light speed. Shocking how few software developers know how to type.

He looks up. John Miller, former football hero, my tormentor. "Let's do lunch, pretty girl."

CHAPTER TWENTY-SIX

Pretty girl. Did you hear that? He called me pretty.

Oh I know that you beautiful people just don't get it. BPs. That's what I call your kind: beautiful people. Oh don't grimace, it's a compliment, doc. You have good bones. My guess is you've always had good bones. So despite all that book learnin' about the affects of physical appearance on social behavior, I bet it never struck you that homely people feel like dog shit, just dog shit, a good deal of the time.

Consider what I've done to alter myself to meet the current standard of attractiveness: I cut, peeled, acid burned or lasered every recognizable aspect of myself. Everything that makes life endurable and enjoyable I blew off to get to pretty: no drugs, no booze, no fattening food, no lazy days, no sugar for the love of God, all to try and make the outside of me look like what people want to see. I would have given up sleep if that's what was required.

"So was it worth it?" Doctor Pepper asks.

I ignore the question.

"Three weeks after my surgery, mom got back from London and we met for lunch. At the entrance to Red Robin, my mom strolled right past me. She didn't blink when passing. I tapped her arm and called her mom. She later claimed that she thought some cracked up supermodel had turned on her. I know this is true because that's how she described it later.

"Eventually she recognized my voice. Then she started crying. Crying with happiness. I mean she was overwhelmed with joy at how much I didn't look anything like her daughter."

"Did you ask her why she was crying?"

"No need. People were doing it all over the place. Practically every person I knew before." I look away for moment, gathering my thoughts.

"I'm just so cheesed off. I watch those makeovers shows. I'm a junkie for 'em. Extreme Makeover. The Swan. Hell, every frigging show on plastic surgery, ever. I watch them all. At the end, the family and friends always tear up and blubber about how happy they are. But think about it: they're happy this person they theoretically love isn't the same. Ergo, they never really accepted them in the first place.

"Do you get it? I was always clear on bio dad hating me, not news. But realizing my own mom never really accepted me? Much worse."

CHAPTER TWENTY-SEVEN

So here I am, a formerly dateless wonder dating the man of my dreams. Or a monster from my childhood. Pick one. The jury's still out.

Elvira believes my mind may be a victim of plastic surgery.

John calls me Alana, which is the name I gave him. I'm sure he thinks I suffer from hearing loss since I rarely respond on the first 'Alana.' It takes effort and focus to adjust to a new identity but this is my doing, so I can hardly complain.

So where shall I go on my first date ever?

A wedding. Heavy sigh. His sister Rachel's wedding, specifically. Could be worse: At least I don't have to wear a bridesmaid's dress on my first ever date. This time I will be a spectator.

A spectator in a blind panic. This necessitates a call to Kennedy J seconds after John makes the suggestion, as I now rely nearly exclusively on his wardrobe choices. My theory is that this conserves thousands of brain cells that may one day cure a dread disease. You're welcome.

"Oh my god, Kennedy, he asked me to his sister's wedding! Isn't that a rite of passage or something? I mean his parents will be there for goodness sake!"

"Don't strip a gear dear, you just met him. This may simply be a man-ploy to avoid deepening a commitment he's got with someone else. As a wildcard, you must remain calm, cool, and oh-so-sexy. Oh you SO need to get over here! We'll trot out some decent formal wear. I do so love formal wear," his voice trailed off dreamily.

"Kennedy I don't have dime one to drop on formal wear, as well you know. The frigging tummy tuck alone will keep me indentured for the next three years. And that's only if I get a bonus this year."

"Now you're just sniffing for freebees. And you shall have them! I have this drop-dead vintage Azzedine Alaia that will just knock his socks off. With your hair color –"

"Sold. Free is my favorite price." I grin.

I hear chuckles on the other end. "You don't even know if it will fit. Let's do drinks and a fitting. Then if it doesn't, we won't care. Come down to the shop around… let's say six-ish. I want plenty of time, but I don't want to miss the tail end of happy hour at Chartreuse."

Several thousand test cases, a couple of hours of bus riding later, I'm at his studio. I must now contend with a Kennedy J dress fitting. It's a pain in the ass. In the good old pre-makeover days, I lived in sweats (cotton) and oversized shirts (cotton). They're practical choices for an oversized body. Nearly everything I owned had elastic in the waistband – if there was a waistband.

My new look, new stomach and certainly my new boobs are high maintenance. I'm still not thrilled with any material other than cotton on my skin, but per Kennedy, there's more to life than cotton. There's also cotton blends, linen, and silk. I now endure a whole plethora of materials that look great and feel... well, icky.

Clothes still never fit me off the rack, but now it's because they're either too small in the boobs or too huge in the waist. "So use a tailor," says Kennedy. He insists, for example, that the simple Calvin Klein sheath he's selected will need tailoring.

He removes a mouthful of straight pins. "The goal is to have the dress hang as though it wants to be a straight line, but simply can't because of the perfection of your bosom and ass."

"My bosom? Eww! I don't think I want body parts associated with Dame Edna." I stop laughing when he stabs me in the butt with a straight pin. "Hey!"

"Settle. I nearly have this pinned up and then we can booze. I've had a dreadful week – and did you see Jefferson's face? – he's such a slut. He's got on more makeup than Tammy Faye."

I hadn't noticed as I am busy admiring Kennedy's notion of business casual: tweedy pants, cranberry silk sweater over a thick pinstriped shirt - the whole mess under a leather car coat. He has on cool shoes, brushed suede. I'm starting to notice shoes. Ugly shoes can trash an outfit - who knew? You can shoot an ensemble dead with a pair of running shoes, no matter how comfortable they are. This is why being a woman sucks. No one expects a man to strap on heels. Except for Prince maybe.

The door swings hard open. "I heard that, bitch. Don't be jealous. Not everyone can have a perfect complexion." Jefferson wanders in for a look-see and pecks me on the cheek.

"There." Kennedy steps back and admires his handiwork. "The line is splendiferous. Boodilicious. Rockin'." Jefferson, at his shoulder, nods in affectionate agreement.

I look at my reflection in the simple – or not so simple – navy sheath. Dang. I look good. With the Valentino stilettos that I refuse to wear till I have to, this will look sensational. "You are a friggin genius, Dr. J."

"Not news. Get your clothes on. Let us imbibe."

I change back into work clothes - not sweats. That was Dot, old school. New and improved Alana Lindell dons a pencil skirt, kitten heels, and an 'I love your bosom' cutout sweater. Since we're post work, I'll lose the jacket so I can show off the signature jewelry piece I have on loan from Kennedy's collection. Jefferson begs off – hot date – and Kennedy and I do the short hop to Chartreuse, an ultra trendy lounge I wouldn't have dared enter a few months earlier. Now, Kennedy and I stroll past the crowds and wave at Gus the bouncer. He drops the velvet rope and we're in.

Chartreuse is...you guessed it, chartreuse: a frosted glass miasma of that weird yellow-green color, heavy with mahogany and flashing enough mirrored surfaces to sedate all the pretty people. As a former teetotaler, it's unnerving how easily I've become an aficionado of 'house specialty' cocktails. This place has a lovely one: a crazy concoction of Midori, Seven-Up, and yadda yadda yadda that they serve in a beaker. There might be lime sherbet in it? Anyway, it's tasty, hazardous and I'm on my second.

My recent transformation has taught me some interesting lessons in finance. Plastic surgery is expensive, which causes liquor to become free. I never bothered with bars in the past, and I doubt free beverages would have come my way, even if I had mustered the courage to show up. Coupled with the prices at the high end establishments Kennedy frequents and you would have found me stuck at home watching The Swan for free. But not anymore.

Nope. At the moment, I'm in a happy haze of green alcohol. I've managed to not let freebees from passing suitors and their glib sweet talk go to my head.

Oh I'm such a lying sack of shit! That's a complete lie. I'm stinky, messy drunk and only the steadying influence of a six-foot plus gay man glaring at me occasionally prevents me from falling into the lap of the gent footing the bill for my Seaweeds, which I switched to an hour ago at the suggestion of the sweet bartender.

Kennedy is reading me the riot act I think. I try

to focus on his running commentary, but the second law of lounge dynamics states that for every base filled thump of the sound system, your hearing is reduced by about a million percent. Of course blowing a .09 probably doesn't help. I smile vacuously and shrug.

Mr. Open Wallet Man leans in from the other side. He mentions something about his place and a nightcap. Nightcap? It's not even eleven o'clock. I think. Then I giggle, because clocks are pretty dang funny. I think my potential love interest might be younger than me. He's kind of cute in an early Miami Vice, Don Johnson kind of way. He keeps talking, but as mentioned, I can't hear. I make 'no hear' motions by tapping my ear, and his lips move to the side of my face to assist.

Suddenly this guy is close enough to smell. He smells nice, an interesting mix of cologne and 'other.' His lips on my ear tickle a bit. The intimacy of the situation suddenly strikes me and I yank my head back. I can feel Kennedy J doing his eyebrow raise thing without even looking over. A part of me wants to stick my tongue out at him, he of the paternal eyebrow, and leave Chartreuse with O. W. Man. This guy LIKES me, can't Kennedy see that? That's two entire guys in a week! Plus untold numbers of free beverages. Clearly a new Dot – oops I mean a new Alana – world record.

Another part of me is just disgusted. Who IS this lame creature, drinking like a fish and flirting like a twenty dollar whore? A wave of nausea overwhelms me and I stagger for the ladies room, totally disoriented.

This is the design extravaganza ladies room. If I wasn't hanging over a toilet, I'm certain I would have been very impressed by all the lovely stone and glass in there. Maybe someday I'll actually look up and make a note of it. Meanwhile, the sounds of Kennedy J's voice, muffled through the walls, echo past along with the percussive blows as he bangs on the door asking if I'm okay. I groan and several Seaweeds take flight.

Light years later, I drag myself to the sink and rinse out my mouth. I look over and to my horror I see the reflection of my next door neighbor, Merry Sooner. Yes that's her real name. Merry is a very angry lesbian. Don't get me wrong, I know plenty of happy, friendly lesbians. Merry just isn't one of them.

She's lived next door for two years. I know exactly how many because that's the number of years I've spent peeking out my curtains before daring to leave my place for any reason. See, you have to make sure her car isn't there before picking up mail or heading for the bus. Before I knew about the dangers of encountering angry Merry, I foolishly picked up my mail at will. Then one day, BAM! I'm rifling through my junk mail when the woman stamps up. She's maybe five feet tall, but she plants her muscled, furry legs in an inverted V and crosses her arms indicating she's here for battle. Her head is wrapped in a bandana. "Who the hell told you to paint your mailbox that color?"

I jump back startled. Her voice reverberates so loudly I think I've been shot. "It's the color the real estate agent said to paint it. She said it's in the covenants."

She snorted. "I don't know what planet you're on, but we're supposed to paint them green. Woodland green. Not that god-awful teal shit you have there. It makes the entire neighborhood look like crap."

It's a mailbox. Pretty sure a person cannot single handedly destroy resale values for an entire neighborhood with a single mailbox. "I'm sorry you feel that way. It's no biggy."

Oh that was a big mistake. My clue is the shifting of hands to hips, the bulging of eyes beneath furry raised brows, and a large 'O' of a mouth dropped in disbelief. "You do understand that you're responsible to the architectural review committee, right? Do you get that if you breach enough covenants you're out?"

I've only met a few people that truly hated me on sight. Oh sure, tons have grown to despise me, and a handful have taken pot shots at me, but more commonly I'm completely ignored. I'm not prepared for fisticuffs, which seems to be the direction this is heading. "Actually I'm a very responsible person –" That's as far as I get.

She pokes me hard in the chest with a pointed finger. "Then paint that piece of crap. Woodland green. You can pick it up at Home Depot."

She turned on her thickly booted foot and stomps off toward her 4-Runner. She needs to hop just to get in the seat, given her diminutive stature. She guns the engine before bolting.

So you can understand why I would prefer no confrontations with the terrifying Merry S.

I stand here like a moron, heart hammering in my chest like I'd recently committed a homicide, the latest victim of PTMS - Post Traumatic Merry Sooner disorder. How the hell did she get past the bouncer? Maybe she killed him.

I try desperately not to look at her. It takes me a full twenty seconds before it strikes me: she doesn't recognize me. Not one whit. Worse, I think she may be...

"You okay? You're a little green around the corners," she says. She smiles up at me. I didn't know she could. I'm fairly certain I don't want her to. The do-rag wrapping her head this time is a bold polyester print. I dodge when her hand moves toward my back.

Oh my god. I think she's trying to pick me up. "One Seaweed too many. I learned my lesson. If it's green, don't drink it." I back up. Surely she'll recognize my voice, and bad things will happen...

"They can be deadly." She nods, a wry smile – yes that's a smile – on her angry pug face. Do you need a lift home? 'Cause if you do – "

"- No, no." Gad, no. "My friend is waiting just outside. I just need to rinse my face."

"You sure?"

She's crowding into my personal space. Her voice has dropped yet another octave and I'm too sick to scream or run.

"No, really. I'm good." I take a shuddering breath.

The door opens a crack. Kennedy J's big head peeks in. "Oh Queen of the Porcelain firmament. Do you need a hand?"

Never have I been so pleased to see a familiar face. I grab for my purse and make an apologetic face at Merry before wobbling out the door.

Where I encounter hurricane Kennedy.

"You're doing your decision making from the lizard brain, Ms. Dotty?" Kennedy J refuses to use my new cool name. I push us away from the restroom. I don't want Merry overhearing.

"The what?"

"Lizard brain. Amygdala. What low life mouth breathers use for decision making. Evolve my darling."

Ouch.

Kennedy presses something into my hand.

"What's this?"

He grins, too hokey a smile to go with his outfit. "Business card from your admirer. He says to call anytime after 9:00 a.m."

"You do you realize this has never happened before? Ever?"

"What? You getting stinky on Seaweeds? Or stringing along a suitor for free refreshments?"

I consider. "Both. I've never been much of a drinker – "

"You don't say!" He slaps both cheeks, doing his best Home Alone impression.

"And until all this –" I point to my everything, " – no one has ever given me the time of day. Let alone paid for my drinks."

Kennedy J looks thoughtful, a good look for him. "You've upped the appearance ante is all. Underneath that perfectly straight nose, good skin and killer bod, you haven't disappeared. You're still

– "

I put up a stop-sign hand. I'm obviously not a completely sober being yet. "See, that's the thing. I'm not the same." I shake my head a few times. Big mistake. The green motif of Chartreuse swirls for a minute. "Can you take me home, pal? I'm not feeling so good."

"See, now I know you're smashed. You're not feeling so well. So well! Don't be plebeian."

"Spare me the erudition, please."

Kennedy J tsks tsks me, but he is a very nice man. He grips my elbow as I weeble and wobble through the elegant bar, preventing me from face planting several times. Everything seems too much, the lights and glass too bright, voices and sound track too loud. Suddenly, we're outside and outside is too cold. The fresh air brings on a new wave of nausea. I put my hands over my eyes, feeling suddenly tearful.

"You okay, girl?"

"Yeah. I just feel stupid. I totally know better."

"You're just a late bloomer. Most of us have worked out the kinks by your advanced age."

I stop in my tracks and face him. "Why are you doing all this for me?" I feel weak and weepy, probably from of the booze.

He grips my shoulders. "Dorothy Alana Lindell, you are a fantastic soul. You were a beautiful tchotchke on a dusty shelf. I simply can't pass by fine objects without wanting to show them off to best advantage. It's my nature." He pets my head. "You're such a goof. Time to go home and take aspirin with plenty of water."

CHAPTER TWENTY-EIGHT

Laser beams shoot through my eyelids, puncturing both corneas. I hiss and try to turn away from the light. Ka-BAM. Iron clamps tighten on either side of my skull and I wince.

So begins the granddaddy of all hangovers.

I dare to crack an eyelid at the clock and note that it is already after ten. I'm supposed to be leaving for this wedding in two hours. That's so wrong.

I'm not a hundred percent certain how I maneuvered my way into bed. Maybe Kennedy helped. Later I will thank him for not simply tossing my whiny corpse to the side of the road. Now, however, it's time to get moving. I give it a shot.

Wrong.

I plop back onto the bed quickly. Trust me, it's the thing to do when in danger of falling off the world. I close my eyelids over burning retinas.

The phone rings. Gad!

"Hello?"

Warm syrup pours through the phone. "Morning, pretty girl. It's John. You up?"

No. No. No! I sit bolt upright, propelled by my school girl crush and a Catholic guilt tsunami over my behavior last night. Oh bollocks and mighty Thor! My head! I take a breath and hope this comes across as more Marilyn Monroe that hang-over. Thank heavens John knows nothing about my foolishness the previous evening.

"Absolutely. I was just going to take a shower." Big fat lie. I was just going to sit here and try not to projectile vomit. And maybe groan occasionally.

"I talked my buddy into coming along. He's bringing a date so you'll have some company when I'm trapped in bridal party land."

"Great."

"Be by around 2:45 or so."

I sit up too quickly and my right eye tries to explode. I flop back down. "I thought you said 4:30."

"Yeah, but I'm in the wedding party and my sister says I have to be there early for pictures and whatever other wedding nonsense she deems necessary. Is that a problem?"

Hell, yes. "No, we're good. 2:45 it is."

"Later."

I close my eyes and the insides of my lids are bright red. I try to envision myself speed healing.

When I open them, Elvira hangs over me, holding a glass of iced tea.

"Ya know, dude, not everyone has the metabolism to handle nightlife. You don't even drink coffee. How do you expect to resurrect the next day without coffee?"

Gratefully I swallow. "Tea has caffeine, too."

"Sorry about barging in. But you said to come over and then didn't answer the door. I kinda freaked. Used my key."

"I appreciate it. It's good to know someone who would dial 9-1-1 for me."

"I'm your dialer, dude. So tell me about this much anticipated date."

I fill her in, then down two aspirin. I moisten a wash cloth and hold it over my eyes.

Elvira considers."So. Like, this is your plan? Hooking up with your former nemesis's evil dude wingman?"

"Plan? Who said anything about a plan?"

She plops into one of the overstuffed chairs, limbs dangling. "I mean, like how do you know he's changed? Did I miss a memo somewhere? Suddenly he's king dude of the year and you wanna hook up with him? Don't know, Dotty. Seems kind a suspect."

I have the good sense to blush, albeit a pale green one."

"Truth? I don't know if he's changed. But I sure have." I veer. "Besides that was a long time ago. High School. I never really knew him in the first place."

"You know who he was hanging with. And you know what he did. You know the names he called you."

"That was his buddy. John didn't do the name calling, that was Jack Weston, not John."

Elvira's voice slows and loses its lilt. "Jack Weston?"

Despite my throbbing head, I drop the washcloth at the change in her tone. "What's the matter buddy?"

"The guy who left the power print on my neck?"

I look into her Precious Moment eyes. She nods.

Our voices blend.

"Jack Weston."

CHAPTER TWENTY-NINE

John arrives at 3:14 precisely. His new nickname shall be Mr. Tardy Man. I am grateful for this flaw as it gives me another twenty minutes of aspirin healing time.

He walks me to the car, already occupied by a couple in the back seat, a man and a woman.

The man is Jack Weston.

I freeze, issue a silent prayer for Elvira to remain in her pre-gig vampire nap. I lock eyes with the demon in the back seat.

John makes introductions, oblivious. "Alana, this is Jack Weston and his date. I'm sorry, I didn't catch your name?"

From the backseat, "Jenny. Jenny Van Buren."

I paste on a smile purchased from Dr. Maxwell Dorfman, dentist to the stars. "Hi all." I swear on a stack of bibles that Jack Weston, arch nemesis from high school, attacker of my roommate, recognizes me instantly. A slick smile tucks into one corner of his mouth. I may barf.

"You look awfully familiar. We've met somewhere?"

"Too bad if you did, buddy," John says, "because, boo-hoo for you, you failed to make that love connection," John smiles over at me. "Because Ally has shocking good taste."

I climb into the front seat of John's Lexus, the muscles in my jaw still locked. I'm too freaked to appreciate that I have a new nickname.

"What are you guys talking about?" Jenny Van Buren looks confused.

Must redirect conversation immediately. "Have any of you been to Chartreuse? I had this marvelous drink there last night."

Jenny smiles "Oh that place is supposed to be amazing." She pouts at Weston. "You never take me anyplace decent, you stinker."

Jack agrees amiably. Internally, I grit my teeth and wonder if this ass had been seeing Jenny Van Buren at the same time he was seeing Elvira. Fortunately for me, he and John start jawing about Manga, those Japanese cartoons they love so much. Grown men, deeply in love with comic books. I don't get it.

Oops, I said it out loud.

"What's not to get? The stories are great and –" John grins into the rear view mirror at Jack – "the female characters are very well drawn."

What was I thinking? I'm going to be trapped with this group for hours. Such a mistake.

I hear Jenny's voice float from the back. "I think it's kind of creepy. Cartoons are for little kids."

Amen sister.

"Well if that isn't the pot calling the kettle. Her bed is covered in more stuffed animals than a Toys R Us. I have to rake them off to get busy.

Jack Weston's voice still sounds like an eel. Why oh why am I in this car?

John chimes in. "I'll cut you a deal, Jen: I'll dump a Manga title for every Beanie Baby you agree to toss."

You have entered the Twilight Zone: trapped in the toddler section of a luxury car...

John smiles his toothpaste ad smile. "What about you, Alana? You have a secret indulgence to spill? Barbies? Unicorns? Fess up." His hand lands lightly on my thigh.

A burning sensation created by the man hand on my leg distracts me. What can I offer up to get the conversation turned? Perhaps my purchase of every 'as-seen-on-TV' diet product ever created including juicers, supplements, the Thigh Master, and the Ab Roller. I balked at the Tony Little Gazelle, but only because it cost in excess of $19.95, which is where I draw the line. If a product claimed to help you lose weight and was under the threshold, I probably tried it at least once. And I refuse to divulge one wit of this within earshot of Jack Weston, resident jackal.

"I do have a thing for self help."

Jack snorts from the back seat. "Girls have this twisted need to be told what to do. Pathetic."

Where would we be without the Jack Weston's world view? "I'm just interested in becoming a better person."

John interrupts, "Relying on a stranger who's never met you to decide your fate? I'll stick with Manga. It's more fun."

Part of me wants to slap him silly. And another unfamiliar part relishes the heat transferred from his hand to my thigh. "You're just Mr. Super Confident, right? Take me as I am? Never a moment of doubt?"

"I don't need Doctor Phil or any other self help guru telling me what my next move is," John replies.

"How handy for you: a lifetime supply of nerve. I'll just wait over here for that next bravura move." I shove John's hand off my thigh.

Jack barks a laugh from the backseat. Jenny hasn't a clue what's going on.

John Miller is connected by virtue of a broken chromosome to that heckling creature in the backseat, that monster who should be in jail. And no one gets to call me needy while rubbing my leg.

Must change the subject before I go postal. "Tell me about your sister, John. Who's she marrying? Do you like him?"

"Oh it's a good story," John sits up a bit. "He's a welder."

"As in Flashdance?" This from Jenny in the back. Ah, Jenny. You're a little bit special.

"As in. Mom and dad are just uber pleased." Now he's laughing.

"I take it that's sarcasm?" I ask.

"You take it correctly. They were expecting something in an M.D. or a J.D. or perhaps leftover royalty."

My stomach somersaults. I may have forgotten my close encounter with liquor at Chartreuse the evening before, but my digestive tract has not. And my head, while less swirly than last night, grows more poundy. I crack the window a hair. "Have you met him?"

"Oh yeah. He's a truck driving, country music lovin bumpkin with huge hands. He wanted a Vegas drive-by wedding, but Rachel put the kybosh on that."

I close my eyes briefly against a bile backwash. "I take it the folks aren't into country?"

John and Jack have a good laugh over that. Jack pipes up from the backseat, "You haven't met Skip and Lonnie, have you... Alana is it?" He snickers. "John's parents are more the symphony type." Jack affects a Southern drawl, "They don't cotton to Democrats, trucks, or plaid work shirts."

"They sound kind of scary." Jenny says.

I quite agree. "So how'd they meet each other?"

"Bart stopped to change her tire."

I love it when guys do guy-things like that. It's so...manly. "He sounds sweet," I try.

"Sweet? He's enormous." This from John, who isn't exactly puny.

Well you go, Rachel.

We've reached the Cathedral (yes, Cathedral. This ain't no country church y'all). John waves me and Jenny toward a group of women in the back while he and Jack connect with the other groomsmen. Happy to steer clear of Jack Weston, I follow the herd of heavily perfumed similarly dressed women to a room on the opposite side, where Jenny and I are left to fend for ourselves.

I easily I.D. the bride: she would be the one in white, surrounded by a pack of pastel princesses who appear to have escaped from America's Next Top Model or maybe the Playboy mansion, bra size depending.

Rachel parts the sea of skirts and comes over to say hi. "You must be Alana, right? I'm Rachel. John's such an ass. He might have introduced us." She shakes hands, friendly, efficiently. She turns to Jenny, who's twirling a tiny beaded handbag. "And you are?"

"I'm Jenny Van Buren. Jack Weston's date."

Rachel, shoots me a look. It seems to relay some concern about anyone who'd hook up with Jack Weston. I am reassured by this look. She turns back to Jenny, places a gentle hand on her back, leading her.

"Jenny, I brought along a bunch of magazines and stuff over there." She waves her other hand. "I know these things can get boring. Oh and there's bottled water and such in the mini fridge. Bitsy! Can one of you get Jenny a water?" Rachel asks a lavender swathed girl. The two of them wander off, presumably in search of a bright idea.

"Do you know her?" Rachel asks when she returns.

Other than her encyclopedic knowledge of Flashdance and a predilection for plush toys? "I just met her. I don't suppose there's anything I can do to help out?" Oh please distract me from yet another wedding, one that comes complete with a bucking hangover?

Rachel smiles widely, showing the same perfect dentistry she shares with John. "Oh hell, yes. My mom is wreaking havoc out there with the flowers. The florist spent hours getting them just right and he'll go ballistic if she moves them one more time. If you could find some way to distract her? Anything? Perhaps an explosion of some sort? That would be enormously helpful."

"Which one's your mom?"

Rachel's head tilts just a fraction. "Look for a bunch of diamonds wearing a woman. That'll be my mom. Oh and keep her away from Bart. That would be better still. If she keeps messing with him, eventually I'll have a runner on my hands. Given the choice between guarding the flowers and rescuing Bart, go with Bart."

"Bart would be?"

"The groom."

"Oh, right."

"Can't miss him. Very big guy. Serious formal wear. Maybe a cowboy hat." Rachel returns to the bouquet of bridesmaids and I wander out into the church proper to track down Lonnie Miller.

Mercy. The place is amazing.

Remember, I've been to a plethora of weddings, so I've seen my share of floral arrangements, decorations and stained glass, but this is surreal. There are tangled arbors of branches, sprayed white and twined with twinkle lights. A canopy of them at the front drips with glass crystal beads that catch every bit of light. There are uncountable candles, unlit at this point, in row after row of crystal holders, some nearly six feet tall. Pink roses, ribbon, and some little yellow flower I can't I.D. are twined around every pew, emitting a powerful scent that reaches clear to the back where I'm standing transfixed.

"You there! Girl! Give me a hand."

Ah, Momma Miller has found me it appears. She's kind of a Martha Stewart type, if Martha wore a disproportionate amount of diamonds. She has a choker of them around her neck. Her hands are heavy with them. She's wearing an elegant berry colored suit and pumps, and when she lifts her hand, bracelets of them slide down into the cuffs.

I'm tugged down the aisle by the force of her jewelry.

"These are all wrong! The crystal curtains are supposed to go behind the canopy, not to the side. What were you thinking? It will destroy the photographs."

Me? I'm thinking I need another aspirin. Or Kennedy J. He'd know what to do. "I'm a friend of John's. I'm just here –" why am I here again? – "I'm his date. Rachel suggest you might need some help - "

"Well let's get started then. Look, just move these – carefully! They're Swarovski – around to the back. Yes. Just like that."

For the next twenty minutes, I annoy every creative type involved with this wedding, all at the behest of Lonnie Miller. She has me moving ribbons, flowers, candles. She alters the location of the liturgical stand. Nothing remains as originally designed. I comply with all her demands and curse John Miller, who I hold accountable for my presence here. I try and keep a particularly servile expression on my face – this is not hard. I've been practicing that look all my life – while doing exactly what she tells me to. Florists, photographers, wedding planners, they all glare at me since they dare not glare at Madam Miller.

The photographer, who by now suffers from irritable bowel, rounds everyone up for pictures. A sea of tuxedos from Gentlemen's Quarterly emerge from the left side of the church, sharing whatever's in the silver flask. They're laughing, elbowing, and drunk as lords. They've forgotten how to behave in church. I'm jealous: I've slipped into head pounding sobriety while they're just hitting stride.

John propels Jack by the elbow as he nearly careens into a tangle of white, spray-painted branches. Jack sees me at the back, hiding behind Lonnie Miller, and raises the flask in a mock salute.

Charming.

A redwood in a tuxedo and a cowboy hat joins them. How on earth did they find sufficient fabric to wrap a tuxedo around that? He towers over John and Jack, (who are not exactly Oompa Loompas), a black suited concrete column. Unlike his posse, he appears sober as a judge - from here anyway.

The photographer says he'll shoot the men first. Lonnie Miller assigns me the task of tracking down Rachel for pictures, so I head back to the crying room.

Rachel Miller stands in front of a mirror. She is perfection. Her cheeks hint at blush, lips suggest gloss. She is high society bridal. But she twists around when I come in, smiles and her face cracks open like an egg, spilling warm and friendly all over her elegance.

She does a little dance, causing the graceful lines of silk charmeuse to sway, catches my arms like we're old army buddies. Using the tune "You Say It's Your Birthday" by the Beatles, she makes up her own lyric and croons, "You Say it's my Hitch Day," at high volume. I think I like Rachel Miller a lot. Maybe even better than her studly brother. Despite the effervescence, she, like her groom, does not appear intoxicated. She's just happy.

"Thanks so much for keeping mom outta my hair. Have you seen Bart? Has he fled the scene yet?"

"Tree wearing a cowboy hat?"

Her smile broadens, as if this is possible. "He wore it? I bet Mom's going postal, isn't she?"

"Not sure. Your mom sent me to track you down. It's time for pictures."

"You are helpful and wise, oh date of my brother, whose name I can't recall."

"Alana. Alana Lindell."

"Well, A. L. I think we need to toast first." She grabs some champagne glasses (yes, real ones. These are not the plastic snap together kind) and a bottle of Cristal. Cristal - as seen on T.V.

"To Bart Hughes. The man I trapped into marriage!" Rachel clinks her glass against mine and we toss them back. Not a good idea, I know, but I'm thinking it might help my head. I saw that on T.V., too.

Just about the minute I start to try and figure exactly what "trapped into marriage" implies, her female entourage returns from wherever they went – probably a mass restroom exodus – and seeing the bottle cracked, begin scrambling for glasses. The volume goes up and up and I suddenly realize I'm in.

I'm in, don't you get it?

I'm not the fat girl taking gifts at the door.

I'm not ugly girl being ignored altogether.

I'm connecting.

Rachel's laugh floats above all the others. I haven't seen anyone this joyful since... since my mom's last wedding.

"Rachel, what did you mean by 'trapped'?" Nosey, sure, but I'm on the champagne. Forgive.

Miss December, dressed in a coordinating rose charmeuse sheath dress, takes the bait, "That's the right word, all right. She locked him up and threw away the key. He kept telling her he wasn't good enough for her. So she told him she was knocked up." Tingly laughter all around.

My face falls. "You did what?" I admit it. I'm shocked. She doesn't seem the type.

"Oh, I had no choice." She takes a deep swallow of Champagne. Closes her eyes. "Hmmm. Nice. I haven't had a lick of liquor since I pulled that stunt. See, Bart's this old school gentleman. He believed that he needed to go out into the world, make his fortune first. Then, and only then, would he return to propose. Please! I'm twenty-eight. I'm not waiting around for ten years while he puts his dimes into a 401K. Especially when he's using my dad as the measuring stick for wealth.

"I could have died an old maid waiting for that. Worse, maybe some sensible shoed Mary Ann wanders up with an apple pie and daisy dukes while he's off making his fortune and BAM, there goes my future husband. Not going to happen.

"So I seduced him. Then told him I was late. And that I was terrified! Just terrified of telling my parents."

Her friends laugh again.

"To be fair, I am often late. Ask anyone. Late for dinner, class, work. Just not that kind of late."

"You told him you were pregnant?" I'm incredulous. Intrigued, but incredulous. People really do that?

She has the good grace to look sheepish. "Well, sort of. Yeah, pretty much. All I actually told him was that I was late, not preggers. But I did clear things up after we got engaged. Of course by then... well, I say by the time I see a doctor, I'm hoping I'll have caught. Meantime I have this lovely ring on my finger –" she waggles her hand.

"And she put a backup one through his nose!" screamed a giggling bridesmaid.

"Now, now. I just don't want my Bart unprotected from you estrogen vultures." Rachel smiles a Mona Lisa smile. "They're just jealous 'cause they're either married to snobs or unhitched." An angry uproar starts.

A tight bun with a woman attached sticks her head into the melee. Do all wedding planners wear the same up-do? "Five minutes, ladies. We're getting ready to start."

I wish Rachel luck and slip out into a pew behind the Miller family.

Two more people throw caution and common sense to the wind.

CHAPTER THIRTY

My headache's long since gone and I'm at my desk trying to care about work. Not happening.

For the past two weeks, I've been dating John Miller, world's hottest man. Oh don't judge. Sure, he got hammered at his sister's wedding (his sister Rachel insisted that she and her new husband drive me home on their wedding day - embarrassing). Sure he suffers from a bad case of perennial Japanese cartoon-itis. And he has terrible taste in friends, because he continues to associate with Jack Weston. We all have our issues.

I, for example, seem to be obsessed with John Miller, which can't be healthy. There is something so compellingly attractive about him that every cell in my body screams "take me" anytime he's within visual distance. And that kind of infatuation cannot be a good idea.

Another few pounds dropped off and my nose has found its final resting place. I have stomach muscles and job security. I have a fresh dent in my sofa where a boy's butt has been, and the fact that a male butt created that dent shocks me still.

I have an ever widening circle of friends, courtesy of Kennedy J and Jefferson, Rachel and Bart, and of course the crazed Elvira, whose band actually is phenomenal.

So why do I feel so unsettled? So tense? I can't seem to follow a thought. My focus is shot. If I were twenty years older, I'd blame Alzheimer's.

Today John gives me a lift home from work. His place is loads closer to Microcosm and has three times the square footage of mine, so you think we'd head to his place.

We do not.

I've been to John's twice. The first time, he insisted on me waiting in the car while he grabbed his laptop. Given my limited history with men, I assumed he had a live in gay lover tied up in the basement, so I said nothing. The second time he had – in his own words – "tidied up." This meant the piles of debris had been raked and groomed into rows.

On that glorious day, I was met at the door by the smell of mildew and decay and ten day old pizza. The pizza in question had petrified, its box balanced teeter-totter style on a pile of black garbage bags. The bags were the heavy duty kind, normally used for lawn care, and stuffed nearly to bursting. They'd been lined up like bean bag chairs. The walls, which had been contractor white at some point, were working their way to a yellow-ish gray pallor and coated with a variety of stains and discolorations every few inches. I looked down the hall into the kitchen and went stalk still.

"Twice a year I hire a service to come in and clean it." John's voice came over my shoulder.

"I'd say that time had come and gone, J-man." A dreadful thought blew into my head and I twisted around quickly. "Look, you didn't ask me out to clean this place did you?" Pre-surgical Dot would assume that was the case. Hell, she'd be strapping on rubber gloves and scrubbing by now. Fortunately, well groomed Alana Lindell shudders. "I should warn you I don't do windows."

"And I don't do Linux, so where does that leave us, since obviously I don't do windows either." He smiled his bad boy smile. It prevents me from running like a frightened rabbit from this gross apartment.

"Given the chaos, perhaps heading swiftly to my place?" I shake my head. "How can you live like this? I mean seriously." I wander - carefully - down the hall and into the combination kitchen living room. There's not an inch of clean as far as the eye can see, just layers of grime and dust. To give him credit, there were fresh scrape marks where items had recently been peeled off, (coming to rest, no doubt, in lawn care bean bags). I creep carefully into the living room side in my danger girl shoes, shove aside a crusty hand towel and some loose pages from last week's Wall Street Journal to uncover a section of sofa I deem safe for habitation. A high-end leather sectional reveals itself and it probably cost more than my nose job. Should have left that leather on the cow where it would have been safe. "How do you find anything in here, John?"

"I'm not here all that often."

"You have to sleep sometime."

"Plenty of warm places to crash." This is accompanied by the requisite flash of teeth.

"Oh you are the razor wit. Why with that pulchritude and this palace of a home," I wave my hands at the filth, "How could the ladies resist?"

I need to use the bathroom soon, but gad, dare I? "Please tell me your bathroom exceeds the standards of my local gas station?"

"Just a sec." John grabs an empty lawn care bag from the kitchen counter. He maneuvers expertly around mountains of bags, clothes, and a pile of soda cans awaiting recycling. I find the cans funny. John's too environmentally conscious to ditch his dead cans in the trash and too lazy to recycle. I watch his back go through a door to the left of the kitchen. There's a flurry of plastic rustling noises, the sound of an aerosol spray deploying. He emerges with the bag half full. Ugh.

"We're good to go."

"That's what Jody Foster said before entering a black hole." I make way to the bathroom and peek in the door. Ooh gad this is bad. In addition to the sharp stink of mildew and mold, John chose to exercise his horticultural interests in the bathroom via a series of very dead plants. "Do you have any bleach? A Hazmat suit? A key on a paddle that opens the restroom at the AM/PM?"

"You think you can hurt my feelings with your callous words."

"John, your feelings are fairly sturdy or they'd have succumbed to the Hepatitis B growing in that stink. And speaking of B, I'm thinking we switch to plan B."

"Where we flee to your place?"

"After a quick stop at the AM/PM so I can use their restroom."

After stressing a high degree of appreciation to the AM/PM folks for one coffee, one bottled water and the key to the bathroom, we arrive at my place.

John follows behind me – too close. I don't realize how close he is and nearly back into him out of nervousness while digging for my keys.

"Sorry." I make a move to step away from him, but he wraps a supporting arm around my waist, forces me back against the door.

"Wouldn't want you falling down over me," he says.

His mouth is too close.

"Not much likelihood of that happening." My voice wavers a bit and I hope he doesn't notice.

"Oh sure there is," he leans even closer, purrs into my ear. "There is a high degree of probability."

He seems much taller, this close. I can smell his breath against my face, including the traces of the coffee he snagged at the AM/PM. His face is so handsome, so foreign. I can't look directly at him anymore and my eyes fall on the stubble darkening his chin, drop further down and come to rest on his chest.

His hand on my back tightens and I'm pulled against him.

"Do you want me to come in for a while, pretty

Alana?" He breaths this into my ear. I can hear it echo in my head - 'do you want me?' - and I don't know, I don't know. Too fast, going zero to sixty in such a short time. I inhale sharply to make my mouth say something banal about how we just met but instead his mouth is on mine, and instead of air, I suck in warm coffee and his scent. One of my hands finds his face, planning maybe to push him away, but instead it slides down his cheek and wraps around his neck, up into the thick hair at the back of his head, surprisingly soft.

I hear an "hmm," like a mantra, like a chant, and it might be his voice, but it might be mine. His hands are on my back sliding, one up, one down, pulling my shoulders to him, cupping my ass. I can't get seem to get any air and I panic. I instruct my hands to push him away and they weakly comply. Then I turn my back to him, and take that breath I so desperately need. He simply advances on me from behind, and lets his arms slide down from my shoulders, along my elbows, clear down to my hands. He clasps them together in front of me, trapping me back against the wall of his chest, his body. I feel him behind me, this man, and his lips are at my ear again. "Are you scared, Alana?"

Well damn him for knowing. I take a raggedy breath. "I think I might be. Just a bit."

He laughs. "I'm not." He turns me around to face him. His eyes lock on mine. "You think too much." He looks down at me and he's so beautiful, those heavy lidded eyes, thick black lashes. He's going to kiss me again and I'll be done for. Then he does put his mouth on mine and I'm drunk on him.

CHAPTER THIRTY-ONE

I wake up warm. My hands and feet are often stiff from cold, but this morning, I'm liquid caramel. My sheets feel softer than usual and I pass one hand over the pillowcase, easing my backside toward the source of the heat where I encounter skin.

That should have been enough to send me bolt upright. Instead, I remain completely at peace, relishing the transmission of heat from his skin to mine. John's skin. My boyfriend's. John Miller, my boyfriend. I had sex with my boyfriend. I want to giggle, and I assure you I'm not the giddy type. I gave it up. My giggles shake the bed and jostle John just enough to raise a groan from behind me.

I lay there for another twenty minutes before remembering its Friday and I have to be at work in an hour. I force myself to leave the warm encampment of my bed and head for the shower.

Standing under the hot water, a light sting at

my crotch informs me that I'm not a virgin. John used a condom (he just happened to have one with him) but I still insist on praying to the patron saints of fertility to give me a pass on this one. Pregnancy had been the farthest thing from my mind last night. Suddenly I understand how women get pregnant by surprise. Condom or not, I could have gotten pregnant. Given our degree of craziness the previous evening, I very well could be carrying John's baby.

Oh my.

My hand finds my tummy. A little mini-John or maybe a little girl as funny and nice as his sister. I'm off in space, pushing a stroller when the shower door abruptly slides open.

"Company's coming!" John, naked, pushes me back out of the stream of water. "I'm sticky and in need of a good soak. Pass the shampoo, please."

"Why of course you can take a shower with me." I try to sound stern.

"You're welcome. Shampoo?"

Why do I bother trying to one up this guy? I pass the shampoo over. "I'm freezing back here, buddy, move over."

His arms wrap around me again and he switches positions with me. Now he's behind me and the shower's beating down on my head. "You can have the front while I lather up."

"Oh, you are so gracious, given this is my shower. What did I do to deserve you? And how do I fix it?" I feel myself smiling like an idiot.

We goof off in the shower, verbally dueling then washing each other's backs. How I can be so comfortable with him? I really know nothing about him. He's handsome, has a job and a bad Jones for Japanese comics. Given my limited knowledge on men, he could also be a serial killer. Or gay. Or a gay serial killer.

But I doubt it.

I decide, under the shared spray of my shower, that every twinge of pain from surgery and every muscle ache endured from working out was worth it.

It's after nine on a Tuesday, a "non-John" night because of the commute, so the banging on the door is a surprise.

A bigger surprise is Elvira's bent head at the peephole. The final kicker is her thin frame flying through the door when I hurry to open it. She nearly knocks me off my feet and slams the door behind us, then leans against it, panting.

"I'm so sorry, so sorry to come here," she begins, her voice thick from crying.

"What's going on?"

She raises her head and there's a swelling egg where her eye should be. Her thin frame leans against the door and shakes.

I catch at her shoulders. "Oh my god, El! I'm calling the police?"

She shakes her head wildly, "No, no, no," but the motions pains her and she winces shut her good eye. "It'd make things worse."

"I'm calling 9-1-1."

Her one good eye turns on me and she grabs at

my arms. "No, please. It'll be okay as long as I don't go back to the apartment for a while- "

"You aren't going anywhere, kid. Come on. Sit down." I gently untangle from her grip and ease her toward the sofa. She collapses onto the cushions. There's a comforter in a basket on the floor and I drape it over her shoulders. It seems like what she needs, given how she's shaking.

"What if he, like... followed me here?"

What indeed. "Let's worry about you first, k?" I grab frozen peas and a washcloth for her eye, then rifle through the cupboard for an Ibuprofen. "You really need a doctor." Her breath sounds wheezy and asthmatic and non-doctor Alana wonders if she's got a punctured a lung.

"No. Just sore. Can I maybe stay here tonight?"

"Of course, but I need to call 9-1-1 -"

She grabs my arm again. "No, please. Listen to me. If you contact a doc or the cops, they have to report it. And if that happens... please just let me sleep. Please." Her one good eye pleads. She gulps and sniffs, horrible mucus-y sniffs.

I owe her so much. "Whatever you need, El. Let me get you a pillow and something to sleep in."

The t-shirt swims on her, a pathetic Dickens waif in an Edna Mode t-shirt. She sinks into my sofa, gratefully accepting a couple aspirin, a mug of hot tea and an ice pack. To my surprise, she conks out in moments. But not before she relays details of the second coming of Jack Weston.

She'd had Mickey T., one of her band mates, over to work on a song. When she heard Jack's voice through the door, Mickey was the one who responded, asking what he wanted. He had a perfectly understandable reason for being there: wanting back his jacket and the t-shirts he'd left behind. Mickey hesitated, but Elvira patted his shoulder. She thought it would be a better way to end things: return his things to him, all civil and respectable, not confusing and... awful.

I know, I know fool me twice, but Elvira, for all her funky charm, is naive as Pollyanna. You don't end up in Dr. Pepper's group because you make excellent character judgments.

Mickey agreed to leave, only after Elvira practically shoved him out the door. Jack, true to form, acted cool and friendly, then dropped that persona once Mickey was out of earshot.

Elvira offered him a seat while she went to retrieve his things. She assumed, incorrectly, that he had taken it. Instead, he followed her to the corner of the studio that she had set up as her bedroom. He snuck up behind her, cat silent, pressing up against her when she reached for the box of his things. She spun, startled, and shoved him, an instinctive move, not calculated.

That's all it took: one shove. She just wanted him out of her personal space, out of her apartment, and out of her life. That's all.

I look at her, fetal curled on my sofa for the third time in weeks, vulnerable as a very long, very skinny kitten. Rage surges through me. What kind of world lets this happen to such a gentle soul? If there's a God, why does He allow innocent women to become victims? And how in the hell do you stop evil?

John, with his movie star good looks, is not responsible for this gritty tension. I chant to myself, "John is not Jack, not Jack, not Jack." But he's still one of them, simply because of that damn broken chromosome of his. And because of his connection to that roach of a human being who assaulted my friend.

———————◄█●►———————

John shows up the next day unannounced, surprised to find a skinny, bruised elf on my sofa eating a granola bar very gingerly, dunking it in a container of yogurt to soften it, since chewing hurts.

"John, meet Elvira Wentz. Elvira, John."

"Hey, hot dude," Elvira offers between bites. She avoids making contact with her good eye.

"What happened to your face?"

"It ran into Jack Weston," I blurt out.

The silence that follows sucks in all sound leaving the three of us pinned by a mouthful of words.

John cracks a hole through the quiet, "He did that?"

Elvira nods, dunks her granola bar.

I wave him in, not wanting him to stand there. I reach for his coat.

He hands it over, but he's still staring at her face. He balls his fists. "I'm sorry. I... "

"Did you know? That he's capable of this?"

He whirls on me. "What? Are you kidding? How would I know?"

"How could you not? How could you not know? He's a bully. And you know it, because you've been thick as thieves with that monster since high school. And he's always been a bully."

Elvira moves from the sofa. "Ah, look peeps, maybe I'd better leave - "

"You stay put and rest." I press down on her bony shoulder.

John's totally baffled by my interrogation. "Why are you dragging me into this?"

I feel my own hand clench tight.

Elvira, nervous tries, "You sure you wanna go there, Dot?"

John looks even more puzzled. "Dot? Her name is Alana."

"Okay. Sure. Whatever works. Mind if I take shower Do- eh... Alana? I really should be getting out of here."

I nod, my eyes fixed on John's confused face. "Sure, El. Go ahead. I left a towel on the hook for you." She escapes behind the door.

John takes up Elvira's seat on the sofa. "So. Dot. Who's Dot?"

I felt a sudden intense urge for Cherry Coke. "Me. It's a nickname. An old one. I don't use it anymore."

"That so?" He seems to take up a great deal more space on the sofa than Elvira did, even now, with his arms across his chest. "What is going on? What did Jack do to this girl? And why do I feel like you are holding me personally accountable for this?"

My arms unconsciously mimic his, tightening over my breasts. "A few weeks ago, she made the tremendous error in judgment of dating Jack

Weston. It only took her a few such mistakes to learn he's a complete horse's ass. This isn't the first time he's hurt her. It's just the latest. Not even mentioning he was probably seeing that Jenny twit the entire time-"

"Allie, what happened to her face?"

I take a deep breath, force my words to slow. "Last night, he went back to her place. His story was he needed to pick up some things he left behind. When she asked him to leave, he attacked her. She tried to get him to leave with his stuff and when didn't act overjoyed to see him, he got mad and punched her in the face. That's where she got the black eye."

He lets out a held in breath. "Shit. "

I turn on him in a rage, "That's it? That's all you've got to say? How many women has that bully hurt while you stood by?"

"Excuse me? I drive for an hour to see you and because your friend's been hurt, suddenly it's my fault? Why are you picking a fight? What's going on? Why is she calling you Dot?"

The sound of running water interrupts us as Elvira starts her shower. Our eyes battle lock for a heartbeat.

Then I stand up. Sitting down doesn't feel right for fighting. "She's calling me Dot because it's my name. My given name. Dorothy."

A deep furrow develops between John's brows. "Is that so? So… Alana. Why Alana?

"My middle name."

His eyebrows hike a millimeter or two. "So what's the whole story? Let's hear it."

Now I'm well and truly pissed. I start pacing a path, sofa to kitchen and back. "Fine. You want, you got it. My full name is Dorothy Alana Lindell. The girl in the bathroom is my friend Elvira. And that asshole Jack Weston punched her in the eye. And I know Jack Weston is an asshole and I am completely unsurprised that he beat up my friend because he tormented the absolute shit out of me all through high school. How could we ever forget the melodious strains of 'Dot, Dot, she'll never eat cock?' And you, John Miller, you of all people, should be well aware of all of it. Because you were there."

"I was where?" His voice drops like a stone. He's totally lost.

"Fuck, John!" I smack the counter. "You were right there when he made jokes about me! Right there!"

He rises from the sofa. He puts both hands on my shoulders. "You two shared a car ride for what - maybe a half an hour?"

"What we shared was four years at Inglemoor."

His arms, drop, he's puzzled. "I went to Inglemoor."

I nod. "I know."

He shakes his head, denying. "You didn't go to our high school."

"I did. You just didn't see me. I was invisible to you."

Now he's bent out of shape, too. "Just tell me what's going on."

"I already told you. You really don't remember, do you? Dot Lindell? 'Dot, Dot, will suck no cock?'

"

His faces drains of color.

"What? Suddenly you're at a loss for words? Your friend Jack never has that problem. Always ready with a verbal backhand, that one- "

He grabs me, gives me a little shake, like everything will settle back down if he can jostle things back into alignment in there. "Is this some kind of joke? Some kind of game? I do remember a girl with that name from school. And I remember Jack being a complete ass to her. But you are not - "

His voice drops off. He looks at me - hard.

His eyes widen with realization."Christ." He takes a step back, his hands drop to his side. "Christ Jesus!" He stares at me for another second.

The running water in the bathroom comes to an abrupt halt. Elvira has finished her shower.

His lips are a thin line, his eyes cold crystal. Without another word, he walks out, the door slamming hard behind him.

Behind me, the bathroom door opens a crack releasing steam into the room.

"Is he still here? Should I leave?"

My sinuses clog like a sink full of bacon grease, preparing for a monster cry-a-thon. "No, no. Please stay."

Wrapped in my ratty robe, she races from the bathroom and wraps her arms around me, causing that last thimble of self control to spill and I pour myself out to her like Northwest rain.

———————◆◗◖———————

Two days later. Elvira is gone and John hasn't

called. Michael, the drummer for the band "Bad Apples," insists she move in with he and the wife until they can find her new digs. I suspect she dreads being a burden, so despite my insistence that she's nothing of the sort, she'll accept Michael's hospitality for a day, then find a way to move. It took convincing to get her to stay put for even a day, her concerns about imposing override common sense. Which is ridiculous. I owe her hugely for dropping everything to help me out when I was hopelessly post-surgical. God forbid, though, that she be obliged, even a day.

Without work or Elvira to keep me occupied, I'm forced to confront what a mess I've made of my first ever relationship.

Hoping TV will prevent introspection, I flip on the news, which proves a big mistake: nothing but global mayhem and disaster. All the poverty, pain, and civil unrest convince me that I've had it too good for too long. And that I should cancel cable.

Stop being glib. Start being honest.

I haven't been honest with John. There. I've said it. And it's because I'm a coward, a coward who didn't have the courage to share the truth of who I really am and what I've done. And instead of coming clean, instead of just calmly revealing the truth, I wield it like a reality TV contestant and sucker punch him with "my truth." What exactly did I expect him to do after this Maury Povich moment? Beg for forgiveness? Praise me for my transformation? Be awed that I've changed?

Mindlessly, I grab a handful of veggies from the fridge. Munching a celery stick, I wonder if I have completely destroyed a relationship that brought so much color to life. What use is there in retelling a story you didn't like in the first place? Did resurrecting that hurt solve anything? Make anything better?

I flip the TV off and stare at the phone. "Explain yourself," says Mr. Phone. "The person you deceived is not required to call you."

Mr. Phone is an ass. Calling seems impersonal. Not quite right.

The phone, apparently realizing how cowardly I am, rings imperiously, causing my heart to do a cartoon jump from my chest. I wait for the second ring to restore sinus rhythm.

"Hello?"

"I've got a milestone in a week, Alana. This little shit storm of yours needs to be resolved so I can think again. I'll be there in thirty minutes." The phone goes dead.

Oh yippy. We're speaking again.

My stomach knots up, very nostalgic. Reminiscent of those confrontations with ex-dad number two where he'd rip me a new one for whatever grievance he fabricated on any given day. This was worse. This was my doing.

The longest thirty minutes in history finally reaches its end when the doorbell chimes.

Ah, that cartoon thump again. When I open the door, my heart nearly breaks open at the sight of him. My eyes can't handle the contact. I step aside so he can come in. Instead of sitting, he panther paces in my small space.

"Why all the subterfuge?"

I wave at the sofa, hoping he'll take a hint. He's too tall and threatening striding back and forth. He ignores the suggestion and moves closer, arms crossed across his chest.

His arms are beautiful like the rest of him, sculpted lovely muscles, my eyes get stuck there, studying the soft black hairs on his arms and how they flow in paths, and I notice how different men's arms are from women's. My insides perform a perfect half gainer.

"Well?"

I'm yanked back to the messed up now by the anger in his voice. My voice trails off, "I was afraid if you knew who I was you wouldn't like me."

He makes a short chuffing noise. "Base on what? Me asking you to coffee?"

"Based on you standing by while your buddy made fun of me for years." I try and look him in the eyes when I say this, which is very hard.

His handsome mouth shuts tight. Then he sighs heavily. "You've got this twisted story in your head where I'm a popular jock and you were a victim. Except I was never popular."

My mouth opens to interject, but he pops a hand up.

"You gave me your side. My turn."

I fall silent.

"I was not some jock people fawned over. I was a weird teenager with a huge head who liked Japanese comics. Hell I'm still a weird guy who likes Japanese comics except my body caught up with my head. But I got the shit beat out of me daily clear through to my freshman year. My interests didn't mesh well with the popular kids. How many popular kids are into computer science. And for God's sake, a backpack full of Vagabond doesn't scream "popular." He adds fingers quotes for emphasis, and that makes it more pathetic. I maintain stony silence, because... well he's correct. And because I haven't the slightest idea what the hell "Vagabond" is.

"Jack stood between me and a daily ass kicking. People were too intimidated to fuck around with him. And of course we shared a secret vice - "

When I grimace, he laughs out loud."I'm talking about Manga, you idiot. Cartoons. Grown men aren't supposed to like them, right? You look like you just learned I have toe fungus. You already know this about me. He liked a lot of the same series that I did. And he was literally the only person who didn't make me feel like a freak. He's the one who talked me into trying out for JV." His eyes wander back in time. "The next year, I made varsity." It's his turn to make the crabby face. "Suddenly people remembered my name. Girls who would have glared at me if I accidentally bumped into them? Well now they intentionally bump into me. And for some bizarre reason, they think I don't remember how they acted a year earlier. Like I'm retarded."

He gets up and wanders into the kitchen, rooting through the fridge for something to drink. I started stocking Diet Pepsi because the man loves his DP. The hiss of escaping gas comforts me. It's a John noise.

"Playing football was fun, but it didn't make me

a different person. He grins, sheepishly. "It did, however, deliver access to Jack's discarded, often broken girlfriends. Very handy when you're shy." I hear the sound of a second can opening and a Diet Pepsi appears by my hand.

Now I make a gross noise at the back of my throat. "Right. Mr. Shy."

He has the good grace to smile broadly. "I was shy. I really was. But I'm not seventeen anymore. Football helped. Getting hired at Microcosm helped. The Internet most sincerely helped, because I discovered there are more than two guys on the planet earth interested in Manga. And Jack helped, because he was my friend."

I take a sip of soda. "Your friend punched my friend in the face."

He swallows hard, stares at the can. "I knew he had issues."

"John, I'm not talking about some minor faux pas here. I'm talking about hitting a woman in the face. A girl really. Did you see her? Can you imagine doing that?"

"No." His face hardens. "No I can't." He reaches for me. "I've known Jack for a long time."

I definitely want to interject here, but again he raises the stop hand.

" - but I'm not going to defend that shit. He's a grown ass man. And that's not acceptable." He takes a swig of soda like it held Dutch courage. "I'll talk to him."

This frightens me. "John that doesn't sound like a good plan." I reach for his arm.

"Let's table that for the time being and get back

to you. What exactly possessed you?"

I get up and pretend to peruse the bookshelf, as if I don't know exactly what I'm looking for. "You grew into your looks, right? Well, what if you never did? What if the universe chose not to deliver the goods? Ever?" I drag my yearbook off the shelf - I know exactly where it is - and thump it down in front of him. "I never had looks to grow into. I was just that unfortunate looking girl with an old woman's name. Dorothy. Dorothy sells carpets wholesale. Dorothy works at a nursing home. Or maybe she's a lunch lady. No one wants to bang Dorothy."

He barks out a laugh, starts thumbing through the yearbook. "So where are you?"

I swallow, take it from him. It flops open to where the spine snapped, at the page my senior picture is on. I point.

"Holy cow! I would never have recognized you. How did you do it?"

The honesty of his question surprises me - and I'm equally surprised that it doesn't sting like I thought it would. "You really wanna know?"

Ah, that smile. "Yes, goofus, I really do. Looks like you did a bit more than give up desserts."

No fighting that smile. My face cracks open. "Let me give you the play by play."

———————◆◆◆———————

John sprawls on my sofa, long legs resting over my lap, compressing me into the cushions, completely at ease. He wrestles the remote from me and flips over to AZN to watch Adult Swim. Damn!

So much for plastic surgery on the Discovery Channel. I squirm.

"Am I squishing you?"

"No. Just antsy." I'm trying to stay positive, here. I focus on the screen, but my leg still bounces up and down, as though an electric current runs through it.

"Ya think?" John indicates my restless leg with his eyes. He swings his legs around to the floor, unpinning me.

I pretend to stare at the TV screen which I can no longer see. "Don't you ever feel like there's something you're supposed to be doing in the world? Something…big?"

"Yes. I'm supposed to be relaxing and watching Inuyasha in a big way."

Sometimes he really pisses me off. "I'm serious, John."

"Why is it that the mysteries of life always need to be resolved when my shows are on?" He sighs deeply, mutes the show using the remote, then sits up. "Have you always been like this?"

"Like what?"

"Like tense angst woman. It'd make a great super hero, 'Tense Angst Woman.' Maybe you should adopt one of those Sally Struthers kids and be done with it, or a Sarah McLaughlin dog."

He thinks he's being witty, but I seriously consider it. Would buying tennis shoes for some little kid in Ethiopia fix this? Is that it? Would that be big enough? Helpful enough? What am I thinking – I'm not sure I even like kids. And I know that while I love dogs, I despise animal hair.

"Jesus, Ally, is your period due or something? You look crazed." His handsome brows draw together.

Now I am well and truly pissed. "That is pretty frigging condescending, ya know." But then I consider: is it hormones? Thank god I blew off the Botox injections so I can still scrunch up my forehead to think.

He sighs, clicks off the TV altogether. "Look, I don't know what you want from me. I just want to watch my show without getting my head chewed off. You seem hell bent on saving the world. Tonight. Immediately. I don't have a clue how that's supposed to happen, or how it suddenly became your job to do it." John gets up, leans over, puts a hand on either side of me and looms.

I'm still not used to this, having a man in such close proximity, one who can be trusted. His cologne smells heavenly and so far removed from me, from female. He's this creature of thick forearms and hard chest. I know what he's doing with that leaning over thing, trying to distract me. I try and dig my mental heels in and try to refocus on misery. I fail.

He buries his face in my neck, inhales deeply, drags one hand through my hair. I'm forced to look up at him, at his icy blue eyes. "Perhaps, you just need a place to deposit all this pent up energy." I'm pinned against the sofa, trapped by his weight and my attraction to him. I hold my breath, a bit put out by my reaction to him. Where was he when I felt unloved and ugly? When I was sad and alone? When was that again?

He runs a hand over my t-shirt, slowly, intently. "You have the most incredible tits." He breaths the words into my mouth, then puts his tongue there, gently, exploring, finding my teeth. "Incredible." His mouth is on my neck and I feel him getting hard, pressing into me, wanting me.

He's saying things in my ear, making me hot and I'm angry again, so angry that I want him, that he can do this to me. "I'm going to fuck you on this sofa, pretty Alana. It's going to be so good." His arms wrap around me, pull me hard to him. I can't seem to think with his hands on my back. "Save the world later. After I have my way with you." He unhooks my bra. He's obviously had practice at it; he has less trouble removing it than I do. Now his hands are on my skin, smooth and warm. He pulls my shirt and bra off. He stares at my chest. "Perfect, perfect," he murmurs, then his mouth is on my nipple. There are raised circular scars there, but he doesn't seem to notice. It hurts a little when he does this. I hear whimpers of protest in the distance and then realize I'm making them. He takes his mouth off for a second, stares down at me. I feel vulnerable and lightheaded and pressed under his weight at the same time.

He doesn't bother to take off his pants, doesn't bother to remove mine. He finds the zipper of mine and pulls down hard, his finger catching my panties, too. One hand finds me, making gentle circles with his finger. The other unzips his fly and he releases himself. He's hard already and when he puts it in me I feel incredibly safe, safe for just a moment. He's groaning in my ear as he takes me and his hands are stroking me.

At this moment, for just this moment, I have a purpose. Maybe this saves the world a little.

And at this moment, I'm content.

CHAPTER THIRTY-TWO

Sex is a great problem solver for those with short horizon lines. John's problem solving technique works fabulously for about twenty minutes at a stretch. Unfortunately, I don't spend every waking moment under him, over him or next to him. Eventually the nagging pull of my own psyche drags me back like an undertow, leaving me freshly angry at John for his seeming immunity to this inner screaming. He seems perfectly okay going through the motions of life, working, screwing, watching his silly anime cartoons. He's reliably smiling and funny, inviting and warm.

I want to deck him. Two times we didn't use protection, behaving like two idiot children. We should be ashamed of ourselves. I smile at his photo, taped to the corner of my computer monitor and keep typing. Apparently shame runs shallow in this girl. Besides, I made an appointment to see a gynecologist this week. We've been lucky so far, but I don't want to press my luck and create problems I'm not ready to solve. That's the story I'm pitching when my mind drifts off, offering a tiny version of John, all huge eyes and dark hair...

"Dot, Milestone Meeting!"

My head snaps up. Greg doesn't pause to chat after his announcement. He doesn't even slow down. A stubborn part of me wants to ignore him. Alana. My name is Alana. Everyone but Greg has been supportive about this. Old habits die hard, I guess. I sigh heavily and grab a yellow legal pad. I travel by shuttle to Building Ten where I'm the only one present without a laptop.

Talk about old habits.

Tim, my project manager, Greg, and maybe six other people are all camped around an oval table jawing about the status of our code and whether or not we're going to meet the scheduled milestone. I'm QA, so the answer is always, No. No the code is not ready. No I haven't finished my test plan revisions. No, I haven't completed a full pass.

It's almost my turn. I'm going to be called on any minute.

"Okay, so dev has released that last set of fixes and dev received them...a week ago. Alana, what's the status?" Tim asks.

I start rattling on about the test pass when a guy busts into the meeting. I don't know him. He's red faced, stocky, and lacks any sense of fashion so he clearly works here. He's breathing hard, like he ran the stairs.

"Sorry about the interruption. Is there an Alana Lindell here?"

"That's me." This is weird. No one ever barges into a Milestone Meeting.

"Can I speak to you out in the hallway?" His pink cheeks grow pinker. He'll catch fire at this rate. Now I'm truly freaked out. I can feel the eyes of an entire room on my back as we walk out into the hall.

The guy is nervous, keeps looking down at the floor, the walls, anywhere to avoid eye contact with me. "Look, I'm really sorry to have to do this, but HR told me I needed tell you. And give you a ride home."

I want to strangle this guy. "What is it?"

"You're friends with John Miller over in Building Ten, right? Well...his sister called from Harborview. He was in a car accident. He was... well... he's dead. I'm really sorry."

For a second, I don't feel anything at all. I stare at him like an idiot since I believe he's nuts. I say something. I think I said, "What?"

Then I do something I've never done before or since: the room swims, the floor rises up to meet me. I'm out before I make contact. I fainted.

ALWAYS A BRIDESMAID. ALWAYS.

Walking down a fifty-foot-long path isn't usually so daunting for people, but when there is a life-altering event awaiting you at the end of that path, feet stumble, knees buckle, and normally very "on it" people completely forget where they're supposed to be.

excerpt from The Bridesmaid's Manual *by Sarah Stein & Lucy Talbot, Page 151*

Lisa Souza

CHAPTER THIRTY-THREE

Rachel Miller Wilson and her tree trunk husband Bart are sitting on the sofa, bawling like kids. Rachel is already three months into her pregnancy and Bart's terrified she'll get stressed and lose the baby. He keeps one enormous paw around her shoulders at all times, just in case.

We are in Lonnie Miller's frightfully uptight living room, and it feels exactly like she wants it too: intimidating. I have never been in the Miller house before. It is a far cry from John's landfill. It is a lifetime away from my empty apartment.

An internal voice tells me this is all my fault, which logically I know is ridiculous. I didn't run a red light and smash into John's stupid Lexus. Shouldn't a car that expensive protect you?

Maybe my envy killed him: he could sleep deeply while I stewed about my inner demons. I cowered at social gatherings while John's friendly demeanor drew people to him. He could be funny and handsome AND do math. How could I not hate him?

Maybe that's why I'm stuck here, dry eyed and hollow in the Miller's over-decorated living room. I feel my jaundiced eyes critiquing every stitch in the room: drapes too heavily tasseled, fussy rococo fireplace, annoying swoops and swirls that bend around anything made of wood, of which there is far too much. Too much everything.

Rachel sobs and Bart rubs her back with one hand, swipes the other across his eyes. Skip leans against the mantel of that damned ugly fireplace. He has something amber in an eight ounce glass. Lonnie looks like dough that's been punched down after a rise, deflated and slowly losing shape. There no hint of the diamond clad Martha Stewart I remember from their wedding.

We're kindergartners, waiting for our parents to come and take us home. We are a gathering of crows, all in black. I long for Elvira's gaudy flair to swoop over the room. Kennedy J found me this suit, since I insisted I wouldn't own a creepy black dress I knew I'd never want to wear it again. Sure as shit I'll burn this suit when it's over.

Lonnie's voice breaks through.

"They wouldn't let me see him." Lonnie sounds bemused.

"Well of course not, Lonnie. He's all smashed up." Skip glares at her and takes another swig of Scotch. "What would be the point?"

"Don't be nasty, dad. She just wanted to... be with him." Rachel and Bart nod in synch.

Lonnie tries to straighten a bit, "I'm not a child,

you know. I wanted to be there. To show I cared enough to…"

"To what? To stare at his mangled corpse?" Skip tosses back the remainder of the glass.

Oh my god. This car accident continues.

"Daddy, please don't start."

"Oh stow it, Rach. She's always been a crappy mother and suddenly she's -"

"Daddy!" Rachel's hand covers her mouth.

" – the queen mum." Skip finishes his thought.

Bart pulls Rachel to her feet, stands with her. He is approximately double her height.

"Skip, I know you and Lonnie are heartbroken as can be, but save it for couples' therapy. You'll mind your manners around Rachel. I won't have her any more upset than she already is." His hand guides her toward the door. "Alana, why don't you come with Rach and me in the limo? Lonnie and Skip can follow when they've gotten themselves squared away."

I'm grateful as hell to Bart and his country boy charm for making good my escape. The three of us ride together in the first limousine, the other will carry the feuding Miller' and the battered body of my dead boyfriend.

We proceed to the cemetery to bury my one chance at happiness.

CHAPTER THIRTY-FOUR

I stare at the hole where they plan on dumping my boyfriend, the only person on this earth who made me question my eternal, everlasting worthlessness. Now there's just this hole.

Short tempered Skip and the newly fragile Lonnie, pregnant Rachel and towering Bart crowd around me. John was a lapsed Catholic (a Catholic in recovery, he'd always tell me) but his parents aren't, so a priest, a friend of the family, does the honors. I don't hear a word. There's just this hole.

The instant the ceremony is finished, Father Dousseau drags a stogie from under his surplice and plants it in the corner of his mouth and lights it. Oddly enough, the stinky cigar makes him far more approachable. He pats my shoulder with a short fingered hand, ignoring the crowd of people still gathered at the gravesite.

"You holding up, young lady? His voice sounds like it's dragged over gravel, like a friendly mob boss.

"The truth, Father?" He nods. "I'm pissed. Well and truly pissed." Where did that come from?

"Makes sense." He nods his big square head. "Be nice if people would kindly give us the heads up before they go and die on us like that. Give us a little more prep time."

I try and smile. He's kind, so I try, but my face feels brittle, like a saltine, and I'm afraid I'll crack. "That's it exactly, Father. John and I… well we've only been close for a few months… he was very kind to me."

He blows out a tidy ring of smoke. "I sense you feel this is an uncommon occurrence?"

"You're a perceptive cuss, aren't you, padre? As a matter of fact, yes. The nice part is fairly new."

He takes a deep drag on his cigar, patient, waiting me out.

"I had known him from before, though. A long time ago. We went to the same high school."

"Our John was quite the big man on campus, then. Excellent running back, wasn't he?"

I wish I could cry. I conjure John's speech about high school, about his shyness. "Yeah. He wasn't so nice to me then. He hung out with these football jocks. They called me names. Terrible names." Mouth diarrhea. Someone should make me stop.

Father Dousseau switches the stogie to the far side of his mouth without the aid of his hands. Quite a trick. "I wouldn't classify that as nice."

"Me neither." He lets the conversation dangle there, a hanging chad. "I'm not the same person I was in high school either, Father."

An enormous smile splits that block of a head, (but the cigar remains securely tucked into the corner). "Apparently, neither was John. Few of us remain the emotional cripples we were in high school, praise be." He looks heavenward with raised hands for the last part, and I hear a dry crackle that I guess is me laughing. A Tim Burton laugh, like bones rattling.

"So you and John evolved."

"I didn't so much evolve as I sort of…rebuilt."

Father pulls a stogie switch again. "That sounds intriguing." His watery blue eyes are amazingly perceptive. He smiles with his eyes.

"I had a bunch of surgeries. Plastic surgery. John… well he didn't recognize me. He doesn't… I mean he didn't even know we went to the same school. I started using my middle name."

"Part of that rebuild program?"

"Pretty much." We've drifted away from the others, and end up surrounded by elaborate grave markers and a surprising burst of sunlight.

That stubby oven mitt of his hand descends onto my shoulder again. "Change is inevitable, my dear. How fortunate that you and John were able to find joy in yours."

CHAPTER THIRTY-FIVE

"John's death was terribly sudden," she says.

I hate this office. It's intended to push a positive vibe with its cheery yellow walls and comfortable furniture. It says 'we're all just chatting here, just having a friendly, folksy get-together. Grab a quilt.

I'm forking over one-fifty a visit to get the voices in my head to shut up. Yellow walls don't help. "Ya think?"

Doctor Devers rubs at her eyes. She looks tired. "You rely pretty heavily on sarcasm to get you through the rough spots, Dot. Does it help?"

I'm pretty tired myself. "No."

———————◀❚❚▶———————

It's my first day back at work after taking the week of John's funeral off. I have absolutely no vacation days left – I used them all for the surgeries

– so I had only two days of "grief" leave available, then I took the rest unpaid - which is pretty harsh.

Greg, my lead, phoned me last Friday to feel me out, trying to determine whether I'm ready to get back to testing before they miss a milestone. I figured what the hell, better than sitting around.

To my surprise, I find I like driving. I'm coming in the back way up Novelty Hill Road and singing along to the radio. No more Community Transit plus Metro for me. Rachel insisted I take John's "other" car, his beloved old Dodge Ram truck. I've no clue why John needed a truck. He didn't haul things, he didn't hunt, didn't fish. Maybe he planned on digging all that garbage out of his place someday.

In any case it's mine now, title and all. As John's stated beneficiary, Rachel planned on giving me the Lexus, knowing I didn't have a car. She let the idea drop when Lonnie pitched a fit and I begged her to drop it. Rather than push on and cause a squabble, Rachel simply pointed at the truck. "You want it? It's yours. Bart has his truck and I won't drive that thing." She patted her round little tummy. "Can't climb up at the moment."

The truck is awesome. It frees me from public transportation for as long as it runs. And the radio still works.

I'm at the light, stuck with my fellow commuters at the Highway 520 entrance. The light changes and I accelerate, but out of the corner of my eye, a car materializes in front of me, barely avoiding my right front bumper. She must have tromped on the gas to sneak ahead of me after the light went green.

Somewhere deep in my soul, there's a snap. My foot depresses the accelerator. I push that old Dodge like this is Talladega. I'm after her, chasing her, that skank in the Mercedes, a big dog after a fast rabbit. She must have felt my intention, because when 520 opens to two lanes, that sleek car begins weaving in and out of traffic. I stay stapled to her bumper, pressing that poor old truck way past its limits and my own common sense, simply crazy with rage. This friggin moron, this bitch, acts as though I'm invisible.

I gun it.

I follow her for maybe another seven miles. Her driving indicates she's aware of me, a pimple on her ass disguised as a truck. Her head twists to glance in the mirror a couple of times, and she weaves off the next exit.

And so do I.

I don't know how many blocks I trail her, into Kirkland somewhere, maybe Totem Lake. Don't know and couldn't care less. At some point, she screeches to a dead stop in front of me. It so surprises me I nearly career into her car, but mercifully the old truck brakes just short, but my head isn't so lucky and smacks against the unpadded steering wheel with a thump, nearly knocking me unconscious.

My rival pulls an efficient U turn and speeds off the other way, just missing an older black lab resting by a mailbox.

I pull over slowly, giving the gray muzzled dog plenty of room.

She might have killed somebody.

Okay, me too. I think my intention was to mow her down, crush that useless hunk of Bavarian junk into next year. God knows, between the two of us, we nearly killed a helpless old mutt and put a scores of lives at risk on the highway. I hyperventilate until the adrenaline drains away. When my breathing slows, I no longer feel compelled to smash s stranger's face in with my dead boyfriend's truck.

What kind of monster does something like that?

I wait another few minutes till my heart stops trying to explode out of my chest. There's a tap on the driver's side window and my head nearly contacts the roof of the car. So much for calming down. I roll down the window a crack. "Yes?"

"You okay?" It's an elderly man, probably the lab's owner.

"Oh, yes, I just needed to take a minute. I'll be on my way."

The old guy looks at me funny. Then he says something to the dog which trails after him back into his house.

CHAPTER THIRTY-SIX

"Is that why you called me? Because of the road rage incident?"

I bet that's what it says in her notes. Probably in caps: The Road Rage Incident. Definitely not a Barbara Cartland title. "Dot and the Road Rage Incident."

"Maybe. Partly." I sigh. I do that a lot. "Look, there's a lot going on right now. Things are messed up at work." I look at those jaundiced walls. She should repaint. Something neutral. Maybe beige.

"You rarely speak about work. How are things messed up?"

"My boss says... I'm having problems focusing. In general, I mean. It's hard to stay on top of my projects." I picture the scene from Raider's of the Lost Ark, Indiana Jones looking over his shoulder as an enormous stone descends from a hidden space, pursuing him, ready to crush him into dust. "I have to make some decisions soon or I think I'm going to explode."

Elvira scribbles in her notebook. She looks up as I exit Doctor Pepper's office. Today her hair is in pigtails. With her heart shaped face and enormous eyes, she reminds me of Christina Ricci playing Tuesday in The Adams Family, only stretched taller.

"All shrunk?"

"Significantly so, practically cured, thank you." We pack up and head out to El's beetle, which barely seats two, crammed as it is with percussion instruments, a guitar, and notebooks full of music.

"Did you, like dump the road rage thing?"

Not one for subtlety. I think Elvira should consider a career shift to counseling. "Yeah."

In that intuitive way of hers, she drops the subject. "On the bright side, I got a great song out of it. Road Rage may be our first number one single." She pulls onto the freeway, while Sherman, her Volkswagen, struggles to reach speed. "Are you gonna be okay? With us on the road I mean?"

The Bad Apples have a tour starting with a Seattle up and comer, a huge deal. "I'm going to miss you, but I'm so happy for you. It's what you've worked. You leave next Friday?"

"Thursday."

Not sure why stomach tightens. It's only a day. But it amps up the sense of loss a tick.

———

Myrna Bosco looks resplendent in a winter white suit. I was shocked to the teeth when she asked me to be a bridesmaid – I didn't think we were all that close. Saying hey to someone while they park their bike hadn't struck me as a relationship. Just goes to show you that I'm not the only isolated person in the world. Which may explain why I agreed to do this: part of me sympathizes deeply with a woman so disconnected that a casual work acquaintance fills in as her one and only bridesmaid. The other part just wants to see the fish Ole Myrna hooked.

Her face lights up when she gazes at her new man. George Clooney he ain't. Zachary Grisham is nearly as thin as Myrna with the same graying hair, and rocks a pair of John Lennon-style spectacles. I keep thinking Grisham sounds like something she'd name one of her cats. My mind wanders and Zach suddenly grows a tail. The resulting image? One of those hairless Egyptian cats of a breed that evades memory. Eww! Clear the vision!

"So Myrna, how'd you and Zach meet?"

Myrna blushes, bringing more color to her narrow cheeks than they've seen in years. "It was the most incredible thing. I finally attended a Scrabble Championship. I've always wanted to go." Her eyes sparkle. She is lit up." – and this year I said 'screw work, I'm going' and I took off a whole week to make sure I'd be there. And I get to the auditorium and the crowd is great. Have you ever watched competitive Scrabble?"

I do a slow no twist of the head. Myrna is totally worked up over her courageous venture into board games.

"Amazing, really. Brilliant. Anyway I see this guy I don't recognize, and I'm pretty well versed on who the real players are. So my sister Miriam tells me its Zach Grisham and I almost faint."

"You knew of him?"

"Well of course! He's just famous is all. One of the premier players ever."

Myrna continues tales of Mighty Zach Grisham's Scrabble prowess while I help her sister Miriam adjust a basket of flowers for the flower girl. I keep one ear hooked to the discussion so I can nod and look riveted when appropriate, but I find the flower petals more interesting. I don't want to be rude, but I don't want to be bored either. It's a complex world.

A little cherub of a girl with a head of oversized brown ringlets twists back and forth, one hand glued to her crotch. She's the flower girl. And apparently she'll soon be a damp one.

"Do you need to use the potty, Bethy?" I try.

She has one finger lodged in her mouth. She drops her chin and raises her eyes. "Umm."

"Is that a yes, or no?" I don't speak cherub, just high school French.

"Just take her, will you?" says Miriam. "I still need to get dressed and we've only got ten minutes."

Miriam is Myrna's twin. They're both rail thin and graying early, but unlike Myrna, who made an enormous effort today, Miriam's wiry frame appears wildly out of place in a plaid shirt and old straight leg Levis. She appears more cowgirl than Jewish matron. Her unpainted face looks ready to cook for the cattle drive.

Myrna, however, does have on makeup, and

this is a first. I suspect she had someone do it, since I can't imagine her knowing how. The touch of color transforms her. She looks luminous and fresh faced.

"Alana, can you take her or not?" Miriam's exasperated voice snaps me out distraction land.

I reach down and take the pudgy little mitt in mine. "Shall we give it a try, Bethy?"

Bethy remains silent, eyes like plates. She nods slowly and we wander toward the restroom. Even this trip is better than a tile by tile description of the Scrabble Championships. If Myrna and Zach wax euphoric over Scrabble, who knows what sex will do to them? That's a fresh nasty image I try and dispel instantly.

"Awana, can you take my dwess so it doesn't get wet?" a pile of clothing plops into my hands. I look down at little Bethy, the Campbell Soup girl. She has divested herself of nearly every stitch of clothing, and stands in undies and tights before me, finger still in her mouth.

"Get moving, Bethy." I open a stall door and give her a small shove in the back. Great. Now I need to redress her from tights to bow in ten minutes.

There's a knock on the outer restroom door. "Are we just about ready in there?"

"No!" shouts Bethy, who apparently has found her tongue. "Need to go number two!"

"Give us just a sec, okay?" I say, trying to gloss over the specifics little Bethy is so willing to share.

After a power flush, Bethy flies out, completely naked. "Loud!" she squeals.

"Where's your underwear?"

She hides behind my legs and points into the stall. I wiggle free and track her stray underwear and tights.

"Okay, little pumpkin, let's get you ready to rumble."

I speed dress her, a talent I hadn't known I possessed. Within three minutes she's in her undies, tights, and dress, zipped and bow-tied. In the flurry, though, Bethy trashed her springy curls into a tangle. I didn't bring a brush, (forgive me Kennedy!), so I finger comb them back in line.

Another knock at the door. "It's time, ladies."

Oh grrr. "Okay. We'll be right out." I look down at the apple cheeked kid before me. "You ready to go now, Bethy? Let's go get your flower basket."

We head outside to watch Myrna tie the knot on Lake Washington.

She and Zach the Scrabble King stand on the dock before Rabbi Koss, who already married them in the temple three days ago under the canopy, solid, Jewish and legal for Myrna's folks. Today, I'm told, is all about the happy couple.

It's freezing. I cannot for the life of me imagine a more inauspicious place, but apparently there's a bike trail nearby which holds sentimental value for Myrna, who has ridden it every day for years. Charming. But why not wait until its warm enough not to freeze a zipper?

Bethy balks at leaving the sanctity of the restroom. It's warmer in there than out here. Who could blame her?

I rub Bethy's pudgy arms for luck and warmth and escort her outside. The bridal party stands at the foot of the dock looking… well, they look resplendent. Honestly. Homely ole Myrna looks just as radiant as a very narrow graying woman can. And now the sun pops out from its hiding place behind the cloud cover and suddenly Lake Washington is the most beautiful place on earth, all azure water, golden sun, and a couple dressed in wedding finery.

Everything is idyllic till the music begins. It pours out of someone's old battery powered boom box. For some reason Streisand crooning a tinny Evergreen strikes me as hilarious. The ceremony is gloriously short, so I'm spared the indignity of holding my sides and screaming with laughter in the middle of Myrna's big moment while simultaneously freezing. The minute it's over, so is my giggle jag. I solemnly plod up the hill in my silly spike heels. The Yarrow Bay Grill, where the reception is being held, lies just up from the beach, but these shoes weren't made for walking even short distances. I think you're just supposed to stand in them till someone carries you to bed.

That makes me think of John. And now I'm seriously depressed again.

I fall behind the wedding party (who are not wearing these shoes) and lapse into my usual coma. When I finally reach the door, relieved to be inside, I'm startled to hear "Fancy meeting you again," said in the salacious tone usually reserved for mating.

I turn to my right and there is Jack Weston.

CHAPTER THIRTY-SEVEN

Up go the hackles. And John's not here to keep him at bay. Behind him are a couple of post fraternity types, well groomed and Zoom whitened.

"Hi, Jack." No sense pretending I don't know who he is. I look over his shoulder for the wedding party. I hadn't been in any hurry to catch up with virtual strangers, yet suddenly it's my duty.

"Don't you look fetching today." His eyes scrape me up and down, opening scars I thought healed over, "meeting someone?"

"A friend from work just got married. The reception is being held here. I need to catch up." My voice sounds glacial, even to me. I make a move to leave but he slaps a hand in the space over my shoulder, connecting smartly against the side of the building, trapping me between his arm, the building, and his buddies.

His compadres grin unpleasantly, making no move to leave. "Oh I'm sure they'll survive without you. Married couples aren't likely to be overly concerned with a lowly bridesmaid on their wedding day, right?" He smiles his salesman smile.

I swallow but my throat's dry so nothing goes down. The last time I had to deal with this guy, I had an ex-football player and car seats to protect me. Now he's invaded my personal space and the only person who might have helped is unavoidably dead, and I can clearly expect zip from his cronies. And why? Why am I feeling so scared? Because some twenty-six year old twice-convicted drunk went on an early morning bender. The only tool I have to work with is a lifetime of greeting unpleasant situations with politeness. I still have no idea how a person extricates themselves from someone they find scary.

Jack Weston's teeth are dazzling white, maybe even whiter than John's, like they've been dipped in Clorox and shellacked. I'm staring at them to avoid his eyes, which have none of John's easy warmth. They're predatory.

A mental picture of Elvira's bruised and swollen eye materializes. "Taking time out from beating up on helpless little girls, Jack?" I slip underneath his extended hand.

He laughs at my exit move. "I'll swing by your place tonight." He says easily and leaves the restaurant. "We'll talk some more."

I panic, then relax. He doesn't know where I live so I'm safe. Then I panic again: he was in the car when John picked me up for Rachel's wedding. That was months ago. He won't remember, right?

Now I'm scared to go home.

I sit politely through the wedding luncheon, mostly staring out at the water, but occasionally trying to snap out of it and be polite to Myrna's sister Miriam who had the misfortune of being seated beside me.

I never realized that invisible has some advantages. People expect things from you when they see you. There are those surreptitious glances from men: a couple of boys in cutup jeans and skateboard hair with their parents, older guys in polo shirts with their wives, business men, even a couple of guys in sportswear, maybe chowing down after a round of golf. Their eyes sway my direction, hang for a two count, then return to their booths, then swing back again. I feel trapped again.

This is one of those Oprah light bulb moment. People, men, find me attractive.

Nausea hits me and I race to the ladies room. I've got it wrong of course. Those men were staring at some glitch in appearance, as usual. Perhaps something stuck in my teeth. A rogue bit of spinach maybe. Or I'll find toilet paper clinging to my ridiculous high heels. I sit down on the elegant padded bench in front of the lounge mirror and drop my head for a second to clear my sick tummy. That gives me a chance to check the shoes: they're fine. Next I grin the false, tooth bearing smile of someone checking for food particles. My porcelain veneers gleam back, devoid of a single speck.

Then I take a chest breath and look at myself in the mirror for real, the way I did nearly a year ago. I'm trying to see what's really there, not what's stuck in my head, playing like an unfortunate pop song, one I don't really care for but can't stop singing. The image in the mirror is a stranger, symmetrical, clear skinned. Beautiful.

I'm beautiful. My stomach heaves a little and I drop my head again.

I didn't know.

Maybe I should have, but I didn't really connect the dots.

I started seeing John just two weeks after my tummy tuck stopped hurting. The window between ugly invisible duckling and newly arrived swan never fully opened. Till now.

Oh sure, there were some stares at work, but I don't encounter many people at work, didn't need to when everyone's a mouse click away. Other than the cafeteria and a couple of meetings, I rarely contact people in person.

Save for my outings with Kennedy J, I still don't leave my place much. And given Kenney's propensity for only the best life has to offer, his choice of hotspots is always chock full of the beautiful people. There may even have been an unwritten minimum attractiveness requirement. In my previous incarnation, I'd probably have been refused at the door.

The only other place I might have encountered people was on the Metro. Faces on the bus don't really register all that much, just a rotating gallery of seniors and rogues like myself, still using public transportation. I don't recall encountering more than a glance.

But no more.

Don't get me wrong: I'm certain that I could dial it down, could return to my makeup-free, dressed-down existence and turn off all the lights again without too much effort. But the thing is, I didn't realize until this moment that the lights were on!

Even with John I hadn't known. We had a sexual relationship, yes, but I always assumed it had more to do with understanding him, maybe with him feeling a bit guilty about high school, not with him finding me physically attractive. And what a relief that was - finally connecting with someone! But he showed respect for my work, too. And we emailed all the time, silly word games. Chatter. I found him attractive. It never struck me that maybe he found me attractive, too. Somehow our outsides, the superficial part, always dimmed into an echo behind this sense of connection. It was not its center.

Now Jack Weston and his frightening friends have alerted me that my outside draws stares.

And this is new. And scary.

CHAPTER THIRTY-EIGHT

I frown at the phone. On the other end, Elvira has her bags packed for the road, blissfully unaware of my recent Weston sighting. And it's ridiculous to consider calling, getting her all worked up before she leaves. What kind of a monster gets her friend all distressed before her big tour? A bad one.

So maybe an email to Kennedy J? Just to let someone know about the threat?

Right. First, he's clear over in Seattle. Second, what threat, exactly?

An internal 'war of the inside voices' ensues. Sparring voice one shrieks: "well it sure as hell felt threatening two hours ago when I was smacked up against that wall." And the second voice props hands on hips, purses its lips and shakes it head, "So if a guy rests his hand in the same vicinity as you, you're in deadly danger? Puh-leeze."

It gets so noisy in my head I decide to take a bath to distract myself. Barbara Cartland's The

Devil Defeated, ought to do the trick. By the time the water cools, I'm prune-y and half asleep, so I change into P.J.'s and decide to get to sleep early.

When the door chimes, my heart slams so hard it practically flings me out of bed. I do what any smart deer in the headlights does: freeze.

The volume of the raps increases, followed by the thump of something dropped on the stoop.

"Don't be an ass... Alana. I've got a bunch of Elvira's things. I tried to drop them at her place, but the landlord said she's gone for the next three months."

This is where I make a mistake.

A few seconds pass before autopilot sends me to the door to silence the noise. I make a rudimentary check of the peephole, apparently for no reason at all because I let him in.

I let him in.

"It's awfully late, Jack."

I let him in!

He swings past me into my apartment, glancing around, dropping an open cardboard box on the floor.

There's not much to see. Since I'm not home all that much, my design style leans toward 'comfortable clean.' There's an overstuffed sofa, a matching chair in some nebulous, non-committal shade of caramel and a generic, pseudo-country coffee table, one that likely graces a thousand bourgeois living rooms. Thanks to my disgusted mom, there's a couple of things on the walls, a big mirror and some generic artwork, which she purchased herself, frustrated that I refused to deal with my inhospitable walls. There are curtains, drawn, so I don't have to look at blackened windows.

Jack makes himself comfortable on the sofa.

"Nice ensemble," he says with a grin, waving a hand at me.

I glance down. I'm wearing my Scottie Dog jammies.

Of all the lifestyle changes I adopted, changing to exotic sleepwear never gelled. Not even for John. A sexy night with John involved me stealing his t-shirt and his taking it back. Since he died, though, I can't bring myself to wear the two he left at my place, not the black one with the Ramones in fading white print, nor the one featuring Sango, some chick from John's Manga obsession. I think she's a character from Inuyasha. In any case, as soon as he died, I dug out my old flannels, now six sizes too large. Thank goodness for drawstrings.

"It's awfully late, Jack. Maybe we could postpone this little talk for some other time."

Jack leans back further into the sofa, clasping his hands behind his head. "Oh, why wait when I've come all this way to see you?" He reveals those too even teeth of his and again I'm reminded of something feral.

I feel supremely stupid. How am I going to get him out of here? A lifetime of compliance programming squashing what I know should be running for the door and shouting. What I actually do is stand there, the way a cow would, a look of dull acceptance on my face. I wait for some magic force to send him on his way.

"I know who you really are." His scary grin widens a fraction.

Tiny hairs on the back of my neck spring straight up. I remain silent, because I have a right to, don't I?

"We went to high school together, the three of us. John didn't recognize you. I planned on enlightening him, but sadly he passed before I could share." Both his legs are now propped up on my coffee table. "Miss Dot Lindell. Something like 'will suck no cock,' right? I may have had a hand in that." He smiles more broadly. It doesn't reach eyes.

"You're a veritable Byron." My voice shakes.

"Modesty forbids me from taking full credit. Gotta save some for John. After all, I doubt it would have made it clear around the school without his getting the word out."

Oh now I'm coasting on pure adrenaline. "It's time for you to go." My voice has firmed up nicely, courtesy of rage, but I'm shivering in my PJs.

He rises off the sofa, a scary creature advancing on me and in an incarnation I don't recognize, not at all. This isn't the smart assed jock I tried to ignore in the high school. He's something conjured, summoned. He's a curse.

While he's all movement, I'm stuck, frozen. There are things I'm supposed to be doing right now, I just know there are, but I can't get cooperation from my voice or my legs or any other part of me. The useful part of my brain, disconnected, shouts and screams in the back of my head, telling him to get out, telling me to run away.

I should do something. I'm sure I should.

The phone enters my field of vision. I stare at it. Pick it up. Call for help. Jack follows my gaze and wanders over to the phone. He yanks the jack from the wall, leaving bare wires. "We wouldn't want intrusions during this conversation, now would we?"

I finally locate my voice, but I'm an instant too late. He's reached my frozen position and quickly clamps his hand down hard over my mouth, smashing my teeth against my lips, my head against the wall. I taste a faintly metallic taste, blood. I'm stunned senseless, as he steers me toward my bedroom.

"Funny thing is, Dotty, I suspect this entire time you've been secretly attracted to me."

Anger floods back in. Energy returns to my hands, and I claw at his face and at the hand over my mouth.

He curses through gritted teeth, then clubs me in the head with a closed fist. There's an agonizing pop of air into my ear. I groan into the hand still clamped over my bleeding lips.

Fingers grip tightly into my hair, yanking my head back and smacking my forehead smartly against the edge of the molding outside my bedroom door. He hisses something into my ear, but that ear isn't working at the moment. His body presses me into my room, onto the bed.

Too scary. Too dreadful. So I disconnect again.

But things happened, terrible things. I know because bits and pieces of what happened are still there, hanging memory chads. Like my missing flannel PJs. I remember putting them on. But now I'm naked and I walk to the bathroom. It's oddly immaculate. The porcelain gleams and the chrome shines. When I spit into the sink, the red is such an intense color and then it fades to pink when I turn on the water and it swirls away.

I look up at the mirror. I inventory my hurts, do a diagnostic. My right wrist hurts more than my left and I hold it up to the mirror. Already faint purple ovals are emerging like a thick bracelet. I raise a hand to my face. I think I got punched in the face. My right eye is going black and my face is swelling. Glad he missed my nose. My right ear is ringing. My backside and crotch have a thousand angry things to say but I can't see them in the mirror and I don't want to. turn the volume down on that pain. I don't want to know about it. My throat feels swollen, too. There's scratch marks on my breasts.

For some reason, my image in the mirror, all that work come to this, sends me to giggling. I can't seem to stop and oh it's such a horrible sound, my high pitched giggles, except they're changing and now I hear a keening sound, far off, like a pup left alone for the first time.

It's me. It hurts my throat. I shush myself.

I want John.

I wander through the apartment. I find my Scottie dog PJs and my pretty girl underwear. I pick them both up, holding them in front of me like a cat peed on them. I stuff them into the garbage pail under the kitchen sink. I stare for a minute. Not good enough.

In a haze, I return to the bathroom. My terrycloth robe hangs on a hook there, and I quickly put it on. There's an old pair of canvas boat shoes by the door, my "garbage taking out" shoes. Kennedy J would pitch a fit. Bathrobe and boat shoes. I gather up the garbage bag full of Scottie Dogs and underwear and God knows what else and walk out to the dumpster behind the apartment building.

With a quick toss, it never happened.

Lisa Souza

BRIDESMAID EVOLUTION

It's not your job to call the groom-to-be to tell him that his bride-to-be is pissed because his mother-in-law-to-be was offended by the bride's sister-in-law-to-be over whatever-the-hell-it-may-be.... or something. You get the picture. Stay out of domestic disputes.

excerpt from <u>The Bridesmaid's Manual</u> *by Sarah Stein & Lucy Talbot, Page 50*

Lisa Souza

CHAPTER THIRTY-NINE

There's this distant banging. I ignore it. Just like I've ignored having the phone repaired. Not like I have anything to say.

I can hear the dulcet tones of Kennedy J. Didn't know that guy had that kind of anger in him. Eventually, I realize I'm no match for an irate homosexual and I pull myself from the rumpled pile of bedding and lurch toward the door.

I make a big play of checking the peephole. Lo and behold.

I let the door swing open. Gust of fresh air wafts in. Strange. I had no idea how stuffy the place had gotten.

Kennedy lets himself in and gasps. "Dear God, Dot. What the hell is going on?" He crosses his arms huffily over his chest. "And what is this getup?"

The getup he refers to is my new uniform. It consists of a T-shirt I got years ago from work that says "That which does not kill me makes me stronger. And if it does kill me, maybe I'll get some rest." Nietzsche I think. Hilarious. I've paired it with an outrageous pair of flannel jammy pants in a blue plaid, sheepskin slippers, and bed head. Quite a combo. I've been wearing it for a few days I think.

He takes in my décor. Empty containers of Haagen Dazs (purchased for Elvira, who could afford to eat such empty calories). Empty two-liter bottles. Empty pizza boxes – well, not completely empty. In each I've left a few strips of crust. They always put too much crust on pizza. I'm about to share this with Kennedy when he wraps his enormous arms around me.

I go rigid. It's reflexive and I hope he hasn't noticed. Then I feel his shaking and realize he's terribly upset. I like ole Kennedy and don't want him to be sad. I fight the urge to say "there, there." It's like trying to care through syrup. I feel lethargic and slow. I just don't have it to give.

He pulls back a bit, putting some space between our upper buddies, but keeping his hands tight to my upper arms. "Why didn't you call me?" He shakes his elegantly coiffed head. "Why didn't you call?

Do I tell him about the phone? I decide it's my problem. No need to burden him.

He drops his arms. Points. "Go take a shower. Now." He twists me like a puppet then gives me a slight shove. "Now."

I'm afraid. Afraid of what I'll see in the bathroom. Yeow it's trashed. There's no paper on the roll, and neither shower nor toilet has been cleaned for a bit. There's a scummy layer on the side of the shower door and no towels. I grab the least filthy one from the floor in the hall.

I do what I'm told, I take a shower and I'm absolutely shocked by a wave of sensations: hot water flowing through my hair, lush lather from shampoo, the fresh, clean smell of soap. I have no idea how long I stand there under the water, hypnotized. I come to and soap up my legs, grab a razor and shave off layers of fur.

By the time I complete these operations, the water is starting to chill up.

I grab the scary towel – hey, it's the only game in town – and wish to God I had a clean one. I start to throw on the same clothes I was wearing when the door flies open and a hand miraculously appears holding a pile of clothes: some jeans, a t-shirt, even underwear. Act of god, or act of fashion, it matters not. I slide them on.

Kennedy J has undertaken the back hoe approach to cleaning: he pushed everything from the kitchen counters onto the kitchen table, everything from the kitchen table into a garbage bag. He must have done a run-through, though, because I'm missing quite a bit of filth. The man works fast.

He doesn't turn around when I come into the room. "You should have called."

I ponder. "I didn't have it to give."

Now he turns around and oh-boy is he pissed. "That's the point, you dumb broad. Despite claims to the contrary, I am not psychic." He shakes his head, returns to sink. "I don't believe you have a single clean towel in this place, so I borrowed one from next door."

I freeze. "Next door? You mean as in hurricane Merry?"

"Come again?"

"My neighbor despises me."

"Apparently not enough to prevent her from loaning a towel. She did suggest buying her a new one."

I laugh – okay I bray like a donkey, a nasty sound. "There's a surprise. Did she snap you on the ass with it as she chased you out the door?"

"My we're nasty tempered. No, she in fact did not. What's all this about?" he waved an elegantly manicured hand in the air. "Is this a reaction to your friend's death? Or is there something else I don't know on top of everything else."

I assess the place objectively for a change. The room is truly a sty. It looks nearly as bad as I did before Kennedy J took me under his wing. "So it sucks. Sucks big gaping chunks of foul. I admit it. Are you happy?"

Kennedy brushes aside towels, magazines and an empty two liter of Orange Crush. Makes a big point of wiping real and imaginary crumbs off before sitting down. "As a matter of fact, I'm very happy a great deal of the time. Are you?"

"Are you crazed? Did you miss the part where the only guy on this planet who finds me remotely attractive just up and died? Not to mention - "

"Excuse me? The only guy on this planet? What special sauce have you been sniffing, dear? There are plenty of people who find you attractive.

That's your excuse for the state of anarchy in this room?" He pauses dramatically. "You need a shrink. Oddly enough, I have one."

I choke. "You do?"

He rolls his eyes. "Oh not for me, silly, for Jefferson. He suffers terrible angst. Or depression. Or some sordid disorder. Anyway, this is the name of his listener."

Wow. What an incredible word. 'Listener.' Not shrink, not psychologist. I look at the card. I know this name. I bark a laugh.

"Hm?"

"Nothing" I say.

"I've called and made an appointment for you. Told them you were an emergency. Who knew I was so accurate?" He gazes around, clearly mortified. "Jefferson will pick you up. After all, he knows the address. And I'd rather not be seen milling around a therapist's office. Bad for my image."

He hands me a card. "Your appointment is tomorrow at 3:45. That gives you... not nearly enough time to dig out of this hole, but I suggest you start digging. It will be therapeutic. It will certainly be better for you than this environment."

He gathered his things together: a crystal handled umbrella, a long black silk scarf. "Get cracking. I'll phone you tomorrow morning to ensure that you haven't found your way back under that rock."

"Kennedy?"

"Yes, my dear?"

I choke on it, that vile word. It burns my throat,

stings like glass shards. "Thanks."

CHAPTER FORTY

Oh my god. This is bad. I haven't seen a place look this bad since... since John's place, that ultimate pig sty.

It's funny, I never thought of myself as a particularly tidy person, but given the ungodly number of cleaners and paper towels stockpiled in the pantry, either I was or I collect chemicals. I start in the bathroom, the smallest room in the house.

When my mom's second husband Curtis taught me to clean a million years ago, the instructions were "top to bottom, left to right, wet, then dry." I look up. Even the ceiling looks like crap. I wander back into the entry room and locate my "magic beans," the wonder mop. I bought it after witnessing the miracle of microfiber on an infomercial. It's purported to remove unseen germs at the microscopic level. Handy. I just hope it can scrape scary crap off my bathroom ceiling.

I drag it back it into the bathroom and

methodically spray and scrub, spray and scrub till the ceiling looks like a ceiling again. I repeat this performance on one wall and foolishly check the bottom of the mop. Eek. Fortunately the fine men at magic bean laboratories kindly included a replacement mop head. I pull of the dead one and stick the backup on.

I wonder how long I've been in the fog. The only date I know is "today," which is when I see the listener. That stops my hand in its slow rotation on the mirror. That's pretty amazing. Usually my entire life seems date driven, milestone driven. But here I stand, trying to find a clean spot through the water stains on my bathroom mirror, not the slightest idea what day it is.

Glass Plus works pretty well. Especially with my super microfiber cloths. This time I purchased their cleaning power from Wal-Mart, which is considerably cheaper than ordering them over the Internet. Saves me the shipping charges. I can see my altered reflection in the mirror now. I don't recognize myself. My inside view of me doesn't match the image I see, with its clear skin and high cheekbones. I didn't buy those over the Internet, either, nor were they inserted through slits inside my mouth while I lay drugged into nonsense. They're the result of the lifestyle change in conjunction with all the surgeries: new eating patterns, a more active lifestyle. No wonder they look foreign to me.

The only things that look familiar are the mouth and the eye color. Even the enormous dark half moons beneath my eyes are strangers. When you're fat, even your eyes are fat. So the dark circles are new.

I'm working top down, left to right, wet to dry.

I finish the ceiling and walls, and the large expanse of mirror. I locate toilet bowl cleaner and squirt a generous amount under the rim. The counters and floor are covered in shit: dead Kleenex, empty plastic bottles, a trashy celeb magazine I must have filched from somewhere – or maybe mom left here last time she visited. Irrelevant. The itty bitty garbage can under the sink becomes my dumpster. First the overflowing contents must get dumped into a plastic bag from my endless supply of garbage bags, then I reline the can and begin to dig.

I'm an amateur archeologist, excavating my countertop. Eventually I uncover a surface but need to reline my mini-dumpster. I spray sink and counter in foaming cleanser. The diminutive room reeks of the combination of ammonia, chlorine, and 'added fragrances,' so I open the window. A blast of damp air flies in. That reminds me of outside. I crack the window a bit further and peek out. Mercy. It's nearly winter. It's raining in great, hoary sheets. I pull my face back.

I spray the inside of the shower stall/tub surround with the same foaming cleanser and remove same from the counter and sink. That part's easy, just a quick swish with a paper towel or two and its gleaming. The shower and tub is a bigger problem. First I have to remove an enormous hairball that clogs the drain. Yick. Thank goodness for crochet hooks and rubber gloves.

It takes me the better part of an hour before I've finally reached the floors. I scrub my way out backwards like dad-number-two taught, then come back in with clean rinse water. All it takes is a final drying with a clean cloth. I, of course, have no clean cloths, so I use another of the ubiquitous Scott Towels.

I step back into the hall and peer in. It looks familiar. Clean and comforting.

The hall reminds me of an overflowing Goodwill Truck. Clothes are strewn from end to end. I push - from the bottom this time - in the direction of the laundry room, but I can't open the door. It's wedged shut, presumably with other clothes. I had no idea I owned this much clothing. I blame Kennedy.

Eventually I burrow my way in and start sorting a load. Instead of darks and lights, I come up with fats and thins. Apparently, I've been wearing all my big girl clothes, since they're all filthy. I figure I'll wash my new stuff first, then wash the old and get a donate garbage bag together. It's a big day for garbage bags.

I continue this way for a few hours: digging my way through the clutter, pushing it into piles, sorting, tossing. Purging. I suppose its cathartic. Whatever. Its sure as hell necessary.

I'm just grateful I'll have a clean place to shower, which I need to do immediately or I'll stink up Jefferson's car.

When Jefferson arrives, he's clearly nervous.

He's also entirely too well groomed for me to comfortably ride in his car. I keep reminding myself how very gay he is, but it's difficult because his bone structure drags my eyes back. He's immaculately turned out in a navy suit, unrelieved by so much as a pinstripe – just yards of fabulously expensive wool blend perfectly tailored. He wears this watch that somehow manages to scream "I am tasteful" but "I am SO edge" at exactly the right pitch and exactly the right time.

The bitch.

We pull up to the curb. "I'll pick you up in a two hours."

I scrunch a face. "Isn't that way long for a shrink appointment?"

"Apparently Kennedy felt an extended amount of time might be required."

How flattering. "I see. Well thanks for the lift, Jefferson."

I'm not a regular visitor to doctors. Scratch that. I didn't used to be a regular visitor until the great gutting of '04 when it seems I paid a visit to every medical professional within a hundred mile radius. Still, this is my first private visit to a shrink (surprise!) so I'm a bit curious what her office looks like.

The enormous paneled door bears a brass plate that reads "Doctor Pepper Devers, Psychiatry." Ring a bell? Yes, it's her. Life is truly comic. I shove the heavy door open. The room is warmly furnished: red Oriental rug, sage overstuffed chairs, sunny wall art. There's only one person waiting, an aging hipster with a granny bag over one shoulder and knitting needles flying in her hands. She doesn't glance up.

But there's a receptionist behind a half wall who does. "May I help you?"

"I have a 3:45 with Doctor Devers."

"Great. You're a new patient? If you could just fill out these forms, Doctor will be with you shortly."

Ah my favorite. A few forms. Second cousin to voice mail. I sit down with the clipboard.

The first part is easy. I know my own name and how I like to be addressed (your majesty works well. I'll settle for Alana). The medical history part isn't too bad – until I get to the previous surgeries. That used to be an easy section. Not so now.

My hand cramps.

On the back of the page, I reach the meatiest part of the form. "What brings you to seek counsel?" I like that. A supplicant kneeling before an obelisk. Not "what sent you round the bend?" I fight the urge to write "The desire to achieve enlightenment." Hey it's what I'm after, but sounds just the teensiest bit smart alecky. Don't want to press my luck before I even get in the door. After all, this woman already know I'm nuts.

I start writing:

A year and a half ago I remade myself, changed myself from top to bottom to become loveable after years of being on the sidelines, always the bridesmaid. I found love. Then he died. Died. Because some idiot with too much money and little sense thought it a fine idea to hand over the keys to an SUV to a junior would- be alcoholic before he could see over the steering wheel. Then something else happened...

I look it over, turn the pencil over and begin erasing frantically. I try again:

A friend thought it might help to talk about it.

There. Better. Safer. Less... exposed.

The receptionist says my name in an elevated voice that indicates it's not the first time she's paged me.

"Sorry. Still filling out forms."

"I'll take the top two and you can bring that one with you." She has a gentle smile. Not too overbearing. Just right for the delicate world of crazy people.

"Thanks." I follow her pointing finger into an adjacent room. This one is warm, too, but a bit heavier. Another Oriental rug, leather furniture, friendly butter color on the walls. Piped in music too low to actually hear. I wonder if it's subliminal. It would drive me batty.

"Miss Lindell? Please come in. Have a seat wherever you're comfortable. I just need to make a couple of quick notes."

I noticed a couple of things instantly about your office, Doc. First, there are two doors: the one I just came in, and the one people exit from. Interesting. Next, I think psychiatrists should look like Ruth Bader Ginsberg: sweet and a bit matronly. In your office environment, you appear to be an even more Candice-Bergen-polished than usual. That puts me on guard. How the hell can someone who looks like you know anything about the human condition? Huh? How?

And those butter yellow walls. Really? A ploy to induce sunny thoughts?

She startles a bit, glances down at the paperwork again, back up at me, making the connection. "It's nice to see you again, Dor... I'm sorry. I see you want to be addressed as Alana. I'll be more careful in the future. Before we start, I normally tape our sessions to help me review. Do you have any objections to that?"

I shake my head. Whatever. Publish it if it gives you a rush, Doc.

"I haven't had much time to look over your history, but I know you lost someone close to you recently."

It's a leading statement. I'm supposed to jump right in I guess. "My boyfriend. He was killed in a hit and run."

"How recently?"

Later it struck me that your voice doesn't match your face, Doc. It's about two octaves lower than your face. Did you train yourself to talk like that? To sound more hypnotic? Maybe you took voice lessons? "September. He died September 3rd."

"Have you spoken to anyone about his death?"

"Yeah. His sister Rachel and I, we talk sometimes."

"What's his name? Your boyfriend?"

I fight the urge to scream, 'He's not my boyfriend, you idiot, he's dead!' "John. John Justin Miller."

Her face looks quizzical. "Skip and Lonnie Miller's son?"

She friggin knows them? "Yes."

She scribbles on her notepad. Glances at her notes.

"You've said that coming here was a friend's idea, not yours. In order for any form of therapy to be effective, I need to know your goals for therapy. What is it you're after? What do you hope to accomplish through therapy?" She's sitting in a high-backed leather chair, comfortable and elegant in a pants suit. She has all the time in the world.

Thinking hurts.

"You seem stuck. Is part of the reason you agreed to see me? To get unstuck?"

I consider. "That might be part of it. I'm very tired. I don't ever remember being this tired in my life. Maybe I have a thyroid problem."

A small smile plays at her lips. "To quote, that may be part of it. How's your sleep?"

"Oh I sleep just fine."

"Define fine."

"Well, according to my friend – to Kennedy, I've slept for the better part of two weeks."

More scribbles. "But you don't feel rested, right?"

"Right."

"Would you consider yourself a happy person? Unhappy?"

"Angry. If I had to slap a label on it, right now I'd say I was a very tired, very angry person."

"Anger is a fairly active state. You appear passive."

"Do I? Okay, here's some anger for you. What's all this for?" In my ears, I realize my voice has taken on a monotone quality.

"All this?"

I sit up, lean forward. "It strikes me how ridiculous this all is. We go through all this work, this pain, and for what? To be crushed like Cheerios under some guy's SUV? To be snuffed out like a candle? To be punched in the face with a fist? Why bother? You asked why I agreed to come?"

She nods.

"I want to know why any of this is worthwhile. I want to know why I shouldn't just curl up into the fetal position. I want an explanation. To understand."

"Was there a point before John died?"

There's this spot right above my left eyebrow where the pressure is building. It feels like the eye is pulsing and throbbing right out of its socket like some sort of cartoon character. Gad it hurts. "A lifetime ago, before I met John, I had an agenda at least. I wanted to avoid dying a virgin. That was the goal. To get there, I needed to get beautiful. So my pre-John purpose was to get beautiful."

"And do you feel you've achieved that goal?"

"What do you think, Doc? Nine out of ten drinking men seem to agree that I'm quite attractive now."

"The question was, 'do you feel attractive'? When you look in the mirror, do you like what you see? Do you feel accepting?"

That eye bulges further. "Who cares? Who cares what I think? I sure as shit don't. This isn't about how I look. It's about this great, gaping chasm of why bother. I need a reason to stay alive."

My voice shakes. I hate the trembling, invalid sound of it.

More scribbles. I want to grab the pen out of her hand and stomp on it. Throw her clipboard across the room. Punch her in the face with a closed fist. See how she likes it.

But I sit like a lump. I just don't have it to give anymore.

Doctor Devers moves the chair forward a hair, makes eye contact. Hers are amber colored, no glasses, light makeup. "Here's what I know so far, Dorothy Alana Lindell. You ask me to use your second name not your first. That's new. Sometimes that can indicate that you feel second best, and sometimes that the first name didn't work for some reason. Whoever that person was, you didn't like her or didn't feel you and the name clicked, so you remade yourself. Your chart says you've had extensive surgeries, all cosmetic. Presumably you wanted to create a new persona, but obviously you're not connecting your internal self to that new external self. You've recently experienced a terrible loss, and as a result of all of the above, you are clinically depressed.

"Additionally, there's a time gap, here; this gap between John's death and your arrival here in my office. So I suspect there's something more that you haven't told me yet.

"In any case, there are a variety of treatment options for depression, which we will discuss. You are, however, are not so depressed that you've lost the ability to question and to process thoughts. You exhibit no psychosis. I don't see any obvious neurosis. What I do see is existential angst. And anger. The anger's good. It indicates energy. Energy can bring valuable insights. Meanwhile, you want an answer to the very personal question, 'Why am I here?'"

"That would be useful."

Big smile with teeth, for that one.

I sigh, that ole grandma sigh. "Look, Doc, I don't know if this is such a brilliant idea, my coming here."

"Because?"

"Well for starters, because this is going to cost a boatload, I suspect. And I'm not all that certain I want to blast my soul to a perfect stranger. Even though I guess technically, you aren't exactly a stranger. The other problem is you're a member of the club that got me into this pickle in the first place."

"Excuse me? I don't follow."

"Oh come on. We've talked about this before in group. You're a BB. Born Beautiful. You won't have a clue what the hell I'm bitching about most of the time, since you have no point of reference."

"I see." Doc finally puts the pen down and steeples her fingers. "Let me address your first point, the cost. The first eight sessions are entirely covered by your company's insurance plan, they have so assured me. So your cost is zero. As to the second concern," she retrieves the pen, begins tapping on the desk again. "As to the second, let's say I grew into my looks. So I'm not completely ignorant of how cruel people can be."

Her eyes pin me to the leather chair. "So, are

you willing to spill the rest of it?"

CHAPTER FORTY-ONE

This is the last one, I swear.

He fusses with his tie using his right hand and flicks ashes with his left. Every so often he takes a deep drag from his clove cigarette, then returns to smoothing imaginary wrinkles. He turns from the mirror. "Do I look all right?" His eyes beg.

"Kennedy J Taylor, you look stunning." I smile at him. He really does of course, but I'm touched at his boyish concern. "That suit is perfection." Of course it is. It's Armani Couture, for God's sakes, which he flew to New York to have fitted. The tie is neither too wide nor too narrow. It lends exactly the right punch of scarlet. "Relax. Have some champagne."

He takes a delicate sip. "I can't believe he said yes."

"He loves you, you goof. Why wouldn't he?"

He puts a carefully manicured hand over his mouth, and proceeds to talk through it. "I can think of a dozen reasons. I have a short temper. I worry too much about appearances. I talk too much."

I pull the arm from his face. "Look, you nut. You are one of the kindest, sweetest people I know. Max loves you. You just have pre-wedding jitters. Now pull yourself together. Our limo is waiting and you look fabulous."

Last week, Kennedy and Max flew to Massachusetts to get their license, so legally they're already hitched. As a card carrying member of the wedding elite, though, I am well aware that the 'big day' occurs when you finally stand up in front the people you care about, and say the words out loud. That day is today.

Once again, I'm in maid of honor garb, but for the first time in history I can honestly say I feel awesome. I've never looked better, thanks to spending hours getting fitted by Kennedy himself. I'm in this fluffy ice blue cloud of chiffon cut up to here and down to there. And gad my hair looks marvelous.

Max and Kennedy have observed the day sequestered from each other, so I haven't seen Max yet. I have spent the last hour convincing Kennedy that he doesn't need to hang over the wedding planner, the caterer, or anyone else. The wedding planner he hired (no signs of a bun) fields any and all issues. An enormous African American presence stuffed into a sleek, tangerine business suit, she assigned me the job of keeping his majesty away from the Chateau Ste. Michelle Winery. She said Max wanted it to be a surprise, that for a change he could just show up and enjoy. I cheated and got a glimpse earlier, and hallelujah! It's just incredible: Long silk panels drape the walls. There are seven-foot high candelabras filled with glowing cream candles, scenting the air with vanilla. Flowers are everywhere, mostly in that same clotted cream color but with punches of long stemmed pink roses and enormous green leaves. Barely visible are the tables, swamped with elaborate fabrics, gleaming china and dozens of lit candles in crystal holders.

Kennedy is going to flip.

There's a knock on the door and I see my Kennedy's hand, still holding his cigarette holder, shaking.

"We're ready for you," the wedding planner calls.

I can't help myself. I wrap him up in the biggest hug I can manage. Like hugging a tree. "I'm so happy for you, buddy. Let's go."

He finally releases me and straightens up his mighty six-four frame. I'm freshly impressed at the cut of that jacket. How it manages to get around his enormous biceps without tearing remains a mystery.

As we enter the hall, I can hear the sounds of a choir, glorious voices echoing off the high ceilings and swirling around the room, all male voices together. It makes me shiver it's so beautiful.

From our position in the back, we can see the place is jam-packed. The rest of the wedding party has gone forward, and it's time for Jefferson and me to make our walk. I hear a gasp from behind me and I turn. Kennedy is sobbing, sobbing in the arms of a man maybe half and inch shorter but with far less hair. I can't hear what they're saying, although they're inches from me. I just hear the wrenching sound of male weeping, something I have heard maybe twice in my life, once on television.

Jefferson leans over and speaks into my ear, "His dad."

I didn't even see the diminutive woman in the ruby dress. She'd been hugging the other side. When she finally pulls back, round faced and warm as a cinnamon roll, she shakes Jefferson's hand. "Thanks so much, sweetie. I know he'd never have forgiven himself."

I get a push from behind by the firm hand of the wedding planner, and Jefferson and I make our walk, stop, and turn to face the back of the room.

With his father on his left side and his mother on his right, I watch Kennedy J march up the aisle to the sound of blended voices. When he reaches the front, the pastor intones, "Who gives this man away?"

And in a strong voice, with just a hint of a quaver, I heard, "His mother and I do."

And then I cried.

CHAPTER FORTY-TWO

"It sounds like a very nice ceremony." I bet she wishes she had a pencil to tap now.

"Well Doc, you might think so. Truth be told, it was the most beautiful wedding I've ever been to, and I've been to more than my share. But seeing it? It hurt so bad I thought I'd vomit. Because bam, there it was again. Everybody connecting up, and me, one step removed, the bridesmaid, still flying solo in the world. It's too scary, too sad to be here. I didn't want to make Kennedy feel bad about hooking up, but…"

I look down. What a fantastic view of the Seattle skyline from here. It's got to be nearly midnight and the city lights are gorgeous. I can see clear to the Space Needle. When my eyes sweep down, they note a significant distance from my concrete perch to the ground below. I stick with the lights. Very festive. Very nice. A nice place to die.

"Why are we up here, Alana?" Doctors Devers

voice sounds strained.

"I can't speak for you, Doc." I believe she would have slapped me if she could reach me. How unprofessional. "I'm out here on this roof because I just don't want to be here anymore. I don't want to be sad and I don't want to be second. And I'm tired of being scared." I think about the hassle for her, getting rousted out of bed by some selfish sap, (yes, that would be me). "I'm sorry they got you out of bed, doc." I let my feet dangle over the edge. I used to be afraid of heights. Now it doesn't seem so bad. Go figure.

My mouth knows no off-switch. "My gay friend is married. Did you know that? My boyfriend is dead. His sister is married and pregnant and I have no one. Oh, excuse me, I forgot about my rapist. Wouldn't want to overlook him in all the excitement. I guess I'll always have my fear of him to fall back on." The sense of being disembodied oozes over me, so when my head shakes from side to side, it leaves a vapor trail, an echo. "I thought about buying a dog, but that seemed so chicken hearted, I just couldn't bring myself to do it."

"What would be wrong with buying a pet? Lots of people own pets."

"Lots of people want to make trouble for themselves. They die you know. Silly pet owners. They're either lunatic PETA pushers who believe animals are better than people, or scary pragmatists with sensible shoes who believe animals are animals. The first group dresses their dogs in goggles and little hats and feeds them at the table. The second drops a bowl on the floor. Now, normally I'm a bowl on the floor girl. But I'm just so… so messed up right now, I'd probably end up dressing Rover like Miss Piggy and pushing him a stroller. That's just not fair to a dog."

"Can we talk about this inside? It's freezing out here."

I chuckle at that, Doctor Pepper revealing a human streak. Sure it's cold as hell, but I'm dressed for dying, so who cares? "I'm good, Doc. You go in if you get chilly."

"We go in together, Alana."

"You might as well call me Dot. My friends do. That's who I really am, you know. Dot Lindell. I remember you making a big deal out of that. My name. Did you know in High School, I was known as 'Dot, Dot will suck no cock?' Guess who penned that juicy moniker? Why none other than my rapist, Jack Weston. Isn't that droll? Isn't that special?" That shadow voice sounds louder and louder. "And oh the irony. I got nowhere near a cock in high school! I mean puh-leeze. But doesn't it make Alana sound a tad more attractive? Thus I switched. Powerfully observant of you, Doc."

My breath is coming hard now, and my chest hurts a little. I glance down. There's quite a gathering down there now. I see the helmeted heads of firefighters and their second cousins, the cops, along with a few nighttime stragglers. Quite a party. I'm waiting for the chanting to start, like in the movies. Jump, Jump, Jump.

"Alana…Dot, listen. Part of you knows this isn't an answer, right? Part of you just wants things to get better."

Bitch. I swipe at a bit of moisture on my cheek. "I opened the door, Doc. I opened the friggin door and I let that monster walk right into my place." I sob openly now and it makes my chest hurt even more and that shadow voice speeds up, the words coming faster and faster. "I'm so tired, Doc. So tired of not doing things right, not getting things to work. I wasn't okay before, when I was ugly, and I know. I know it. Dad left me and Mom reminded me all the time. And Conrad." I shudder. "He told mom to 'get ole ugly out of the house before he went batshit.' Told her that all the time. So I fixed it. I did everything they said. I ate the right foods and did the right exercises and it was so hard, so hard. I even paid people to make me do it differently, do it better and I tried so hard. But it didn't matter, did it? John's gone. You're never safe, never. No matter what. Elvira wasn't safe. God knows what all happened to her. No matter what you do, things go wrong. Oh hope runs high, it does, but things never quite work out."

"Things worked out with John. His death was accidental. It had nothing to do with you being good enough."

"I'm not so sure, Doc. I think maybe God's in on it, too. I think he's a man. He made me ugly and not good enough. God's a man and it explains the whole menstrual thing, and childbirth pain and stupid boobs. I think God's a man and he doesn't like me very much. He keeps punishing me for not doing it right. And I keep trying, but I just can't." I hear a keening sound far off. I hug myself tighter.

There's a scuffle in the window behind Doctor

Devers and I hear muffled voices.

"Alana!"

"Alana? Alana, God Damn it get in here!"

The first voice is Kennedy J. The second, I think, is Rachel, John's sister. Rachel Miller Wilson's very pissed. "Get in here this minute. I'm big as a Holstein and shouldn't be clambering on a roof. My gynecologist specifically prohibited roof climbing at the last weigh in. I'm supposed to be on bed rest. Now damn it, get in here so we can talk from a bed somewhere."

Rachel's head pops out the window behind the Doc. Her sweet face is swollen with pregnancy and stern as a tax accountant's, even in this poor light. Someone is restraining her, since I can see her wiggling to free herself. She frees an arm, points a school marm finger at me. Then does it again, in case I'm slow witted. Like she's impersonating John Travolta's dance moves from Saturday Night Fever.

I stare at her finger. Maybe it has magic powers. I sheepishly edge down the roof's steep slope, manage to get one foot on the ledge before an enormous hand grabs my wrist and yanks me inside. I plop on the ground on top of a fireman.

Rachel tries to lower herself to the ground next to me. I think she's trying to hug me, but I'm still tied up with the fellow in the fire fighting getup. She can't pull it off – her belly's too big to reach me. She ends up kneeling down next to me. "You forget how to use a phone?" she shouts between sobs, "a simple phone call? You know. Something like 'I feel shitty, Rach, let's get liquored up and bitch.' You could have called."

My entire body shakes with sobs. I roll off the fireman. "You can't drink. You're pregnant."

"I know that, you ninny, but you can."

For the first time, I notice two policemen standing behind her. And suddenly I'm scared silly. I wasn't afraid of dying, not at all – but I'm terrified of prison. They look very authoritarian in their uniforms and badges. I feel all my strength drain into my feet, leaving me lightheaded. "Am I under arrest?"

Doctor Devers, dressed in a bathrobe and winter coat, leans heavily against a wall, answers for him. "Attempted suicide is not a crime in Washington, Dot. They're not here to arrest you." She waves off the smoke trail from Kennedy J's cigarette. "They're here to help keep you safe." She inhales slowly, "However, I'd feel much better if you agreed to some time in treatment. Right away."

"Which you will do!" shouts Rachel.

Kennedy J nods sternly over his cigarette, "Indeed."

"Just a couple of weeks." Dr. Pepper looks pensive, like I'm going to get difficult. Waits, tugging her coat more tightly around herself.

So tired. I just want to sleep. I'll agree to anything if they'll let me sleep. "Sure. Whatever." I let all the fight and strength drain out of me and curl up into the fetal position on the floor. Doctor Devers injects something into my arm. I sleep.

CHAPTER FORTY-THREE

I'm allowed no visitors for the first week, which is just as well. I don't recall much of the first few days. I sleep mostly. Or at least that's all I recall. That changes, though, becoming a marathon: sleep, talk to the doc, take medicine from a little paper cup, walk the hall, sleep.

Nurses hang over me to ensure I swallow - no tongue hiding, no palming. It's touching in a way, insisting I down what is surely an antidepressant. I don't notice a difference. I take a shower though, unprompted, so I guess it's doing something. The second week I return to group. Not that group. This is in-house. No one here is overly concerned about dating anytime soon.

A day later my mom phones and I'm allowed to take the call. She and Rupert Rooney freak out over the phone, full of concerns and regrets. Elvira calls from the road, chews me out. "Seriously, dude. Next time take a Zanax and give me a jingle. No roof diving."

Kennedy J shows up two days later, holding his cigarette holder – sans cigarette. No smoking at the hospital. For the first time since I've known him, he's visibly nervous. I wave him toward the only chair in my room.

"How's married life?"

The skin around his eyes relaxes. "Fabulous. I knew Max was the man for me, but coming home and not having the place be empty… it's marvelous. I thought I'd need time to adjust, to get used to having someone in my space? Not with Max. We're two peas in a pod." He takes a breath. "So what the hell happened?"

I'm prepped for this by now. "It wasn't one thing."

"Did it have anything to do with your makeover? All the pressure we put you under?" He's creating a crease between his eyebrows. I didn't know he could still do that.

"Heck no. Well, not exactly." At moments like this, I wish I smoked. It would give me something to do with my hands. Instead, they have no place to land. "It's lots of things. I still haven't figured it all out yet. People treat me differently. Part is how I look and part is how I act. Then John died. I was so mad at him. He liked me. He could make me laugh." I take a deep breath.

"And suddenly, I was all alone again. Like nothing had changed. All that work and I felt like I was right back where I started. Then… this guy showed up, at my apartment. John's buddy." I think I'm going to drop the whole subject, but instead

ramble on. "And he raped me. I was such an idiot."
I look up at Kennedy, his handsome face shocked,
drawn. "I let him in. I let this guy into my
apartment."

"You were date raped?" His voice is
incredulous, but his hands reach out to hug me.
"You never told me. Do I know this man? Should I
call the police?"

I let myself be enveloped by this by a giant
married gay guy. And I feel something tight inside
my chest relax at his concern. For a minute, I rest
there. But I need to deal and I can't do it from here.
I disentangle myself, turning my back on him. "No.
It was no date." I wrap my arms around my chest.
"He knew me from a long time ago."

He watches, patiently, for me to continue.

I swipe at my face to get rid of rogue tears. "He
used to be part of this troop of football monkeys
that tormented me. And he was a friend, a good
friend, of John's."

Kennedy's refined expression tightens.

"He came to Rachel's wedding. John's sister's.
But I didn't think he recognized me."

"Understandable."

"He didn't say anything about it, anyway.
Maybe just because John was there. But it turns out
a friend of mine went out with him. Elvira. He... he
beat her up. Probably raped her, too. Punched her in
the face. But she didn't say anything. Didn't call the
police or anything."

I hesitate, waiting for him to take me to task
over not phoning the police. He stays quiet.

"Then maybe two weeks ago, he showed up at

my place. Said he wanted to drop off some of her stuff. And the worst part..." I hiccup, fight the onslaught of additional tears. "The absolute worst part is... I let him in."

"That's not criminal, Alana. Just poor judgment."

By tracing an imaginary path on the ceiling, the liquid at the corners of my lower lids stays put. "True enough... doesn't make me feel any better. I still haven't adjusted to people noticing me. Well, other than to make fun of me. Being seen... having people find me attractive? It's so strange. I don't know people's motives anymore. And suddenly... suddenly this guy isn't just making eye contact. Do you get it? I have never had to turn someone down. Not ever. I didn't have a clue how to..." I face him.

"Escape the situation?" he supplies.

"Exactly." The moisture at the outside corners threatens to overspill, so I tilt my head a bit to settle it. "He beat me up."

"Oh my god, I heard nothing about this. Did you call the police? Did they catch him?"

I shake my head. Kennedy starts to get that cranky look and I cut him off. "I could just see the whole thing: some nice officer asks why I let a guy, practically a stranger, into my apartment. At night. There's no case. The whole thing would just be a tremendous mess. I'm a mess."

"No, that's messed up. Since when is it okay to beat someone up? To assault them?"

"Kennedy, people do it to me all the time. Usually they use words for weapons. No fingerprints."

"Oh such bullshit!" He waves the cigarette holder wildly. "Aren't these people supposed to fix this wrong thinking of yours? Where on earth is your therapist? Since when are you responsible for the behavior of some steroid fueled monster? You were aggressed on, dear. Did you invite this man to your bed in any way?"

I think about that for a minute. This is loads better than group. "No."

He pauses. "Good answer. When do you get out of here?"

"Ah, a subject change. Greatly appreciated. Day after tomorrow, if I pass my basic sanity class this afternoon. Honestly I could walk out now. I'm voluntary."

He chuckles at that. "Sure you are, dear." He gazes around. "They need me here. I've been thinking about expanding into interiors, but it appears that healthcare may need me urgently. How can one heal in this environment? All these weak pastels and hospital smells?" He gathers his jacket from the chair and smiles at me. "Phone Jefferson when you get out and he'll give you a lift home, yes?"

He hugs me hard.

CHAPTER FORTY-FOUR

Rachel calls, telling me I'd better hurry up and get released. Her baby shower is coming up and she wants me to attend the planning session to ward off potential disaster.

"You don't know these women. I'll end up with nothing but marabou covered baby clothes. You can't dress a boy in marabou."

"How do you know it's a boy?"

"My tarot reading. Why take chances?"

I tell her I have one more night and one more day. Then I'll be released. But right now, I do what I'm told.

It's so calming. Just one more night, one more day.

I blink to the sound of my name.

"Alana? Did you hear?"

Nope. I'm totally AWOL. "Sorry, no. What was the question?"

Doctor Jim takes a deep breath, which is tough

for him, given he's a chain smoker - and can't smoke during group. Can't smoke anywhere inside the building, actually. "You're going to be leaving us tomorrow. Are you prepared for the challenges of living outside?"

He acts like I've been in here for years. Some people have, I guess. "Mostly." I look around at the faces of group part two. It sure ain't D.A.

A grim faced middle-aged woman shakes her doomsday head. "You'll be hopping off a building in a week."

"Excuse me?"

"You don't talk in group. You palm your meds, a week, tops."

"She whats?" Dr. J. Lefkowitz is not a happy camper at this news.

"You sit around all glassy eyed when someone body slams you. I don't see you hoppin on the success train out of here on the basis of all that shit."

Suddenly I miss group. My old group, I mean. Susan and Miss Anna and oh God do I miss Jasper, with his silly patched elbows and laconic style. This dower woman with the heavily lined face would be no match for Elvira's up-beat surfer Goth.

Lefkowitz twirls his glasses, a nervous tick I doubt he knows he has. "What do you think she should do, Edythe?"

"Me? I think she should buck the fuck up. Get busy living or get busy dying, right?"

Now I actually am pissed. "How very Shawshank Redemption of you. Glad you have it all figured out. Which is why you and I are having this little chat in this little gated community."

Her horsy face actually pinks up a bit. "At least I'm in the game. I get that I have changes to make. New choices. And I'm at least trying to make them. You?" She snorts. "You're just hanging out."

Fred nods sagely, uppity guy wearing a hospital gown. He's quite comfortable agreeing with anything that takes me down a peg since I threatened to unsex him if he hit on me again. He's nearly seventy. Paul stares down at his sneakers through thick glasses, not wanting to be the bad guy. Patrick, who believes he's the patron saint, holds his arms out beseechingly. "Engage, Alana. It's difficult, I know, but put yourself out there. Take a risk."

I feign ignorance. "Be specific. What exactly is it that I'm not doing that I'm supposed to do?" That's me. Just the facts, ma'am.

Dr. Lefkowitz fields this one. "Do the work. Actually take medications that might help you. Eat right. Sleep regularly. Exercise." His voice softens. "Decide that life is worth living. Find a reason. Some little thing. Every day." He smiles broadly. "Here's reason one: make Dr. L. feel like a decent doctor."

CHAPTER FORTY-FIVE

And just like that, I'm on the outside. I'm got my little wheelie suitcase that Rachel or Jefferson must have packed and I'm waiting for the bus back to my place, which will require two transfers. Kennedy offered to send Jefferson for me, but I wanted to normalize. I'd take the truck home, but it's waiting for me back at the apartment. I figure if I took a bus to my suicide attempt, I'll take one home. Rachel asked me why I went clear to Seattle to attempt suicide. I pointed out there really aren't any tall buildings in Monroe. Which made her laugh.

Before they let me escape, however, they present me with a parting gift: a bill for over three thousand dollars. Federal cutbacks. My portion after insurance, etc. etc. Can you imagine? Here you are, so mentally wobbly you end up in an institution, a complete psychological melt down. After heavy meds and significant therapy, you claw your way to a semblance of sanity, and BAM! Financially ass whooped. This is your prize for the luxury of going nuts. Can you cope? I guess this is the acid test.

I write in my journal: Reason for living #2: pay off staggering in-patient bill.

A less mentally healthy person might consider this bill an inspiration to jump, so I'm glad I took my antidepressants. Of course they've probably been tacked onto my bill. Wasn't there a recent article about some Prozac users attempting suicide? They probably got their hospital bills.

Note to self: next time I decide to take a holiday from sanity, climb aboard a cruise ship. Same price, better accommodations, easier exit.

It's cold as hell. Bone chilling. The Northwest at this time of year just sucks. Like the Eskimos and snow, natives of the Pacific Northwest have hundreds of names for rain: showers, buckets, sheets, pellets, drops, oozing, drizzle, dripping, plopping, the straight down kind and the rain that shoots at sharp angles. It finds its way inside water resistant shoes, crawling from the socks up, and behind an umbrella it sneaks in and tickles the edge of your collar and creeps down your back in small rivulets. It smells thick and wet and mossy. I dread it. Why in the hell do I live here?

Reason for living #3: research warmer places to live.

The minute I get home, I throw the deadbolt on the door. I'm scared shitless. For a second, paralyzed, back against the door, sopping wet, I'm too afraid to move. Fortunately, I'm too wet to remain.

I shed every stitch of clothing in a pile where I stand, then race for the shower, slamming the door behind me and locking it. I stand under water as hot as I can tolerate, one of Dr. Lefkowitz's 'little things.' Shooting jets of water burn off that icy crust of cold. I could stand here forever, feeling the numbness floating away. Nirvana. The water sounds terribly loud and I'm fascinated at how it changes tone depending on which way I bend my neck: higher pitch, lower. Water as problem solver.

I grab a towel and get dry. Glorious. Clean. The towel smells of Downy fabric softener. I dig through the medicine cabinet and find some Oscar de La Renta, the olfactory part of the Kennedy transformation. I take a tentative sniff. Delicious. I dab it like my mom always did, wrist, wrist, back of the ear, back of the ear. Don't crush the scent, just dab. I raise my wrist to my nose and inhale.

I wander to my closet and I'm amazed at what's inside. I'd forgotten all about my crazed cleaning attack – how long ago was that? Weeks? A month? Nothing looks familiar. What happened to my Scottie Dog jammies? Oh hell. That's right. I dig deeper. The nearest relatives are: 1. a sort of lounging outfit, a pair of yoga pants and matching T in powder blue, or 2. a cobalt blue negligee. Yoga it is. Not feeling the Jean Harlow nighty.

I check my messages and shocking true stores, the machine is full! Elvira is in Phoenix and while it's not Seattle cold, "it isn't like crazy warm either." Kennedy J and his now husband Max the bartender ask me to call when I get in. Rachel called three times. Mom has left scads of messages, mostly complaints, with Rupert Rooney telling her to be nice in the background. My shrinklet, Dr. Devers, tells me to make a follow up appointment. My boss Greg Larson called to chew me out for leaving him short staffed. Even Ginny Lake Tibbets Johansen phoned.

Perhaps I should threaten to take my life more often. How else are you going to know who really cares?

I look around the kitchen to insure it's empty. No signs of Jack Weston. It's a bit grubby from my absence, but since I'd been on that cleaning binge so soon before my exit, it's just surface stuff, not too bad. I wipe the counters with a paper towel and fight the urge to look behind me.

I pop popcorn on the stove. Its smells like my childhood – the good parts, for a change - with me and Curtis Mayer in his cheery kitchen. I'm propped up on a barstool while Curtis does the actual popping, a bottle of soda in my hand. To hold onto my connection to the past, I decide to use a brown grocery bag from under the sink to hold my prized kernels, splurging on melted butter and overdoing the salt, (neither of which I will record in my food diary. Take that, Nancy Meiser, Nazi nutritionist).

I survey my tiny living room: sofa still there, old chenille throw still tossed over the back, TV on the same stand. Still no sign of Jack Weston.

I plop down on the sofa with the remote and the bag of popcorn. I crack open a soda (diet this time, in a nod to Ms. Meiser's mental stink eye) and begin channel surfing for a trashy romance movie.

Where there is the Lifetime Channel, there is hope.
Reason for living 4: the possibility of romance.

CHAPTER FORTY-SIX

I'm deep in the heart of the most incredibly vapid conversation I've ever had. Having suffered through group therapy, a mental institution, and private counseling, this is a bold statement.

The discussion revolves around the games required for Rachel's baby shower. The room is knee deep in pulchritude, an interesting mix of pageant girls, Playboy bunny wannabees and debutants. I play the part of the outsider.

Don't get me wrong, I'm now officially beautiful enough to wear a sash or possibly even pose for the magazine, but as usual I don't belong to any of their girls clubs. This is the down side of befriending John's sister, especially since Rach isn't here to bail me out, given she's the subject of this planning commission.

Despite being past the religious renaissance, there are an ungodly number of Mary-somethings at this gathering. My guess is a boatload of guilt ridden lapsed Catholics got busy, then hoped to recover their ticket through the pearly gates with an homage to the Holy Mother. Thus, to my left is Mary Theresa, then Mary Margaret (known as M-squared), and finally Bitsy whose given name is Mary Elizabeth. A holy mess of Marys.

Jenna, a fine mix of sorority president and mob boss, controls the crowd gracefully. We've already decided on menu (no alcohol, enormous platters of dim sung and a variety of green teas catered by Kim Lee), decorations (a Tonka Truck theme, since Rachel's expecting a boy, all yellow and black, men working signs, everything but the dirt, and yes, I think it's strange, too), and the guest list. That's Tonka sized as well. All that remains, per Jenna, is to determine the games, which are ritually played at such a fête.

I had thought bridesmaid land was painful, but at least alcohol is served. One rarely need participate in bizarre rituals involving diaper pins (Incidentally, I had thought diaper pins obsolete, what with the invention of the disposable diaper. But eco is in so cloth is in. A diaper service makes an excellent gift, and only the dark lords of Satan and trailer trash use disposable. So I'm told).

This is a planning meeting and not the actual event, so Jenna has supplied plenty of booze (god bless Jenna). We're swilling Chardonnay and chowing on a selection of glorious little appetizers on elegant crystal platters. The chasm that rests between these women and myself becomes more apparent at such moments. They throw a party to plan an even bigger party. They have funneled a mountain of cash into an event to plan an event.

Bitsy (alias Mary Elizabeth) tries to convince Jenna that Speed Diapering is a great game. When Jenna puts the kybosh on that plan (it requires men, no dice), she attempts to frown her displeasure, but sadly, copious Botox injections prevent it. It's pretty clear though that Little Bits is well and truly pissed. Unattached at the moment, she very much wants this to be a coed shower. With her frown muscles paralyzed, she's moves to plan B: sniffing air with what remains of her patrician nose after a plastic surgery or two. Jenna insists that the only man invited to this shindig is currently in Rachel's uterus. Bitsy can host a second coed shower at another time, if she cares to.

Before Bitsy can raise another objection, Jenna selects five games involving clothespins, diaper pins, Rachel's ex-boyfriends and a psychic named Lucca (very haut courante) who will enlighten all present about their futures.

This is my first alcoholic beverage in months, and it's hitting my like a ton of bricks. I'm slumped over the arm of an over padded sofa. My dress, a careful floral print, has disappeared in the much larger floral print of said sofa. M-squared, lounging next to me, wisely chose yoga pants, a t-shirt, and sneaks, the only one not in a dress. As a result, her feet don't ache and her mood is high. She also looks as fish out of water as… well, as I used to before Kennedy J got his paws on me. Unlike me, however, she doesn't require an alcohol injection to hush her noisy feet.

Jenna asks me about my dress. I confess that

Kenned J picked it out.

A hush descends.

"You know Kennedy J? Oh my god he is just awesome! How did you get in? I've been waiting on the list for a year!" whines one of the Mary-somethings. I think it's Mary Theresa.

"I met him at my cousin's wedding. I think we're distant relations."

"You are so lucky. It's impossible to see that guy and he does such an incredible job." Bitsy's narrowed nose looks even more profoundly out of joint.

"He's helped me quite a bit. And he's been a good friend."

"I got as far as that guy Jefferson, his lieutenant, once," Mary Margaret shares. "He told me Kennedy was not taking clients and showed me the door." M-squared seems well recovered from the experience and I tell her so. "I got over it. It's not world hunger."

I'm warming to this gal.

"Jenna, if you don't need me for anything more, I've got to get to sleep or I'll sleep through rounds tomorrow." Mary Margaret is full of surprises. Not the gad-a-bout I had cast.

I turn on her. "You're a doctor?"

"First year resident."

"I thought about becoming a doctor."

The grin stretches to Cheshire cat. "Many people think about it. Usually after watching an ER marathon. Less stressful than years of student loans and memorization followed by people bleeding, puking and dying on you."

Indeed. My mouth opens. Maybe it's the booze, but like a burp, I hear myself, "I know this is a bit weird, but is there any chance I that they would let someone follow you on your rounds?"

She eyes me speculatively. "Are you a writer? The only people who ever want to tag along are writers."

"No. It's just that... there was a time in my life when I seriously thought about med school, but I chickened out. I'm interested is all."

Dubious. That's how I'd describe that expression. It's the 'what are you up to?' face. Finally she decides. "Look I can ask the attending, but if he says no, no fuss, right?"

Now it's my turn to smile the stupid cat smile. "Absolutely understood."

I grab for my purse to get information on where to meet her the next morning. Turns out she's on a surgical rotation and they do rounds early - super handy because then I won't be crazy late for work. Don't want to press my luck at my day job. We use the opportunity to grab our things, make our apologies to Jenna and company, and head for home.

———————◄●●►———————

Bright and early - five a.m.! - I meet up with Mary Margaret just outside the hospital. She explains the plan: we swing by the front desk and pick up a visitor's badge for me, then she visits the call room to find out if anything happened overnight on the service. That should take about fifteen minutes or so, then it'll be time for patient rounds.

Until that time, I need to take a chair and cool my jets.

The hospital feels oddly familiar. Until I started my body makeover regime, I'd never been inside one, but now, it's old home week. The place is full of barely controlled smells: bodily fluids, medicine, antiseptic, and a pervasive layer of room deodorizer meant to mask all of the above. The color schemes are all muted, beiges and sages I assume are chosen for their ability to calm and avoid offense. Heaven forbid someone becomes color startled into a coronary. The inane background Muzak from *One Flew Over the Cuckoo's Nest* cues up in my head. Kennedy would be horrified.

A computer monitors hangs outside each room. Is that why I feel at home? The staff is easy to spot: they're healthy. They walk at a brisk clip, wear comfy shoes, and their facial expressions a mix humor and tension. They all look like they're either going to laugh hysterically or announce a time of death, sometimes, simultaneously.

M-squared is no exception. The attending grumbled briefly, but after she promised I'd stay out of patient rooms and keep my mouth shut, he agreed on the hospital equivalent of a ride along. To minimize disruption to patients and staff, I'm given a set of scrubs and told to hold my questions. I'm ashamed at how thrilled I am to put them on, to join the gang walking the halls.

This is a teaching hospital, so I guess a bunch of hooligans in drawstring pants crowding around the sick is the norm. Mary Margaret's boss is a squat, angry guy with enormous arms. He's wearing the requisite long white coat, a stethoscope, and two days growth of beard. The coat makes him look even more stumpy.

"People let's rock. Robin Sterns, 56, smoker. Who's got him?"

A gaunt kid with rooster hair steps forward. "Mine. Thrombectomy. Surgery's at ten today."

"Who's doing the surgery?"

"McConnell."

They rattle back and forth, question, answers. Staccato words. Oh my god, this is so fascinating. Some of the language is foreign, some shakes dormant neurons at the back of my brain. I remember some of this.

They move as a group from room to room, and following instructions, I hang back, just outside the door. Still, I connect with these would be investigators, learning the darkest secrets of people's lives. What's broken? Are their organs functioning? Are they getting better? Worse?

It takes around an hour. I'm exhilarated, but in that short time my feet are sore since I neglected to wear the sensible footwear. Computer science lends itself to long periods spent stationary, with only the fingers moving like crickets over the keyboard, so I usually kick my shoes off. It's a lazy person's profession.

Mary Margaret needs to start her shift, so I thank her and head out to the truck. My head swims. That was an absolute blast.

While driving to work, for the first time since John's passing, my head's full of possibility. What if it's not too late to go back? I'm not even thirty yet. I have my bachelor of science. No debts. I'd still qualify for loans and I have a job to pay for part of it. Maybe there are scholarships for crazy women who suddenly feel compelled to pursue their dreams of medical school.

All that memorization. The endless tests. So much work. But what if I could learn to help people like that?

MADE OVER AND OUT

"Think of yourself as a model," says LA-based celebrity makeup artist Daniel McFadden. "You don't get to pick what goes on you. The bride has an overall 'theme' and your job is to work it!"

excerpt from <u>The Bridesmaid's Manual</u> *by Sarah Stein & Lucy Talbot, P 104*

Lisa Souza

CHAPTER FORTY-SEVEN

"Slow down, Alana, I can't move that fast."

Rachel barely resembles Rachel and I wonder if she'll make it to her own baby shower next week. Her face and ankles are swollen grotesquely. Her belly is so distended I swear a brush against a sharp surface will split her open, and despite her fashionable fitted maternity wear, which is supposed to give you that "I'm gloriously pregnant not at all fat" vibe, she looks frumpy, totally abnormal for Rachel. Only her hair, amazingly sleek and shiny, and her bright blue eyes remain familiar. We're heading to her birthing class at Overlake Hospital – the last one – and I'm acting labor coach. Any excuse to be at the hospital.

Bart, bless his pink cowboy heart, can't stomach the thought of his sweet Rachel in pain. Per Rachel, he'd attended the first three classes full of enthusiasm. At the fourth class, he'd been forced to endure a short film on childbirth. After which, he promptly fainted. From that point forward, he begged Rachel to reconsider the entire 'being pregnant thing' and asked to be relieved of any requirements to be in the delivery room. Rachel wisely agreed. I'll cover the last few classes and the actual event.

I switch the pillow I'm carrying to the other arm. "Sorry kiddo. I keep forgetting."

She stops next to me, takes a few shallow breathes. "I'm just wasted." She pushes a hand into the small of her back and tries to ambulate. "And I waddle like a friggin duck."

She does, in fact, seriously sway, back and forth, like a listing ship.

"Don't be silly, Rach. You look fine." Hey, I'm trying here.

She smiles through her extra-plump cheeks. "Right." She inhales sharply, and her lips purse. Her frightened eyes bulge.

"You okay?"

"I've got to sit down." There's a stack stone fence holding back the plantings at the front of the hospital. She eases down onto it, not speaking, still doing that sharp, shallow breathing thing.

I count to seven before she finally gasps out, "Something's wrong." She looks down at herself, at her lap. A tiny spot of blood appears on her maternity pants.

That's not good. "Well at least we're in the right place. I'm going to run in and get some help, okay?" She says nothing, tightens her eagle grip on the stone wall. I waver for just a second, afraid to just leave her there. "I'll be right back."

My heart pounds as I race inside, grabbing at the hand of the first unsuspecting creature in scrubs I encounter. "My friend's outside. She's pregnant and I think she's starting to bleed."

The doctor may be surprised, but he acts calmly. I think the situation warrants screams and rending of hair, but he strolls his way over to a laminated counter manned by an older woman in polyester like he's going to order a latte. "Amanda, can you page the OB on call? Tell them we've got a pregnant bleeder coming in. And send a couple of orderlies out front with a gurney. Oh, and tell Prescott on line two to push back our tee time ten minutes."

"Certainly, Dr. Simons," the woman has already begun pressing buttons and spinning in her desk chair. His work finished, the guy in scrubs heads for the elevator, so I grab his arm and start pulling.

"She's out here."

He pats my arm, but makes no moves for the door. "We'll get your friend taken care of right away. Why don't you go outside and wait with her till the orderlies come?"

I'm indignant. "Aren't you going to come out and check her? Something's really wrong. She's bleeding."

"Then we need to get her in here where we can help her, don't you think?"

Oh my god, mom was right. Doctors are jerks.

He turns and leaves. Leaves!

I have the urge to scream at him, which I suppress. I race back to Rachel, still sitting on the concrete, her hands now wrapped tightly around her large middle, her face growing pale. My eyes are drawn to the small puddle of crimson staining her crotch.

"Hey sister. They're sending some orderlies to bring you inside. Do you want to wait, or do you think you can walk?"

Rachel ignores me, eyelids at half mast. "I don't feel very well," she mumbles.

The wait seems interminable, but in fact only seconds pass before a couple of orderlies arrive to assist Rachel onto a gurney. The process seems slow and unwieldy, Rachel whimpering and moaning as she tries to find a comfortable position. She doesn't want to lie down – it hurts – and she fights their attempts to get her that way. Eventually, though, they strap her in and inside the hospital. I breathe a sigh of relief. We're inside, right? Now everything will be all right.

I hurry to keep pace with the orderlies, carrying Rachel's things, including an overstuffed pillow that would have been used in her prenatal class. They whisk her through a couple of double doors, behind which sits the woman – Amanda? Was that her name? – who'd been manning the front desk. Apparently considering their mission completed, the orderlies leave the same way they came in, through the double doors.

Armed with a clipboard and a complete lack of emotion, Front-Desk Amanda grills Rachel with questions. My suffering friend barely responds to between groans. Finally, Amanda is satisfied with her myriad of forms. This is fortunate as Rachel has turned a pale greenish gray. A phone call later conjures a quiet man in scrubs. "Freddy, can you take this young lady to Labor and Delivery? Here's her chart."

Freddy, a mustachioed Hispanic man, isn't much of a talker. He simply takes the clipboard and pushes the gurney out of the room. I stumble behind him, feeling ridiculous and in the way and still carrying that stupid pillow, like I'm on my way to a sleepover.

We arrive on the third floor and make our way to the nurse's station, a brightly lit, laminated L shaped desk. Two more nurses man the desk, a solid looking black woman and an older woman with a stethoscope around her neck. The African American woman catches sight of us, picks up yet another clipboard from the counter. "Hey Freddy. You got some visitors for me?" She turns her gaze to Rachel on the gurney. "I'm Shirley. I'm the day nurse on this floor, Miss..." she glances down at her own clipboard, "strike that. Mrs. Wilson. This way Freddy, 308."

She and Freddy assist Rachel onto the edge of the bed. Shirley smiles over at me. "I'm going to have you wait outside for just a minute while we get Rachel into a gown, okay?"

It's not a question. She shoos me out the door and it shuts in my face.

That's where I'm standing when a hand taps me on the shoulder. I turn and Jasper Atkins, Mr. Elbow Patches himself, stares down at me. He's traded the English teacher look for scrubs, a stethoscope and a look of utter exhaustion. He needs to trim the goatee.

"You're a doctor? I thought you were a plumber. Or a basketball player."

"Excuse me? Why would you think I was a plumber?" He shakes his head, closes his eyes and wipes a hand across his face, like he can push aside some of the fatigue. Coffee might be better. He motions across the hall to a pair of cushioned chairs flanking a small table "Why don't you take a seat, Dot, and I'll be out in a minute."

Then the guy I mistook for a plumber enters room 308, shutting the door behind him.

CHAPTER FORTY-EIGHT

Time stretches out when you're trapped in a hospital. I don't dare use my cell phone, since there are signs posted everywhere telling me not to. At the nurse's station I ask about a pay phone only to discover I haven't any change. I end up making a collect call to Bart, which makes the business of delivering bad news even more depressing.

I finish the call, read half of an antique copy of People, and pace the hall. Nurse Shirley exits room 308, but shakes her head no, as in "no, there's nothing to tell, so don't pester."

So I say nothing and keep pacing.

Another ten minutes elapse before Jasper – that would be Doctor - Atkins steps out and looks around. He spots me, and motions me back. "You can come in now."

Rachel is held hostage by medical equipment. Tubes extend from her left wrist, splitting in two and connecting to bags of liquid on a pole. Tubes directly under her nose feed her oxygen. She has a belt around her swollen middle attached to a thick cable in turn attached to a monitor. She looks dreadful.

"There you are, Dot. Didn't want to be stuck here all alone." Her voice comes out like syrup.

I swallow hard.

Jasper starts talking. "Rachel signed a release form, so I can talk to you about her condition. It appears that at least a portion of the placenta has pulled away from the walls of the uterus." He pauses briefly. "Probably her platelets are sick. Coagulopathy. She's probably bleeding internally and we need to get that bleeding stopped right away. That means delivering the baby now." He rubs at his eyebrows, stifles a yawns. "I'm terribly sorry. Long day." He takes a deep breath. "This is a very serious condition."

"How serious?" my voice sounds hollow.

His eyes are on Rachel. "Life threatening. Rachel knows we need to move right away."

"So she needs surgery?" My voice sounds hollow.

He nods. "They're prepping the room now. Dr. Ness, the anesthesiologist, will be along any minute."

"Are you doing the surgery?"

"That's the plan. I've called in a friend to do the neonatal side of things, since Rachel's only thirty-six weeks along. Dr Jenner. She's excellent." He stands up, sets a long fingered hand on Rachel's shoulder. "I have to make some calls and get prepped for surgery, so I'll see you shortly."

"Jasper? Be careful, okay? And drink some coffee."

He smiles grimly. "I'm careful every single time." Then he's gone and I'm left with Rachel, who appears to sleep.

Life threatening.

Bart bursts through the door, and I quickly shush him, pointing at Rachel's sleeping form. I make him sit down before quietly updating him on Rachel's condition. I temper my language: no one benefits from Mount Bart crashing to the floor.

Rachel perks up a bit, reaches a hand out. "Hey Barty. Wanna rub my back? It's killing me."

Bart's face nearly crumples, but he rallies. "Oh darlin', I'm so sorry. If I could make it go away I would."

"Guess what? We're going to have a baby, today. Cool huh? No more waiting."

Bart makes a choking sound and starts to cry in earnest. I back out of the room.

CHAPTER FORTY-NINE

I'm in a daze. I had expected to be washing my hands and donning scrubs and booties when this moment arrived. Bart would wait outside while I'd hold Rachel's hand. Instead, Bart and I sit side by side in the surgical waiting room. Neither of us is allowed in the operating room, because this is a serious operation, not a simple birth.

A nurse comes by some time later to share that the baby (Joshua John Wilson) was doing great, but we wouldn't be able to visit him just yet. Bart leapt off the chair, nearly knocking the poor girl over, and began peppering her with questions. What about Rachel? Was she okay? How much longer? The poor nurse looked strained, but shares only that the surgery was progressing as planned. It would probably another hour or so.

Bart sips coffee from a lidded cup while Skip and Lonnie station themselves on the generic upholstered furniture so popular in hospitals. I hope Jasper got coffee somewhere.

"God, how much longer do you think?" Lonnie says to no one in particular. Skip reaches out and takes her hand.

I'm surprised by the gesture, which is tender and supportive, not the behavior of an insensitive brute. Not the same people I witnessed verbally scratching each after John's death. I guess people can change, or maybe I saw them at their worst.

We wait.

It seems forever, but it's only about an hour and a half before Jasper emerges. If possible, he appears even more drained than before. When he spots us, though, and smiles broadly as he approaches. My heart does a little jump. Smiling's good. Doctors don't smile if things are horrible.

Bart speedily introduces Lonnie and Skip Miller before pressuring for news.

"So far, so good. The surgery went well and it appears we have the bleeding under control. With some rest, she should be just fine. We do want to keep her around for a few days to make sure she doesn't start bleeding again, though. The baby's with Dr. Jenner down in the nursery, and she tells me that he appears to be a healthy, loud little boy. No apparent complications."

Bart's face shines. "Can I see her now? And the baby?"

Jasper does a scan of our faces. "Rachel needs to rest and be kept very quiet while she heals, so

I'm going to ask that everyone but Bart keep their visits very short. She'll be back in the room shortly, and they'll bring baby Wilson up, too.

The relief is palpable. I turn to Bart intending a quick hug and he nearly snaps my spine in two with his enthusiasm. Just as quickly, his back is to me and he's racing down the hall, Lonnie and Skip trailing behind him.

I face Jasper. He's leaning against a wall propped up on one leg. He swipes at his face again, a gesture I'm becoming familiar with.

"You should go to bed."

His hand falls away from his face and he looks startled, a deer in the headlights. "Pardon?"

"Bed. You should go to bed."

He grins tiredly. "Alone?"

Now I wear the shocked face. "Jasper, have you lost your mind?"

He lets his eyes fall closed. "Possibly. I've been up for... what time is it? Nine o'clock? I think I've been up for over a day. I had a patient decide to go into labor weeks ahead of schedule, a scheduled C that refused to reschedule, and bam this... this mess." He comes to and apologizes. "Sorry about that. Your friend scared me. It's not my favorite condition to treat. Too unpredictable. I prefer those smooth sailing deliveries so much more."

"This is not the right time to ask, but I've got to know. Why were you in Dater's Anonymous?"

"Group?" He keeps his eyes closed now, too weary to keep them open, but a small smile still lifts the edges of his mustache. "Pepper and I went to the UW together. And she's married to my best friend.

She asked me to sit in and keep the testosterone balance in check since Gary – that's her husband – refuses to have anything to do with her group. Says it's pathetic."

"We kind of are."

He waves a hand in the air, yawns. "No, Gary's a shit. He's too lazy to get involved when he could spend that time playing tennis at the club."

"And you don't play tennis?"

"Sure I play. I'm crappy, but I play. Better than Gary, though. I think Pepper's a sweetheart. She really wants to help people. So what's an hour between friends? Besides relationships are tough so why not take notes? Figure I'd learn something. Not like my phone's been ringing off the hook."

"Except for Ms. Tiffany of the scary fingernails. She has no objection to you cavorting around with the relationship challenged?"

He looks puzzled. Tired and puzzled. "Who? Oh wedding date woman. I don't do much cavorting. I don't have enough available hours. Besides it's none of her bees wax."

I hesitate. "Look, you're off now, right? I'd offer to drive you home, but I don't have my car here. I came with Rachel."

He closes his eyes. "Got a plan. You can drive mine. Then I won't endanger others. And it saves me cab fare. And it's the least you can do since I saved your friend's life."

"Not pulling your punches, I see." I consider. "How will I get home?"

He frowns. "Oh. Good point. You can stay at my place."

I give him the stink eye. Through closed eyelids he apparently senses it.

"I have a guest room. No hanky panky. Too tired for hanky. Or even panky for that matter."

"Done. It's still a better option than riding the bus. I bet your place is closer to my office than mine."

We walk down the hall in silence, stopping briefly at the doctor's lounge for Jasper to retrieve his clothes, keys and wallet.

"What? No tennis racket?"

"Hardy har har. Use your mouth for good, not evil." In the parking lot it's raining (surprise!) but Dr. Smarty Pants has an umbrella. We finally pause in front of this behemoth of a car. Range rover? Explorer? I don't know cars. It's dark, the car's black and it's raining. The ole Dodge truck seems diminutive in comparison. "You want me to drive this? You're sure?"

"It's an automatic. Not rocket science." He waits till I get in the driver's side then appears in the passenger side. "Wake me after you take the Kirkland/Redmond exit. We're going to Kirkland."

I snap on the seatbelt and make major adjustments to the seat and mirrors. You never realize how much taller someone is till you reposition the seat forward several feet in search of the pedals.

I turn to ask Jasper for more specific directions. He's asleep.

I hope I don't crash his car.

We reach the exit and I give him a shake. He's only half awake, mumbling answers but managing to navigate us to the condo. It's just a block from the water. I park where he tells me, and a short elevator ride takes us to his place. He lets us in and flips a light switch and mood lighting floods the place. An enormous picture window reveals a sweeping view of Lake Washington, which reads black with silver speckles at this time of night, very romantic.

Silly thoughts.

I follow him through the beautifully appointed foyer, into the living room. Nothing like my own dorky place and certainly nothing like John's dumpsite. It's a sea of dark wood and cool colors, with hints of brushed metal. Here and there, someone has strategically placed a lump of perfect coral or a sheaf of curly willow branches.

Not a place for bunny slippers and Scotty dog PJs.

Jasper practically staggers down the hall opens the door on the next door on the left and mumbles something.

"What? I didn't catch that."

"You can take this room." He steps in, points at a door at the far wall. "Bathroom's in there. I'll throw you a t-shirt to sleep in. Unless you carry PJs with you at all times. Wait a sec." He reappears seconds later with a man's white t-shirt in his hand and no shirt on himself.

Oh my.

He's still muttering something, so I force myself to listen. I drag my eyes from his bare chest, instruct myself not to notice the smattering of dark hair working its way down his front.

"This one's clean, I promise. It should work." He yawns hugely, this time not even trying to cover it up. "Sorry. Gotta sleep now." He shuts the door behind himself.

I stand there like an idiot, holding a man's t-shirt. I hold it to my face, inhale. Smells like Downy fabric softener.

What in the hell am I doing?

I collapse onto the edge of the bed. I've never stayed in a high end hotel, but I imagine they look like this. There are matching bedside tables and matching lamps, all very modern and sleek. There's a dresser in some sort of black wood with chrome handles. There's even a television on the dresser, remote on top. There's an over-scale painting of a woman's torso from the back, all in shades of blue.

It's a woman's vision of a man's room. No flowers, real or fake. Nothing pink. I inhale, no overly sweet potpourris, but it smells clean.

Crazy.

I'm helping a friend. Staying the night at Jasper's place. His condo. Doctor Atkins's condo.

Doctor Atkins.

I must be nuts.

I drop my clothes in a half hazard pile and pull on the t-shirt. Cotton is the greatest fabric ever, and Downey, the best smell.

I sleep.

CHAPTER FIFTY

I was wrong. Bacon is the best smell.

Oh my god I haven't had bacon in a year, and it's the real thing: fat drenched, smoky pig flesh, sizzling and popping, none of that fake soy and turkey based Nancy Meiser substitute crap. The aroma will be my undoing. I predict I will weigh an additional five pounds if I dare to draw the scent into my lungs.

"Dot! Chow time!"

Gad. How can people be cheerful in the morning?

The morning? Oh my god what day is it?

I race out of the room, unmindful of my state of dress, and come to halt in front of Chef Atkins. I grab the arm that isn't busy flipping bacon. "What time is it? What day is it?"

"Nice outfit." He grins.

I look down and note that I'm wearing exactly one white t-shirt.

I look up at Jasper (and since I'm barefoot, it's definitely up I must look). Oh my god he looks adorable first thing in the morning. There is this hint of whiskers on his unshaven face and he smells like warm sheets and bacon. His hair's all mussed up and his facial hair could use minor adjustments. And those blue eyes. My, my.

Recover, Dot. "Honestly is it Friday? Am I late for work?"

"Truth? I don't know. Just a sec – he grabs his watch from the counter – "nope. Saturday. Almost nine. Need to be somewhere?"

I lean back against the kitchen wall, relieved. "Not anymore. I couldn't remember if yesterday was Thursday or Friday. Rachel's class is on Friday. I don't know why I forgot."

"Last night was a bit crazy." He turns his back to flip the last of the bacon. He's still shirtless (thank you Jesus) but he's replaced the scrubs with flannel pants. He looks awfully good in those stupid flannel pants. "Do you realize I didn't get one page all last night? That's the best night's sleep I've had in weeks."

He removes the frying pan from the heat then embraces me, a monster bear hug. He's a warm furnace of a man. His voice is muffled in my hair, "That was incredibly nice of you, driving me home last night. I haven't been that wasted since I was an intern."

I could faint. I'm still a little iffy on men and Jasper's a stranger. A stranger who smells really good first thing in the morning. A combination of man, cotton and bacon. Delicious.

He relaxes his hold and returns to the issue at hand, plating bacon, taking toast from the toaster, pouring orange juice. He asks about coffee and when I decline he fills a couple of glasses with water.

"What would you have done? I mean if I hadn't been there to drive?"

"Stayed at the hospital. I've done it often enough. Hate to, though, when I'm off. Bad habit. Pretty soon you start to look and smell like sick people. Not good for my patients." He reaches into the cupboard and grabs a handful of bottles, sprinkles an assortment of pills into his hand.

"Fish oil, B-complex, Protein, good ole H20." He flexes a bicep and makes a tough face. "Make Tarzan strong."

I can't help it. I laugh. "So you're on the saturated animal fat and vitamin diet. Okie dokie, artichokie. That and a few more weeks at Dater's Anonymous and you'll be good to go."

Jasper sets our plates on the granite pass through. It serves as a counter with barstools on the other side. I follow Jasper who plops down on a stool and motions me to the other one. I pause long enough to wrap myself in a chenille throw stolen from the back of the sofa. It's about ten degrees too cold in here. I guess furnace men don't get cold.

"Don't knock DA, Dot. Pepper made it quite clear that beggars such as myself might benefit tremendously from the group experience. And see? I have." He wolfs down some bacon while I consider this. "Dating was a lot easier in college, don't you think? More people around. Didn't have to search high and low for unattached women. Not that I have the time to do any heavy searching. So much easier delivering babies."

I choke on my O.J. "Oh poor you. Must be rough trying to connect wearing a white coat and stethoscope. God knows it nearly destroyed poor George Clooney."

Color creeps up his cheeks. "I'm hardly George Clooney. Besides he's an actor not a doctor. In real life, women get creeped out at the thought of hooking up with their O.B.s. They worry your interests are too clinical. Or worse, that they're not." He munches his toast, no butter no jam. "Besides most of the women I meet at work are quite obviously involved."

"Point taken."

He pokes me in the side. "Come on. You know I'm right. It's harder meeting men at work than school, right?"

I laugh out loud. "I work at Microcosm, Doc. Hardly a breeding ground for the overly dateable. Except John. He – " I stop. I wait for a pang of guilt, but it doesn't arrive, which surprises me. "He was the exception that proved the rule. An oxymoron. A handsome computer scientist." I smile thinking of John's beautiful features. And for the first time, it doesn't hurt to do so.

Jasper looks thoughtful. "Pepper told me that you're boyfriend died a few months ago. Car accident was it?"

I nod. "About six months ago."

"You two were pretty serious?"

I pick up the water glass and take a swig,

pause, another. "I think so. I was, anyway. Who knows what John was feeling? Sometimes I thought… it doesn't matter now." I let my eyes connect with his, a foot above my own, blue and intelligent, softer than John's eyes, more gentle. "Men are hard to understand. At least John was. He didn't do a lot of heavy sharing about his feelings or his childhood… I tried to fill in the blanks. Men are awfully complicated."

Jasper coughs a bit trying to chew his bacon and laugh at the same time, which surprises me. His eyes are merry.

"Pretty simple machine, really: work, sex, sports, sex, food, sex and done. There. The book of Men, by Jasper Atkins, M.D."

"You're a helper, Jasper. Maybe you should write that book."

He nods sagely, smoothes his facial hair with his right hand. "Yeah. I thought about it. Decided to stick to medicine. Don't want to spread myself too thin."

"So just medicine and interior decorating, right?" I take a final, imaginary sip of juice. The apartment is just too well designed. If he's gay let's get it on the table now, shall we? If not, well… I steel myself to dismount the barstool wearing a t-shirt and chenille throw.

He watches calmly as I try and keep the throw from slipping "You're kidding, right? I paid a small fortune to Pepper's friend Tellis to do the place. It was so strange walking into my own home and being afraid to move anything. At first I had to fight this urge to fold my clothes before throwing them in the hamper. Which, the decorator had to point out to me, because I couldn't find it. I swear she disguised the damn thing." He waves a hand at me. "You're losing your blanky, there, Dotty." He comes up behind me and lifts the trailing edge of the throw back over my shoulder, letting his hand rest there for just a moment longer than necessary. "Toga, toga, toga." He smiles.

My mouth refuses to stay serious. "You're demented, you know this? What if I'm a crazed serial killer who prays on overworked OB/GYNs? Like Sharon Stone in Basic Instinct?"

"Then you're overdressed." His smile widens as he closes the distance between us.

Nerves get the better of me and I break eye contact. "Nah, just under washed. Can I use your shower?"

He pauses, still looking at me with that steady gaze. A hint of a smile tugs the corner of his mouth by his mustache. Makes me feel more naked. "Alone?"

"You already had your shower. Your hair's wet," I tell him. Those blue eyes are definitely laughing now. "Oh my god, Jasper, you are totally flirting with me."

"And you are clearly out of practice. Pepper was right. Talked about that at group. That's what happens when you miss meetings. Besides, how often do you find yourself chatting with a girl wearing nothing more than your t-shirt?"

"Rarely. My friends wear clothes."

"See? Kismet."

I punch his shoulder. "Well I need a shower,

Kismet man. And I think I'll try this one solo, thank."

"Suit yourself. There's one in your room. All the stuff you need should be in there unless my cousin used up all the shampoo on his last visit." He gives me a little shove and starts loading the dishwasher. "Don't tempt an old man. Off you go."

I take my shower, acutely aware of a handsome doctor just outside the door. Mom would be so proud.

I dress again, wearing the same clothes I wore the day before. Thanks to Kennedy, though, everything remains pristine, even the second day. Fabric and cut matter, my friends. The clothes are casual – after all I was headed to a birthing class – but they in no way resemble the sweats and running shoes of my former life. I slip on casual trousers with just a hint of Lycra over my undies, (not the granny panties of old, no sir!), just the thing for bending and stretching. I add a raw silk shirt in a glorious robin's egg blue and track down the crystal and silver beaded necklace that got dropped on the bedside table the night before. Sport slides in the same blue are the perfect finish. I catch a glimpse of myself in the mirror and burst out laughing: Mama Kennedy would be proud, too.

Jasper's dressed when I reach the kitchen, polishing off the last of a glass of water. He's dressed in jeans, tennis shoes, and a blue chambray shirt with the sleeves rolled up. My eyes get riveted to his arms, dusted with dark hairs and thick through the forearms. His fingers are long, the nails short and clean. They're the hands of a musician, an artist. My stupid mouth moves before I can prevent it. "You have lovely hands, Doc."

"Now you're flirting with me." The distance between us closes. One of his long-fingered hands cups my chin, the thumb sweeping across my lips. It travels to the back of my neck. There, it tangles in my hair and compels me to look up. When his mouth finally descends to mine, it's in slow motion. It takes weeks, months for his mouth to reach mine. I smell something smoky and the mint of toothpaste and then some other scent, darker and warmer. I try to breath and instead I inhale him. The kiss is sweet and gentle. It's too much. I can't let myself feel good. Not yet.

I break the kiss and there are Jasper's eyes, his soft blue eyes, and they're smiling at me, those eyes.

"I'm glad it's Saturday." That's the best I can do.

"You don't know the half of it." He gets a funny look on his face. Then he steps back and reaches into his pocket. His pager's vibrating. Jasper stares at it as though he's never seen such a device before. "You have got to be kidding," he mumbles, grimacing. He glares at the phone on the kitchen counter for only a second before dialing. "Atkins." There's a brief pause. "Start her on 100cc's of magnesium. I'm about thirty minutes out. Call me on the cell if she doesn't stabilize. Tell Mitch – Doctor Webster – that if he needs to take it C, just do it. Don't wait."

He snapped up the cell phone charging on the counter, his wallet and keys. "Well Dot, thus ends the closest thing to a date I've had in a year." He pockets the wallet and clips the cell phone on his belt loop. "Back to the hospital I go. Your car is still there, right?"

CHAPTER FIFTY-ONE

I check my messages. Mom, Mom, and the library announcing that my latest Barbara Cartland is ready for pickup. Yahoo. Elvira's voice tells me that they're "like, playing a gig in Portland on Thursday... and a solid citizen would, ya know, drive down, given your transportation situation has changed." For someone bopping from town to town, she sounds upbeat, not wobbly and terrified. It's a relief to hear the confidence has returned to her voice.

I consider returning mom's phone calls for about ten seconds, then choose, coward that I am, to postpone. Let Rupert Rooney entertain her for a bit. Instead I proceed with my latest project: growing a life.

My previous hobbies, (reading romance novels, ruminating on my sad lot in life, and crying about John), are losing their appeal. Rather than create a vacuum, something needs to replace them. When you do the math, there's seven and a half hours a night for sleeping, work only takes up nine or so hours even with the commute, then an hour for exercise and I'm left with far too many empty hours to fill.

Since I had to pick up my book anyway, (I said they had diminished appeal, not that I'd given them up for Lent), I took the opportunity to wander the aisles of the local library in search of an elusive something. Do you have any idea how many books are in the library? On absolutely everything? Gardening to money management, popular fiction to mosaic design. As I pass the children's section, a magnetic force draws me forward. When the propelling urge stops, human biology reveals itself.

Every conceivable aspect of medicine. Anatomy, physiology. Subsections on endocrinology, obstetrics, genetics, medical research, pharmacology, in hard cover and paperback. Holy mackerel! There's so much to learn about the human body! No time to waste! I grab a volume and pop it open. Behold, a diagram of the lungs. Check out the little cheese holes and the air sacs that look like bubbles of cauliflower. I open a different one and reveal a carefully drawn fetus in its mother's womb. I inhale sharply. Could there be anything more amazing? Consider how many things have to go right to cause a baby to be born, all those agreements between cells, hormones, body parts; such a cooperative dance of chemicals.

I snap that book shut and tuck it under my arm next to "The Taming of Lady Lorinda." The next section over holds MCAT Study Guides and I grab two. What can it hurt? I hoist the enormous things out and stack them under Lorinda and the obstetrics text.

I exit the library with my stash, feeling ridiculously excited and terrified. At home, I prop up the MCAT Study Guide next to a glass of Earl Gray and dig in. When the phone rings it startles me so badly I nearly wet myself.

"Hello?"

"Dot, it's me. Jasper. Jasper Atkins. You may remember me from such moments as 'you look good in my shirt.' How's the rest of the Saturday going?"

My face splits into an enormous grin. "Better than yours, from the sounds of things. Your patient okay?"

"The Mrs. and her underweight pal are doing fine, although she did scare the bejesus out of me. Everyone should stay healthy so I can get some exercise. I think I'm getting a gut."

"Now that's a big fat lie, Doctor Liar Pants. I have seen your stomach."

"See that's why I'm calling. You've seen my stomach but I haven't seen yours. Just your legs, which are the loveliest things."

I blush to the roots of my hair. Ah, the anonymity of the phone. I'm trying to come up with a cutesy response when the doorbell chimes. "Company's coming. Can I call you back?"

"Sure. Just need to figure out when we're going to see each other like normal people."

I holler at the door while I'm digging for a pen. I write down Jasper's number then scurry to the door.

"Who is it?"

There's a mumble on the other side. I can't make it out. I'm sufficiently paranoid that I step closer to the door, but don't throw the bolt. "Speak up, please."

"Your new boyfriend, Dotty. Or Alana. Or whatever the fuck you're calling yourself these days."

My heart spasms and I slide down the door to the floor. It's him. It's Weston. "Get out of here, Jack. I'm calling the police."

I can hear laughter. "Like you did the last time, right?" The voice drops three octaves and the tone changes completely. "Don't fuck with me, Dot. Open this damn door before I kick it in."

Why didn't I buy a gun? Pepper spray? A friggin dog? I search desperately for a weapon of some sort, something to defend myself with. There's my flimsy table lamps. That would hurt for about a second. I dig through the coat closet and come up with a broom. It'll have to do.

The door handle shakes. For a second, I'm so scared I can't string thoughts together. Finally I remember the phone. I race to the kitchen and grab the phone. I stare at the numbers. For a second I can't recall how to dial 911. Then the operator's voice is on the line, asking the nature of my emergency, but before I can respond, the door behind me snaps, splinters, cracks. The frame is giving way. It's still daylight and this nutcase, this monster is breaking into my home.

I rattle off the information the operator requests

but the final splintering sound behind me grabs my undivided attention. I drop the phone and hoist the broom in front of me and a damn good thing, too, because he's through the door.

He's dressed like we're meeting for dinner, except that he's wearing running shoes under his expensive trousers. And he's carrying an ax in his right hand.

"Dot. Great to see you again. You've been missing me, no doubt." His face splits into what I suppose passes for a smile, but it reminds me of Jack Nicholson in "The Shining." He's breathing heavily and his narrow face has a sheen of sweat on it. My eyes become glued to the ax. "I missed you last night. Where were you?"

"I see you brought your own key." Levity. Always my strong suit.

That dreadful slash in the middle of his face widens. "Never know what reception you're going to get." He glances at the broom in my hand. "Tidying up for me, sweetheart?"

A noise outside, coming from the porch. Merry Sooner, still sporting a bandana, this time in lime green. I'm so relieved to see her, tough Merry.

"God damn it, Dot. What's all the noise? I'm trying to prune the – "

The flat of the ax blade impacts the side of her head before I can yelp a warning. When the sound breaks free, it's a whimper, an exhalation. Merry drops heavily to the ground, landing on the broken jam.

"What's with all the company, Dotty?" He drops to his knees beside her, calmly ripping the bandana off her head. Jack wrestles a bit to tie her hands with it. It's a bit small to be used as a binding. I stand there like an idiot, staring at Merry's body blocking the exit, watching him tie her up.

Some sensible part of me strains to hear a siren, but it's silent save the rush of blood in my ears. Weston makes a motion likes he's going to get to his feet. When he does, he's going to pick up that ax. I come to.

I swing the broom as hard as I can, using both hands, planning to crack him in the side of head just like he did Merry. Instead he takes the impact with his arm, which is considerably larger than mine. He swears, gives the pole a hard yank, nearly taking it out of my hands. I time it; wait for the next big tug before releasing it, but when I do let go, I let go big time. He and the broom fly the other way. While momentum carries him, I make a play for the door.

I mentally apologize to Merry as I straddle her motionless torso, trying not to stumble while getting out the door. The bottoms of these shoes haven't been roughed very much and my groin gives a fierce tug when my back foot slides on the carpet. My stylish flats, which I've owned for exactly two days, were not designed for flight. I ignore the burning sensation and keep moving. On the second of three porch steps a hand clamps down tightly on my shoulder, wrenches me back, pulls me clean out of my shoes.

Jack has recovered the ax. He hooks the handle around my stomach, catches the blade end and uses the tool to press me hard against him. He's got an erection, and I think I'm going to throw up.

"Dotty, we're so not finished." The noise temporarily startles me out of nausea, but then I'm flung right back by his breath. It reeks of Scotch, a stench I'm intimately acquainted with, thanks to a few worthless stepfathers. The edge of the ax presses into my newly lifted left breast. It cuts me slightly, the pain forcing me back against him to avoid the sting. "Well, look who's hot for Jack? Be a crying shame to cut that off when you went to such lengths to get 'em, right?" He snickers. "At least not right away."

Where is everyone? He begins backing me up the last stair and for a second I let this happen because my mind hasn't come up with an alternative. Then I flash back to his last visit. And what he did.

I snap my head back as hard as I can, trying not to pass out at the awful impact when my head crashes into his nose, the crunch of cartilage, his shriek of rage. My voice finally returns and I scream, scream, scream. The ax, which had been tight up under my breast drops and the handle bounces off my foot with an agonizing, dull thud.

I use the moment to give one final, barefoot mule kick behind me. I think I hit something, but who cares? I run.

I'm with Trainer Joe. He's chuckling and laughing at my efforts. It's raining and I'm getting drenched as I huff and puff through about five minutes worth of labored jogging. I slow to a gasping walk, spent. He grabs my hand, smiling and supportive. He drags me forward till we complete a mile. I wake up the next day with shins on fire, long strips of aching sirloin beneath my knees. My butt hurts in twin dimples behind me and the balls of my feet are sore. And it's the same the next day when Joe propels me forward again. But by the second week, it's better. Not much. A hair more endurable.

Flash: Trainer Joe teasing and taunting by turns, running backwards, facing me. My lungs, which initially were twin fireballs, adapt. The sound of my running shoes slapping the pavement soothes me. Joe pressures me to run on grass – easier on the shins and feet – but I need the repetitive lull of impact. I've begun to run with an iPod plugged in, another Trainer Joe don't. "You need to be aware of your surroundings, and the people around you." Don't care. So lovely to have Sheryl Crow crooning in my ears, or Micky Dolenz, or Eric Clapton, upbeat or bluesy.

No music today: I'm running for my life, barefoot. The grass feels notoriously slippery and I switch to pavement as quickly as I can. It's bitterly cold against my feet and wet and in no time my feet are cut. I feel tremendously better, though, when I feel concrete tearing at my feet. Now they're not slipping. Jack may have been stunned by the head butt, but my guess is he's more pissed than injured. And he's wearing running shoes.

I run with arms pumping, unaware of my open-mouthed screams. Faces peer from windows and neighbors step out onto porches. I ignore them. I barely register the flashing lights and sirens. I run till I careen into an enormous blue wall, a wall with arms which snatches me by the upper arms. Since I don't plan to stop ever, I struggle hard, try to surge around. The blue wall's saying something, but the words are thick, blurry, like they're being filtered through a wall of water. The tone is perplexed, maybe even a bit frightened. Maybe that's because I'm screaming at the top of my lungs? It repeats, over and over, that slightly thickened voice, "ma'am, it's okay. It's okay. You're safe now. Please stop screaming. Please."

Time gets stretched and messy. How long did I thrash, poised for flight, held immobile by a frightened policeman? When I finally stop, my knees buckle. I collapse, leaving the poor cop stuck with my entire body weight. Bless his heart, he keeps me from falling face down. Later on, I'll regret that, because I'm bleeding a little from the cut under my left breast which stains his uniform. I become present enough to feel the sharp sting there. Then all I can feel is cold.

CHAPTER FIFTY-TWO

The nurse is so nice. Her name's Mindy. Mindy asks if I want to see Dr. Atkins. When I say yes, that would nice, she tells me he'll be in shortly. She brings in a blanket that's been run through the microwave. For a hopeful second, I'm warm, but it quickly fades. My teeth snap against each together. My stupid boob hurts. The door opens and it's not Jasper, but a woman. She introduces herself as Detective Cynthia Madden, and she shows me her badge. She's wearing a camel hair coat and jeans, not a uniform. Too bad. I'm very fond of policeman blue.

She's got eyes like a beagle, round and liquid. Her voice is higher than expected, but competent. She explains that she needs to run a rape kit in order to gather evidence. I tell her he didn't get a chance to rape me this time.

Her eyebrows disappear under heavy brown bangs.

"This time?"

That's how I get stuck rehashing the rape. Cynthia Madden probes for details. I answer the best I can. She explains the current charges against Jack Weston when there's a quick rap on the door. Jasper enters.

The detective holds up a hand, "In a minute, Doc."

I interrupt her. "He's a friend. Let him in."

She ignores Jasper. Removes a business card. "My name and number. We'll need you to come by the station for your statement and to sign some documents." She pauses. "They'll also want you to identify Jack Weston, so you might want to get that scheduled at the same time. You know he's in custody, right?"

I nod. The movement causes the back of my head to pound.

Detective Madden continues." We have enough evidence to charge him on at least five other rapes-"

"Five? Five others?" Elvira's heartbroken eyes appear unbidden into my thoughts.

"So far. Five women have come forward identifying Jack Weston as their attacker. The D.A. believes there are more. Jack's court appointed will probably try to plead it out, but I can't guarantee it. We'll make it as painless as possible.

"Thanks, Detective, I appreciate it." She glares once more time at Jasper to show who's the boss, then leaves.

An uncomfortable silence fills the space left by the detective. I can't handle it. "I've been told I'm not pregnant and I don't have an STD. At least not at the moment. The doc says I'll need to repeat the HIV test a few times to be certain. Oh and I don't have hepatitis. So other than some stitches, I'm in the best of health. Are you here to discharge me?"

Jasper sits in one of the uncomfortable chairs provided for visitors. He's wearing a white lab coat over dark blue scrubs. He looks so... medical - stethoscope and everything. Gad I love blue. He grins. "I'm not your doctor and can't discharge you. I could offer you a free exam?"

I laugh and it tugs at the stitches under my breast. "You're a sicko, you know that, right? I think we need to keep our relationship... what the hell exactly is our relationship anyway?"

His smile is grim. "No idea, Dot." He looks down at his shoes. "Not particularly comfortable chatting with victims of violent crime. Gary threatened to kill me once when we were playing tennis. Otherwise, my life's been pretty smooth sailing." He reaches out and puts a long fingered hand on mine. I stare happily at the dark hairs on his arm. "I'm happy as hell to see you, Dotty."

"Right back atcha."

He pulls the hand back, prepares to leave.

I blurt out, "They're going to discharge me any minute, now."

"Then you'll need a ride home." He glances down at his wristwatch. "But I'm not off the clock for another three hours. I'll talk to your attending and see if we can postpone your departure for a few hours. Then we can swing by your place and get some of your things."

"Excuse me?"

"Can't stay at your place for awhile." Jasper stuffs his hands in the pockets of his lab coat. His mouth thins between mustache and goatee. "Rumor has it you need a new door."

I forgot about that. "I do. I guess I need a new door."

Then he leans over and hugs me. The warm furnace of his body heat melts the chill from me. His mouth is at my ear. "Stay at my place. You already know the floor plan." He remains there, till I nod into his neck. He straightens up. He digs around in the pocket of his lab coat and retrieves a small paperback. "Almost forgot. Got you something." He hands over the book.

I laugh out loud. "The Ruthless Rake," by Barbara Cartland.

"It was the only one I could find. You always carried one around at Daters Anonymous. Figured you could use a distraction. Although I was concerned that the title might be in poor taste."

I smile a watery smile. "So it's not about you?"

He blushes. How cute is that? "Hardly. Not a ruthless guy. Oh! Except when I'm playing tennis. Then, no promises." His hip makes noise and he retrieves his beeper. "Gotta go. Cross those fingers that I make it back in three hours." He drops a kiss on my forehead.

I blush. "Okay."

TIME FLIES

It's a little depressing, isn't it? The party's over, and you've got a wrinkled chartreuse dress and credit card bills to think about. Are you going to grow old in your one-bedroom apartment with just your cat for company? Stop right there!

excerpt from The Bridesmaid's Manual *by Sarah Stein and Lucy Talbot, P 187*

Lisa Souza

EPILOGUE - SEVEN YEARS LATER

"**P**ush, Rachel! More, more, more…"

"I hate you so much!" Rachel shrieks, but pushes with all her might.

"Come to mamma, pretty thing." I coax a tiny head out of the birth canal, careful to loop a thumb through the umbilical cord. I twist the tiny body gently, but the baby remains trapped like a cork in a wine bottle. I exhale deeply. The attending doesn't jump in, but he does glance at the monitor.

Rachel has the worst luck with babies. Baby Wilson originally presented breech, planning to exit tail first. At the last minute, and with some encouragement, the baby did a dive forward roll, thank goodness, but still she refuses to join us. Rachel's moaning above me, but it barely registers. This isn't my first difficult delivery, but Rachel's a dear friend and the last thing I want are complications.

Finally, on the next contraction, both shoulders

spring free and the rest of her slips right out. Thank goodness. Rachel insisted she wanted a vaginal birth and she got her wish.

I give Little Miss Wilson a quick swipe, clamp and clip the cord an place her on Rachel's chest. My favorite nurse, Suzie chats with Rachel for a bit before she takes the baby for a quick check up and bath. I join in the banter about the incredible beauty of Rachel's daughter while waiting to deliver the afterbirth. A bit of suprapubic pressure and it slips right out, alien, silvered blue. I didn't have to do an episiotomy and surprising to me, find no tearing at the site of the last one. Suzie shares the latest Wilson's APGAR score. I turn my attention to Rachel, wasted and sweaty, but beaming like she just won the Super Bowl .

Then there's the final Wilson in the trilogy. Poor Bart. He nearly suffered apoplexy watching the delivery. He barely remains on his feet, ashen and trembling. "Bart? Bart! Have a seat, partner, and you can hold your daughter." He drops heavily onto the chair. Another nurse pushes Bart's head to his knees. "How's it going, Suzie?"

Suzie pronounces, "Her majesty is pageant ready." Suzie brings the pink cocoon to her mama. Bart raises his head back up for a closer look, His eyes well up. "Daddy's girl, pretty Katie Grace. Oh my gosh, Rachel, she looks just like you. Drop dead gorgeous." He continues to croon at his latest addition stroking her tiny cheek.

Rachel smiles. "Sweetie, can you tell the crowd out front? Josh and Mikey are being so good out there, but Grandpa and Grandma are a mess."

I finish up, chatting with Rachel, and taking deep breaths. Not only am I thrilled for Rachel and Bart, but boy was I pleased at the opportunity to do the delivery. Rachel's not my patient, but Jasper's trapped across the hall with an emergency C-section. Just think: if she hadn't been early, and Dr. Bernard and hadn't been busy with a preemie, I would have been with the low risk mommies down the hall. Who knew a shortage of OB docs could be useful?

So much more fun than last week, spent practicing endometrial biopsies and inserting IUD's into unsuspecting papayas. That's what you get for being shaped like a uterus. I spend a few minutes congratulating the couple, and Lonnie. Then it's finally safe to seek food.

I plow into Jasper leaving the other delivery room. We untangle.

"Well?" he asks.

"Katie Grace. Eight pounds seven ounces. She did turn but at the absolute last minute. I owe you five bucks."

"Told you."

"Yeah, yeah. Smart ass. You?"

"They still haven't named the big guy yet – over nine pounds. Easy C, though. Very little bleeding. He swipes at his beard, sprinkled here and there with silver. "Wanna grab something to eat?"

I smile at him. I love him in his blue scrubs. "Absolutely."

We head to the cafeteria, a fetching couple in our matching outfits."My mom's not speaking to me. She told me so when she left a message on the machine. And I think Kennedy's going to throw us under a bus."

Jasper's in profile. When he smiles, it pulls back his salt and pepper mustache.

"He got gypped out of a chance to throw a party. Maybe we should let him." He takes an enormous bite of burger. Think it would pacify your mom? If we threw a bash?"

I grin. "Can't hurt. She does love a wedding." It had been my choice to elope. But a party might be fun. I stop to take a spoonful of soup. A sea of faces pass through my mind and for the first time in a long it hits me that I have a wide circle of friends. So blessed. I smile when Elvira's doe-eyed face pops to mind. "Maybe the Bad Apples could play."

"Are you kidding? We'll be paying off student loans for the next ten years. I doubt we can afford them."

I reach out a conciliatory hand to pat his."I have an in with the lead singer. Don't you remember Elvira? From group?"

His jaw drops. "Oh my god that's her?" he shakes his head. "I didn't realize she was that Elvira. She looks so... "

"Happy? Confident? Awesome?" I polish off the soup. "She's doing what she loves. It does a body good."

"Then why are we doing this?" He waves at the hospital cafeteria.

"Must be 'cause we love delivering those babies. So it's time to play."

He thinks briefly, then between bites of burger offers, "Got one off Reddit.com. A father-to-be says 'as a man, I have always simultaneously looked forward to the day my first child is born and dreaded it, because that's going to be your favorite person coming out, but shit, that's also your favorite vagina.' "

I burst out laughing, an odd sound in a hospital cafeteria. "Okay, okay. How about this one from last week? A Brit. My husband asked his workmates for advice when I was due. One of them told him just don't look at her bits. It's like watching your favorite pub burn down."

It's his turn to laugh. "You win."

My smile couldn't be bigger. "I sure did."

Lisa Souza

ABOUT THE AUTHOR

Lisa Souza is a Washington State native and a terrible multi-tasker who enjoys the company of her incredible family, her cohorts at the Fairgrounds, the amazing Hypnochicks, the supportive Wet Coast Writers and a permanent spot on the family room recliner.

Sitting there, trapped beneath an overheating laptop, she drinks copious amounts of iced tea and eats bottomless bowls of popcorn while dreaming up screenplays and the next, great American novel.

But *this* is her first novel.